A GOD OF MOONLIGHT AND STARDUST

DAUGHTERS OF CHAOS
BOOK 1

MINA BROWER

DELPHINUS STAR PUBLISHING LLC

A God of Moonlight and Stardust is a work of fiction. The story, all names, characters, and incidents portrayed in this book are fictitious and are products of the author's imagination. Resemblance with actual persons (living or deceased), places, buildings, and products is entirely coincidental.

First edition 2024.

Copyright © 2024 by Mina Brower

All rights reserved.

Published in the United States by Delphinus Star Publishing LLC.

Hardback ISBN 979-8-9912482-3-5

Paperback ISBN 979-8-9912482-2-8

Ebook ISBN 979-8-9912482-5-9

No part of this publication may be reproduced, distributed, or transmitted in any form or by any means, including photocopying, recording, or other electronic or mechanical methods, or any information storage or retrieval systems, without the prior written permission of the publisher, except for the use of quotations in a book review, or as permitted by U.S. copyright law.

Visit MinaBrowerBooks.com to learn more about the author and her upcoming books.

Editor Jeanine Harrell

Proofreading by Cayla Cavalletto

Book Cover by Hampton Lamoureux

❀ Created with Vellum

To anyone who has felt like they are a burden to love.

A GOD OF MOONLIGHT AND STARDUST

DAUGHTERS OF CHAOS BOOK 1

By: Mina Brower

INTRODUCTION

Like many before me, mythology and science fiction have always fascinated me.

This book is part of a series and is set in a fictional, futuristic universe where humans have abandoned the Milky Way galaxy.

This story takes place in the Andromeda galaxy, some 2,000 years after the extinction of Earth.

Religion is banned, and humans are under the rule of the Planetary Council, a group of humans who have decided to rule all human-inhabited planets.

The gods and beasts of old are no longer worshipped but remain in hidden realms. Only some know of their existence...

Magic is shunned as technology is favored.

Trigger and Content Warning:

The characters you are about to meet go through various mental health struggles. Some of the triggers of this book include mature sexual content, PTSD, references to alcohol abuse, characters battling anxiety and depression, off-page suicide and murder, and mentions of physical and psychological abuse in the form of flashbacks as told by the survivor.

THE LEGEND OF ARIOS AND AM-RE

In the beginning of time, Source, the creator energy of the universe, created three enclaves of gods to oversee its creation: the Celestial Enclave, the Spirit Enclave, and the Elemental Enclave.

Chaos always followed the Celestial gods from galaxy to galaxy.

Two chief gods existed in the Celestial Enclave: Arios, God of the Sun, and Am-Re, God of Darkness.

Arios and Am-Re were twins, each god providing a balance to ensure order in the universe.

Am-Re resented Arios's power to provide light source to all and his ability to help create life. Am-Re could not see the value of darkness and its vital role in rebirth. No one ever paid attention to the dark, and Am-Re craved notoriety and fame.

In time, Am-Re waged a war with his twin, hoping to topple the god of the Sun and take his powers.

Am-Re lost the war and was exiled to a planet far from everyone he loved.

Banishment to that planet was meant to be a punishment for

the god of darkness, as the planet was full of lawless criminals and the worst supernatural creatures.

However, in exile, Am-Re gained notoriety and grew stronger. He became a feared, ruthless leader and lobbied hard to gain support against Arios and the gods under Arios's rule. Through his hatred and use of dark magic, Am-Re became a wielder of chaos and destruction.

Arios saw the evil created by Am-Re and set out with the Celestial gods to destroy the planet.

During the initial years of his exile, Am-Re had a daughter named Renna. She was his heir. In time, Am-Re adopted a son, and he became Am-Re's right-hand soldier and assassin.

But all would not fare well for Am-Re, the feared Wielder of Chaos, for his daughter would betray him by pledging loyalty to his enemies.

This is her story.

1

RENNA

"Hey, *watch it!*" I yelled, slamming my right hand on the expensive motorbike that almost ran the crosswalk and me in the process.

My palms tingled with electricity. The sensation was like small pinpricks just below my skin, and it happened every time I became angry. I felt like a freak of nature. It was ironic that the girl who seldom took risks in order to appear normal and nonmagical was a walking hazard.

Magic was not discussed or entertained on the planet of Andora. People who were found using magic were sent to be reprogrammed. Some were never heard from again ...

The young student on the bike shrank into his leather seat and apologized with an embarrassed finger wave.

"I better not see you in the Classics building!" I yelled after him, my hands fisted to contain my magic, as he quickly sped off.

Early in my childhood, I learned to never point at people when I was agitated because magic, when uncontrolled, was dangerous. Since I had intentionally stopped training seven years ago, my magic was unpredictable, at best. I had no one to pressure me to use it now . . . Who knew what would happen if my magic got out?

As I regained my composure, I zeroed in on the building in front of me. The reason for my temper today.

The building had an offensive new sign: ARAMIS CLASSICS BUILDING. It was home to my college, where I was a doctorate student. The college was the smallest on our university campus. All universities on Andora were funded by the Council, and because the topic of Classics was not science based, our college received very little money.

Last week a man named Hector Aramis donated an undisclosed amount to save my college from closure, which would have jeopardized all students from graduation—including me. Aramis was an art tycoon from across the sea who had a niche for collecting ancient art from various planets but mostly from Earth, an extinct planet filled with rare ancient art finds for those daring enough to venture to the abandoned Milky Way galaxy. Rumors said that the galaxy had become a place of lawlessness as it was unregulated by any governmental council. Aramis's extraterrestrial finds brought him many lucrative opportunities and notoriety.

Hours ago, my school named Aramis president of the college, and he had wasted no time firing faculty members and cutting budgets from different areas of study to make the college run more "efficiently." He then wasted no time appointing his own professors. It was madness.

Among the people he fired was my thesis advisor. Without a thesis advisor, I ran the risk of not graduating on time.

As I stormed up the steps of the Classics building, my undergraduate students gave me a wide berth. Aramis was going to get a piece of my mind.

Once I was inside the building, my friend and colleague Helena beelined toward me.

"*Oh-kay*, this is happening," she said in a high-pitched, nervous voice.

Her blond curls bounced as we made our way up the stairs, two at a time.

Helena Troyes and I had become friends during undergraduate orientation. We both came from fractured backgrounds and naturally found comfort in each other. She was also a doctorate student in the Classics.

She agreed to accompany me to demand Aramis reverse some of the changes he made to our college. Nobody had the courage to stand up to him in person, but that would change today.

As we stormed through the building, my magic continued to stir.

But as I turned the corner that led to his office, all my momentum began seeping from my pores as my hands became sweaty and my heart pumped loudly in my chest. The realization washed over me that confronting him could jeopardize my trip to Xhor.

"So," Helena began gently as we stopped outside his office, "I realize you know *what* you're going to say to him, but what if he tells you to get lost?"

I turned to face my best friend, her model-esque frame in stark contrast to my unimpressive petite height. Helena blushed and adjusted her glasses, which she didn't need, but she thought they made her look more serious.

"We are not asking for the moon and the stars here. People whom we worked alongside with are *gone*. Livelihoods—*gone*. He is an impostor. He doesn't belong here."

"*Breeeeathe*," Helena said, now gripping my shoulders soothingly. "We won't know what to expect until we see him."

"I know *exactly* what to expect—"

Suddenly his office door opened with an ominous screech that echoed in the hallway.

No one stepped out.

The hair at the base of my neck stood in anticipation, but just as suddenly, a wave of calm seemed to emanate from the office into the hallway toward us.

I froze. I hadn't encountered magic from anyone other than myself since I had arrived on campus seven years ago. My magic thrashed inside me, protesting my refusal to act upon what it recognized as a threat. My body began to tingle with a low hum that only I could hear.

The magic coming from his office felt like a piece of silk blowing in the wind, slowly enveloping me like a physical caress. It smelled of lavender and cinnamon, scents used to soothe.

Did Aramis know I was coming to see him? And was the magic coming from him?

Helena, unaware of the magic surrounding us, touched my arm for reassurance and gently pulled me toward the office. My feet followed absentmindedly as I tried to grapple with the fact that, for the first time in seven years, I was about to meet another person who knew how to use magic.

As if waiting for us, Hector Aramis sat at his desk, his large fingers steepled under his chin, his face expressionless. He wore a black cashmere sweater with the sleeves pushed up, revealing strong, tan forearms. He was far more casual than the previous head of our department, who had looked like an ancient scholarly source of knowledge with wide-rimmed glasses and white hair. Aramis had black wavy hair that was haphazardly pushed back from his face like he had just taken a bath and only managed to run his fingers through it.

A young woman in a beautiful blue dress with gleaming silver waist-length hair sat perched on top of a set of drawers to Aramis's right. The calming energy that had greeted us seemed to be flowing from her. Her eyes were focused on me, and I couldn't look away from her as I stood dumbfounded. The only other person I knew who had used magic was dead . . .

Hector Aramis drew my attention from her by speaking. "*Galene*," he said, looking toward the woman, "it seems your siren's talent for calming the roughest of seas was successful."

I hardened my jaw to keep my magic together as it protested at the mocking comment.

Taking a seat in front of him, I addressed him. "Mr. Aramis."

Helena was still standing by the door, her eyes fixed on Aramis, as if she was mesmerized by him.

"*Helena!*" I whispered furiously and motioned her to sit next to me.

Helena apologized and joined me silently.

"What brings you here today, Miss . . .?"

Gods, even his voice was sexy.

"Renna Strongborn."

Out of the corner of my eye, I could see Galene shake her head and furrow her brow. She murmured that something was off about my name as if there was a mistake.

Aramis looked to her and then turned to me.

"*Strongborn?*" Aramis tilted his head. "A unique name. Who are your parents?"

I didn't like to talk about my past, so I paused before answering and gave the driest answer imaginable. "I was dropped off at an orphanage hours after I was born. They didn't think I would survive the night. The orphanage named me."

"I see." Aramis continued to look at me like I was a specimen. "Miss Strongborn." He sat up straighter. "Why are you here today?"

I filled my lungs with air and sat up closer to his desk. "I am here on behalf of many of the hardworking professors, teaching assistants, and graduate students—"

"*Ah, yes*," he said dismissively, waving his hands around. "You are not the first person asking me to reconsider my changes. You are wasting your time. And mine."

My eyebrows rose, mimicking the anger slowly boiling to the surface.

"Mr. Aramis, I am to complete my doctorate in a few months. I am completing a thesis on—"

"The ancient weapons of Xhor and their impact in the region. You are traveling to Xhor next month to complete your research," he finished for me.

I furrowed my brows. I hadn't expected him to know anything about our college, much less its students. I was expecting him to be a pretty figurehead for the college and nothing more.

"Well." I nodded. "As you probably know, my supervisor was let go. You can imagine how *deeply* that impacts the completion of my work." When Aramis began to shake his head in disagreement, my heart sped up as I tried to reason with him. "I do *not* have the funds to remain at this program another year if I don't finish—"

"Your supervisor was incompetent. He also engaged in an unsavory relationship with a student, a topic which I will *not* discuss with you." He cocked a brow and tilted his head. "Find someone else. You are dismissed," he said, getting up as if my concerns mattered little, which, I guess, to him, they did.

Helena stood, her eyes still glued to Aramis.

Aramis had barely spared her a glance.

Anger surged within me as I fought for my career. "No," I said firmly, standing from my chair.

As if on cue, the lighting in the office began to flicker.

Aramis's mouth made an O shape, and he put a finger up to

silence everyone as he curiously looked around from where he stood.

I began to slow my breath to control the anger and energy within me.

When the lights stopped flickering, he narrowed his eyes on me. My face was blank, void of any expression.

Aramis shook his head. "Good day, Miss Strongborn," he said, shooing us off.

"*No*," I said again, more anger coursing through my veins, warming my arms as if my feelings would spew from them.

I had always been robbed of an opinion and say on things that directly affected me. I needed to take a stand. My doctorate degree was at stake.

Aramis began speaking with Galene about another topic, ignoring Helena and me. As if the room felt my anger, the lights flickered again, and a shiver ran down my spine.

My energy was causing this.

Fuck. I closed my fists to control the prickling sensation in my palms.

Aramis looked about the room curiously. He turned toward Galene, who sat with a peculiar expression directed at me.

I shifted on my feet, my face prickling with anger and shame for making myself noticeable.

"Do you *see* something, Galene?" Aramis asked in a low tone.

Galene nodded, her eyes still fixed on me. I stared back, unflinching as she assessed me. I had grown up with a monster. Her stare was nothing.

I sighed and straightened my shoulders.

Then her observation turned intrusive. She looked at me as if mentally trying to pry me open with pliers, trying to understand my truth and magic. My body tensed with self-awareness as her energy prodded me, as if someone was putting both hands on each side of my shoulders, trying to rip me apart. I pushed my energy outward from my body, mentally putting an invisible shield of protection around myself.

Galene lifted her brows, likely feeling my protective shield. *Good.*

I felt out of my element. That there were potentially others like me shook me to the core. My world was tilting on its axis.

My mentor, a nameless man dressed in black who had entered my life when I was six, was interested in teaching me how to wield energy. At first, I thought he was another social worker sent to evaluate me, but he was different. He had taught me how to protect myself from what he called *energetic attacks*.

As Galene's concentration deepened, I stood my ground. My protective dome began to expand, pushing into the rest of the room. I imagined my shield made of black obsidian stone and gathered thoughts of anger and hate for anything and anyone that would threaten my career.

One of the lights in Aramis's office exploded, and Helena screamed.

"Miss Strongborn!" Aramis said, his eyes fiercely focused on Helena, as if assessing that she was okay.

I turned to my friend, and seeing her cowered on her chair, I lost concentration. My energy zapped back into me like a rubber band, and I collapsed onto the chair behind me. Helena stood to help me up.

"You are dismissed from my office," Aramis said hard. "*Again.*"

I narrowed my eyes at him.

A cough came from the hallway, and I turned to find a professor outside the doorway.

"That's my next appointment, Miss Strongborn," Aramis said, pointing to the door.

"Excuse me?" I said, my face prickling with anger.

"I will review your file to see what we can do about your

supervisor and will be in contact with you soon." He looked to Galene as if silently asking for some sort of confirmation. When Galene nodded, he turned toward me once more. "We have much to discuss."

Unease filled me as I left his office.

I had run from magic for seven years, and in a matter of minutes, my mask had slipped.

2

RENNA

After my years in foster care, I spent my adulthood carefully crafting a normal life. I had never wanted to learn magic as a child. All it brought was never-ending abuse. Its presence represented pain and the perpetual shadow of fear that was my mentor. As an adult, I craved the mundane. The more cookie-cutter my life could be, the better.

Magic had no place in my day to day. It only ever brought out a darker side of me, demanding I explore feelings of anger and hurt—which I had a lot of. And I preferred to keep all that tucked away. There was safety in self-control and predictability.

The training was brutal, and my lessons always carried a sense of urgency, as if my mentor was running out of time. Wielding energy to create magic required intense focus, so my mentor had forced me to practice mental exercises for hours until my eyes became bloodshot from exhaustion.

Because anger was the catalyst for my magic, I was required to gather hateful thoughts about the world and injustices done to me. Once I had sufficient emotions built up, I could channel that anger into a glowing black ball of energy in my mind's eye. The ball of energy could then do whatever I asked of it, including molding a protective shield or something more nefarious, like sending energy someone's way to ruin their day.

My training exercises evolved from causing someone to trip as they walked to causing someone to fall down the stairs—which he forced me to do more than once—and ultimately, causing death.

Death was always the goal. I would lie in bed for hours after he left, with a raging migraine and weary bones, hating my mentor for making me into something despicable and my foster mother for allowing him into my life.

Since I had left home for university, I shut my childhood and the memory of those years under lock and key. I didn't want to be a freak. I wanted to fit in and find people who could love me. Magic had robbed me of my life.

Now, however, when Galene's intrusive energy violated my boundaries, my mental shield had kicked in like a reflex. I didn't care if she knew what I was.

After my encounter with Aramis, the new professors' looks lingered a little too long when they thought I wasn't looking. I was granted short conversations and polite, clipped smiles, highlighting wariness toward me, not disgust. It seemed as though the exchange in Aramis's office had somehow spread, and I wondered whether the new hires also wielded magic.

Being judged before I even had a proper chance to meet the new faculty was uncomfortable. After a week of awkward and stilted conversations, I had had enough of academia, and for the first time in a long time, I needed a break.

Which was how I found myself silently cursing as I stared at a neon sign of a tattoo parlor with Helena.

With my trip to Xhor coming up, this would be the first year the two of us would spend a university break apart. We normally stayed on campus every break as we had nowhere else to go. Due to packed schedules, we hadn't been able to spend a lot of time together. So we agreed to have a night of fun before I left for Xhor. However, my idea of fun was staying in, watching movies, baking, and reading with a good glass of wine. Helena thought a night out drinking cocktails and dancing was better, and because I could never say no to my best friend, I let her plan the night for us. But she hadn't shared that getting tattoos was part of the plan, and I groaned at the prospect.

The tattoo parlor was located on a less prominent side of town. Other Side Tattoos glowed red in the night. Two purple neon dice decorated the sign, and it made me think twice about taking the gamble of getting a tattoo while inebriated.

"I don't know about this, Helena."

"Aw, c'mon!" She stood in front of me with both hands on my shoulders. "It's not like you've never gotten a tattoo before. You have the lotus flower on your side."

I thought of the lotus flower gracing my ribs, just beneath my breast and wrapping around to the side. "That meant something, you know that. We're drunk. I don't even know what I would get," I grumbled.

I wanted my tattoos to mean something, and I only had one so far. For the past seven years, lotus flowers have randomly appeared—physically and in imagery—when I felt hopeless. It always felt like a sign. So I got the tattoo as a reminder that no matter what I'd been through, there would always be hope in some way.

"Well, I can't force you to get one . . ." Helena sighed. "But I really want one, so come in with me?"

"Fine." I smiled and linked my arm through hers. Once inside, I paused. "Opera music? This is fancy," I noted, looking down at the polished marble flooring where I could see my reflection and then at the glittering gold sconces on the walls. "Almost too fancy," I said more quietly, feeling like something was off.

"You don't think it looks a bit . . ." I looked around at the tattoo artists, who looked too dressed up and stiff. ". . . Staged?"

"If by staged you mean this doesn't look like the other run-down, shithole parlors in town, then yes. Would you rather we go to a seedy place?" She chuckled.

"Well, no—"

"Come, help me pick out a tattoo."

My eyes widened as Helena pulled me to a tattoo design book. "You're joking, right?" I laughed. "What if you hate it?"

She chuckled and indicated to her arms, which were covered in small, dainty tattoos. "You know I love tattoos, and you know my style."

I groaned. "No pressure, right?"

She grinned. "I'm sure I'll love it."

By the time it was Helena's turn to get a tattoo, I had picked out a protective sigil for her. As much as I hated everything my mentor stood for, he had taught me about sigils and their ability to provide protection. While Helena didn't know of my magic, I wanted her to be safeguarded this summer. When I shared the tattoo design, Helena approved with a huge grin, and we waited to be assigned an artist.

Her tattoo artist was a woman with fiery-red waist-length hair dressed in all black. A black corset cinched her frame, high-lighting her curves, but it was her impressive tattoo that commanded attention. A black and silver serpent extended from her left temple down to her fingertips. Complementing her tattoo, her eyes were serpentine-like and citrine in color. Although I assumed she wore contacts, I was mesmerized. Helena, however, seemed unimpressed and acted as if she didn't notice her.

Once introductions were made, I explained Helena's tattoo to the artist. Helena settled into the chair, and one of her friends was getting work done in the station next to us. Helena turned her attention to her friend, and the tattoo artist focused on me.

"You're a long way from home," the tattoo artist said, cocking her head, looking me up and down in a more curious manner than offensive.

Her statement was odd.

"Aren't most people on this campus?" I smiled politely, feeling a bit self-conscious.

I hated reminders of home or my lack thereof.

The woman studied my face, her eyes seemingly cataloging every nuance and muscle movement as though I were her prey.

"Why did you pick this tattoo?" she asked as she started working. "It's a very unusual choice."

"For protection," I said automatically.

The woman halted slightly. "Smart girl." She smiled, curiously looking sideways up toward me.

"I overheard some girls talking about the meaning of this tattoo." I lied seamlessly.

She nodded and continued working on Helena. "What do you study?"

"Weapons."

I never went into details about my life with strangers. The foster system had taught me that relationships were never permanent, so there was no point in trying to make new friends. Helena had been my only exception.

"That's interesting," she said lightly. "What kinds of weapons?"

"Ancient weapons." I crossed my arms.

"Anywhere in particular?"

"I'm currently focusing on weapons from Xhor. It's a recent discovery."

"Don't get me wrong, but I seldom hear women become

weapon historians." She shook her head. "I'm sure you're brilliant at what you do. You're not what I expected, is all."

Another odd comment. The woman spoke to me like she knew me.

"I know men typically study weapons." I shrugged. "But that field of study is what called to me."

She nodded. "Keep 'em guessing is what I always say." She winked playfully. "That mentality will serve you well on your journey—mark my words."

"My journey?"

The woman paused her work as if reassessing what she was saying. "*Life*," she quickly said. "The journey of life."

Unsure how to respond, I hugged my arms around my midsection and nodded.

When the woman was done with Helena's tattoo, Helena stepped away to chat with a group of friends who had just come in. It seemed everyone in the parlor was preoccupied with someone they knew. As laughter rose in the air, my world tunneled around me. I felt lonely for the first time in a very long time.

"I'm Etara, by the way," the tattoo artist suddenly said, snapping me out of my snowballing thoughts.

"I'm Renna—"

"*Renna.*"

We both said my name at the same time, and I furrowed my brows.

"I overheard your friend say your name," she explained.

"*Ah.*" I nodded embarrassedly.

"Why are you here, Renna?" Etara asked me, her citrine eyes suddenly glowing.

I blinked, and her eyes were normal again. I was reminded of Galene, whose ice-blue eyes seemed to glow. Except unlike Galene's intrusive energy, I felt no threat from Etara. In fact, I felt at ease in her presence. Like she could convince me to tell her anything . . .

I shook my head to refocus as I felt my vision blur. How much had I had to drink?

"My friend dragged me here," I answered Etara's question.

Etara smirked. "You lie," she said, her golden eyes boring into mine. "Why have you come *here*?" Etara tried again.

"I'm here with my friend." I gestured to Helena.

Etara lifted her eyebrows. "Sit," she said, her citrine eyes dancing as she challenged me.

My body automatically sat at her command while a little voice in the back of my head reminded me about my mental shield of protection.

"I don't believe for one second you walked in here just because of your friend," she said while cleaning her station. "We all have free will."

"Maybe I was curious," I offered.

"For whom?"

I thought about her question. I had entered the parlor out of curiosity despite my feelings of getting tattoos on a whim because, in a way, I supposed I wanted to see if I could be fearless.

"For me," I answered truthfully. "To be honest, I wouldn't even know what tattoo to get. I feel like tattoos should document something, and at this time, I have nothing worth memorializing. I doubt working extra shifts to pay for school or studying in the library till they close when I'm not at work counts as anything special."

Etara looked at me for a moment, her eyes searching mine.

"Sometimes we think there needs to be substantial shifts in our lives that are tangible and evident for them to matter." She smiled slightly. "Oftentimes, in the stillness, we make the most strides. To not acknowledge the silence is a disservice to our growth."

Her words left me frozen as I internalized what she was telling me.

"Have you ever heard of intuitive tattoos?" Etara asked, looking away.

"Um...no," I confessed.

"You let your tattoo artist choose a tattoo that best suits you at that moment."

I sat up, unsure. "What if it's a design I don't want?"

"You need to enter a state of deep relaxation. You will tell me what you see or are feeling. I will tattoo what you ultimately tell me based on intuition."

Helena walked over then with a huge grin on her face. "I knew you'd get one." She jumped up and down. "What are you getting?" She wiggled her brows.

"Not sure." I shrugged. "An intuitive tattoo?"

I looked to Etara, who nodded and explained the process to Helena, who proceeded to excitedly convince me to get something.

"I'll sit next to you the whole time if you pass out meditating," Helena promised.

After I agreed to the whole ordeal, Etara gently eased me back onto the chair. "Close your eyes," Etara whispered, her citrine eyes dancing like a serpent.

I felt captive in her gaze, finding myself unable to look away. "Relax..."

A few moments later, my eyes became heavy, and her golden orbs seemed to continue to dance as I settled into the chair until my muscles felt limp. The opera music began to sound like a far-off echo, and the loudest sounds were my breathing and Etara's melodic voice carrying me into a state of suspended nothingness. I felt like I had fallen into sleep paralysis, where I lingered between consciousness and another place.

My eyes fell closed, and cold smoke caressed my skin, sending goose bumps over my body. The smoke felt like it was settling on my skin, forming a layer over me, laying claim to my body. I felt weightless.

As my vision focused, I was inside a dark tunnel full of smoke. Golden light shone up ahead, and I felt compelled to follow it. As I walked, the ground trembled with vibrations. Approaching the opening, I realized the vibrations came from noise.

I stepped out of the tunnel and found myself outdoors. The sun blinded me, so I brought my arm up to shield my vision. The noise I had heard was thousands of people sitting in a pavilion, perhaps thirty stories tall, with rows upon rows of spectators cheering and pounding their feet in rhythm, creating a powerful crescendo of sound. As the cheering continued, I felt disoriented.

Where was I?

Two hands grabbed my waist from behind and spun me around playfully.

I was met with a wall of gold armor. Despite not knowing for sure, something told me the armor covered the body of a soldier. He must have been at least seven feet tall, but when I looked up to his face, it was blurred.

I blinked and shook my head, hoping to clear my vision, but his face remained fuzzy.

"What do you see?" Etara's voice suddenly said from somewhere far away.

I focused on the armor in front of me as it gleamed in the sunlight. I reached out, the metal cool beneath my fingertips. Two symbols were etched on the breastplate. A crescent moon on its side with moonbeams below and an *X* in the background.

"A soldier," I replied to Etara, trusting she could hear me. "I can't see his face."

I traced the symbols, and a sense of familiarity ran through my bones as my fingers rose and fell through the grooves of the embossed symbol. The soldier grabbed my waist possessively, and delicious tremors ran throughout my body. His hold felt comforting, and I wanted to lean into him. My skin prickled.

"What else?" Etara's voice echoed.

"I see two symbols," I said. "A crescent moon atop an *X* . . ."

Moments passed, and suddenly Etara's voice got closer. "Wake up."

Her voice startled me, and I was plucked from my dream, the scene dissipating like smoke.

I blinked several times as my eyes adjusted to the tattoo parlor lights. Etara quietly observed me, her eyes sharply assessing me. Helena's face loomed next to hers, examining my tattoo with a grin.

I massaged my shoulders, which felt stiff. How long was I asleep?

"I'm sorry if I dozed off." I apologized to both women.

"It happens," Etara assured me and began to wipe my sternum with a cleaning solution and paper towels.

I panicked and looked down, only to see the symbols I saw tattooed on my skin.

"It's so beautiful," Helena squealed. "I'm so glad you got a tattoo, Ren." She hugged me. "A crescent moon and an *X*? Odd choice, but I don't hate it."

"Yeah, it was a symbol I saw. It was so quick I barely felt her tattooing me." I tentatively touched my skin, finding the area sore.

I lightly traced the design, and electricity built in my veins, as if my cells were rising to the surface of my skin. Was the tattoo reacting to my magic? I looked up at Etara questioningly, but she was quickly standing from her seat as if she couldn't get out of the parlor quickly enough. I felt like I would never see her again.

When Etara began to walk away, I stood up. "Wait!" I called, but as soon as I started after her, the music began to skip like a broken record, and a row of sconces began to explode one by one, quickly shrouding the parlor in darkness.

Patrons shrieked and scurried to the exit, and I lost Etara in the chaos.

"We should probably get going," Helena said, squeezing my arm as her eyes darted back and forth. "First the lights exploded in Aramis's office and now *here*?" She shook her head, pulling me to the door, but I halted with her words.

I had caused the lights to explode in Aramis's office because of magic.

And then all the lights in the parlor went out.

That's when I felt *it*.

It was a strong wave of magic. I could feel it weave its way toward Helena and me. Heavy and viscous, it moved through the parlor like a serpent. The magic felt somewhat . . . *familiar*. It was laced with electrical currents—like mine.

My body was frozen, tuning out the screams of the patrons around me and resisting the pulls from Helena.

My protective shield.

I had to put up my shield, but my energy was nowhere to be found as fear—not anger—coursed through my veins.

A man slammed into me as he was running to the exit, snapping me out of my frozen state, and Helena and I were pushed out with everyone else.

3

KHELLIOS

A wave of energy hit my body at an unnatural speed.

I was seated in my study, going over ancient texts with a glass of Ambrosia in my hand. The drink was potent enough to help me forget what today was—the anniversary of Renna's death and the destruction of Xhor.

I had planned on a quiet night inside my home to wallow in memories that would not cease, and I was unprepared when the powerful burst of energy blew through my house.

Magic.

The force had been strong enough to cause pain to my chest. I rubbed my sternum.

This was no ordinary magic.

The force felt like a blood summons, one that humans had once employed in our temples. Calling upon a god with blood was the equivalent of a blood sacrifice, and it bound a god to respond. Not many dared to conjure a god this way, as there was no guarantee the response would be pleasant.

I moved to stand, only to be pushed back down by a second debilitating wave of energy, leaving me screaming in pain and grabbing my head again as it pulsed with the impact.

Who was calling for me, and why was it affecting me in this manner?

Only the energy of another god or divine being of higher or equal power could debilitate a god. If a god was summoning me, the question was *why*?

This energy was dense and had an electrical quality to it.

I braced my body on the armchair, my knuckles white, and I closed my eyes, anticipating the third wave.

Behind closed lids, a hazy image began to form. It was a memory.

My memory.

Her hand lazily trailed the sigil on my armor breastplate. We were at a friendly tournament, and I was to fight that day against other gods as a performance for our people.

As she trailed her finger along my sigil crest, I caught her wrist in my hand and pressed her body against mine. My eyes trailed up her arms, up her elegant neck, and to her hazel eyes.

Her eyes communicated wicked things her mouth would not allow her to say in public.

Renna.

I squeezed my eyes harder, trying to hold onto the memory of her face—a face I had not seen in over two millennia. A face I had made a point to forget. A woman I had tried to escape, whose memory haunted me every day of my life. Whose love I tried to replicate by marrying two human women after her passing. I tried to forget her, to no avail.

Why, gods, was I seeing her face again?

I let the third wave of energy envelop my body with Renna's face in mind, my brain recalling her essence of lotus flowers. The energy called out to me.

"Renna?" My voice echoed in the room, my body shocked from speaking her name after so long.

The energy around me took on an animated quality, waves of

gold dust forming the shape of a woman. The image sent chills down my spine, making me sit up straight.

"What magic is this?" I whispered.

Renna was the offspring of the god Am-Re, but she had never shown any magical talent. She could not manipulate energy like this.

Echoing voices suddenly filled my library, and it was hard to pick out anything specifically from the fodder at first.

"I'm so glad you got a tattoo, Ren," a female stated. "A crescent moon and an *X*? Odd choice, but I don't hate it."

At the mention of Renna's nickname, my heartbeat came to a halt, and I felt as if my body had been doused with the frigid waters of the Nordaluns.

I rose from my chair to listen for a response.

It couldn't be her. Her soul was never found.

I held my breath, anticipating her voice. And then I heard her as if she were standing next to me.

"Yeah, it was a symbol I saw. It was so quick I barely felt her tattooing me . . ." Her voice softly echoed in the room.

They spoke of my sigil, the one I had taught Renna countless times. *She had tattooed my sigil on her skin?* Renna's blood calling to me could perhaps explain the energy I felt.

As I grappled with the fact that my beloved was alive and the implications of her resurfacing and summoning me, I stood frozen to the spot, my body in shock as two millennia worth of emotions coursed through me.

"Renna," I said, my voice frantic.

The voices continued to echo around me with no response. I walked to the gold dust and ran my fingers through the magic. It felt cold to the touch, and I shivered.

Unsure how it was possible to hear her voice, I knew one thing was absolutely certain: Matter was neither created nor destroyed. Matter simply was.

Renna had a physical death all those eons ago. But her spirit, her soul, had not gone through the normal underworld channels for reincarnation. Her soul simply vanished. Her disappearance had confounded me for centuries. The only conclusion I could come up with was her father had hidden her soul for none to find.

But she was alive—*now*.

I did not know how or when her soul resurfaced, but I would find her.

For Renna was mine.

Her body and soul belonged to me as much as I belonged to her.

And I had never stopped loving her.

"How could she be alive?" Ukara, the Goddess of War, asked as she paced the length of the gathering hall in Arios's palace. "We searched for her countless times."

Arios spoke to me from his throne dais. "Are you certain it was Renna who summoned you?" Disbelief and caution were etched in the furrow of his brow and the pursing of his lips.

I did not blame him for his doubt. What I was proposing was fantastical. Our inability to find her soul was a failure for the many who searched for her. Our community was fractured after the attack on Xhor, and finding Renna became a symbol of hope after the chaos unleashed by Am-Re.

"I felt her essence linked to the magic that summoned me. I" —I paused—"I heard her voice clear as day. She spoke of tattooing my sigil on her skin. It was Renna."

"And were you able to locate her after she summoned you?"

I shook my head. "There was a strange quality to the summons. It was as if the magic was deliberately blocking my ability to locate her." I cupped the back of my neck. "I can't explain it. Renna never learned magic before."

"Khellios," Arios began carefully, giving me a polite smile. "I have known you for eons. You are my right hand in the enclave. You are like the brother I wish I had, and I remember the pain you went through at losing Renna." He looked around the room. "We all remember. I understand the passing of Renna was *profound* . . ."

I followed his gaze. The gods seated around me refused to meet my eyes, looking anywhere but in my direction.

They did not believe me.

"We *all* lamented her passing." Arios continued. "You the most, which is *understandable*. Do you not think, perhaps, that in your grief, you may have been . . . *confused*—"

"I believe him," someone said from the hall's entrance.

Everyone turned to meet the new visitor. Draped in a black and gold linen robe, slightly open to reveal an abdomen with scratches surely from his latest love conquest, was Cylas, the God of the Planets.

Cylas met my eyes in the usual lazy annoyance, and I didn't bother masking my judgment.

"Nice of you to join us," I said, my voice void of any emotion.

Cylas liked to cultivate an unreliable, devil-may-care attitude that alienated most gods. As a creator god of planets and the flora and fauna on them, Cylas had a laid-back, laissez-faire approach to ruling. I suspected he had experienced too much loss from seeing his creations repeatedly destroyed to continue caring.

He had also developed a deep attachment toward Renna all those years ago. Although he never attempted to seduce her, I knew his attachment was because of his attraction to her. Renna never returned his feelings, but given the chance, Cylas would have claimed her for himself.

Although I never saw him as a true adversary, I would have expected him to show up on time to hear about Renna's reappearance and what that meant for us all.

"Cylas," Arios began, getting up from his chair. "*Surely* you understand the grave implications of backing Khellios's claim."

Although no one had mentioned his name, Renna's presence begged the question of whether Am-Re was back.

Cylas leaned against the doorframe of the great hall and crossed his arms, his tone dripping in arrogance. "He's telling the truth. The serpent demon's spawn is back."

I tightened my fist at my side at his tone.

Murmurs swirled in the room as the gods shifted uneasily.

"Pemira?" Arios called to the goddess with bronze skin, draped in an aquamarine gown and a headpiece with aquamarine gemstones.

Pemira was the Goddess of the Written Record. All that had and would transpire, she knew.

Pemira turned to me, observing me with a look I did not understand. Her brow looked troubled. She would have known of Renna's return and how her story would unfold. That her expression was not joyous at Renna being returned to me at last irked me.

"The daughter of the Prince of Darkness and the siren lives," she confirmed.

Pemira looked away from me.

The room broke out in chaos as gods stood and demanded she elaborate. I knew it was futile. Pemira only revealed what was absolutely necessary so as not to interfere with the future.

"*Enough!*" Arios said, attempting to calm the room. "Pemira, is it really *his* offspring that roams this planet?"

Pemira turned to Arios and nodded silently. "His *children* live."

"*Children?*" Ukara asked, gripping the spear she seldom went without. She turned to Arios, her face pale with fear. "Father, does that mean—"

"Am-Re's adopted son must be alive," Arios answered.

The room broke into even more chaos.

My fists tightened. Am-Re had scooped his adopted son from the wreckage during one of Am-Re's wars. Am-Re had trained the youth in his magic, and eventually he became his right-hand man and leader of Am-Re's troops. He was a ruthless assassin.

"I just told you all Renna was alive." Cylas interjected, pinching his nose in annoyance. "But does anyone listen to the god who literally feels the energetic footprint of life on all planets?"

"Where is she?" I demanded, rising from my seat.

Cylas smirked. "Wouldn't you like to know?"

"*Cylas*," Ukara warned.

"She's only been dead for over two millennia." Cylas rolled his eyes. "And he stopped looking for her, oh I don't know . . ." He began counting on his fingers.

I was at his throat in seconds, pinning him against the wall.

"Where is she?" I gritted out.

"Down, boy, down," Cylas said, pushing me off. "Not sure she will like the whole macho persona—times have changed, you know." He straightened his robe and rubbed his neck. "I didn't think you cared to know where she was, given you married two mortals back-to-back to replace her after her death. Is she going to come with you to place flowers on the graves of your dead wives?"

Red filled my vision, and I charged at him, only to find the spot where he stood empty. He was now across the room.

"That is enough!" Arios bellowed. "I will not have you both make a mockery of what is happening."

"Father, what does this mean for us?" Ukara asked Arios. "I can mobilize a militia if he attacks."

"You will wait for my command," Arios said dryly.

Ukara's face reddened, and she had a white-knuckle grip on her spear.

"His children may be alive, but we don't know if *my brother* is back," Arios assured the room.

I looked to Cylas, silently asking if we needed to be worried about Am-Re's return.

Cylas's tight jaw and hard stare told me everything I needed to know. Cylas had felt Am-Re's presence.

I had no time to waste. I needed to get to Renna before her father or his wretched son destroyed her life and ripped her from me once more.

"You will take me to her." I pointed to Cylas.

"I could." Cylas shrugged with a grin.

Suddenly, a violent turbine of black mist entered the room, revealing a lone goddess at the other end of the hall. Livina, Goddess of Fate, made her dramatic, resplendent entrance in black silk.

"Take care, God of the Moon and Stars," Livina said to me. "The daughter does not recall what she lived."

My heart sank.

"She has no idea who you are. Or who she truly is."

"My sister speaks the truth." Pemira interjected, standing beside Livina.

Both Goddesses worked together. Pemira knew how someone's fate would end, while Livina knew exactly how events would progress and if they changed course at any given point in time to get to their final fate.

Filled with rage, I looked at both goddesses. "What am I supposed to do?"

"For now, you wait," Livina stated. "Let the events of how you reunite with her unfold as they must. The daughter will return."

"You cannot expect me to sit idly! Her life is in danger."

Cylas cursed. "Liv," he said, rubbing his face in frustration. He was the only one who ever called her by that nickname. "Can't you give us something to go off? You cannot expect us to just *wait*."

For once, I agreed with Cylas.

"If Renna does not know who she is, then she does not understand the danger she is in. Her father can get to her at any moment. She is unprotected," I argued.

"Khel," Arios said carefully, "her reappearance can mean anything. We don't necessarily know if *he* is even back."

"For goodness' sake," Cylas drawled. He held the bridge of his nose in frustration. "Just say his name. His name is *Am-Re*."

A collective gasp filled the room.

"Is *he* back?" Ukara asked Pemira and Livina, gripping her spear closer to her body.

"Open your eyes, Ukara," Cylas spat. "How could he not be? His kids are back."

The room broke out in uproar.

"If you have felt my brother's presence on this planet, when were you going to tell us?" Arios accused.

"Could *you* all not feel him?" Cylas argued, looking around the room. "You are all so preoccupied with luxury and idleness as of late that you have forgotten what you are here for. You sit in this fucking dome of protection thinking you are untouchable." Cylas gestured to the lilac sky, visible through the opening where a roof might normally be. "However, you are all here to do a job, which is to oversee this galaxy. *This* planet included."

Arios stuttered as he tried to come up with an explanation as to why the signs of Am-Re returning could have been missed— *especially* by him. Arios knew his brother best of all . . .

Pemira spoke loudly over the many voices. "The father brought forth the daughter." The room immediately quieted. "He is not what he once was . . . his form is altered . . . Am-Re is weak. Renna and her magic are meant to strengthen his kingdom. She is meant to be used as a pawn."

Gripping my hair at the roots, I tilted my head back to look up at the sky and released a harsh breath. I wanted to scream. Am-Re would never let his daughter live in peace. With her father being weak, she was in even more danger because that made him desperate.

"What do we need to know?" Cylas put up his palms in frustration.

"The daughter will return," Livina said.

Cylas groaned. "For fuck's sake, Liv."

Arios sharply cut off Cylas. "Thank you, Goddesses, for the messages. My brother will stop at nothing. I will begin reinforcing our borders here to protect the people of Taria."

As Arios barked orders about reinforcing the barrier shield around Taria, I pulled Cylas into the hallway.

"So, what will you do, lover boy?" he asked, crossing his arms with a lower voice.

"I need to know where she is. You need to help me track her. We need to bring her here."

"Wouldn't Am-Re assume this is the first place you would bring her?"

I narrowed my eyes and clenched my jaw before I spoke. "There is no better place to protect her, and you know it."

Cylas pinched the bridge of his nose. "So what?" he said, crossing his arms. "You're just not going to let her leave Taria? Is she to be your prisoner? *True romance.*"

"Fuck you." I surged forward, inches from his face now, my voice louder. "I'm trying to keep the love of my life alive. I don't need *any* of your bullshit."

Arios and Ukara stepped in, likely having heard us.

"Enough!" Arios said, exasperated, stepping in between us. "We will solve nothing with your constant bickering."

Cylas lifted his chin and glared at me. "She comes here and what? Are you going to tell her who she is to you and that her father wants her dead?"

"She wouldn't remember." Ukara shook her head.

"Wow, you're smart," Cylas drawled, rolling his eyes. "It's almost like Liv just said the exact same thing."

Ukara launched herself toward him, and Arios held his daughter back.

She laughed with an edge in her voice. "How sweet that you use a nickname for her. *Liv*."

"What about it?" Cylas narrowed his eyes and took a step toward Ukara.

Trying to get us back to what was important, I spoke. "I will tell Renna who she is when she returns. It is *my right* to share her past with her as it involves me."

All eyes turned to me.

Arios nodded after a long while. "I agree," he said. "Better it comes from you than any one of us." He sighed.

"Fine," Cylas said.

Ukara nodded.

"Now," Arios said, straightening his robes. "If you will excuse me, I need to continue planning for reinforcements at Taria's borders."

Cylas and I stepped away from Arios, and Ukara silently followed her father.

Cylas leaned against the wall behind him and crossed his arms. "You don't deserve Renna."

I had heard it all before from him.

I put my hands on my hips. "Yes." I sighed. "I realize that, at times, I may not be enough for her. But *you*"—I jabbed a finger in his direction—"will never be."

Cylas stepped up to me so we were chest to chest. "If you hurt her," he whispered, a deadly tone in his voice, "I will make sure that your presence is wiped from this universe."

"Deicide." I tsked. "My, you and Am-Re have a lot more in common than I thought."

"At least I'm honest with my intentions."

"Take me to her," I gritted out.

"I am only doing this because I want her safe. It's not for you," Cylas said, opening a portal to his domain and gesturing for me to follow him.

I didn't respond.

"Let's go get our girl." Cylas smiled lazily.

4

RENNA

As an adult, I hated the dark. There was a vulnerability in darkness that asked me to trust in the unknown.

Which was why, in the present moment, I stood frozen in the middle of my campus quad.

One by one, the lampposts surrounding the quad flickered and exploded, starting with those farthest from me. In an almost controlled synchronicity, the darkness advanced on me.

Students and faculty crossing campus screamed as the light was violently snuffed out. Glass shattered and electricity popped. An odd emerald-colored current seemed to arc from each point of explosion, and an ominous feeling began to settle within me.

This was no ordinary occurrence. This was magic, and like the tattoo parlor, it was not friendly.

My palms, as if responding to the danger, tingled in waves, anticipation reverberating throughout my body. I hyper-focused on the lamppost closest to me on my left as it flickered. Concentrating my energy toward it, I willed it to stay on. As people continued to shriek and dodge falling glass, I focused on the anger within me of students and faculty being harmed by unfriendly magic.

At my efforts, my magic warmed my body, and I felt as if a rusty engine was slowly starting. My body began to vibrate with the exertion. Perfecting magic took years of constant training. I was at a disadvantage.

The lamppost I had been focusing on shattered the loudest, as if mocking my efforts, and then fear overtook my body like a light switch as glass rained down over me. My hands instinctively came up over my head to try and protect me from the falling debris.

I was no good at magic. I couldn't keep myself or those around me safe.

I surveyed the quad, and some people were huddled on the ground while cries rose up in the air. We needed law enforcement and medical services in case anyone was injured. But my CommsPad battery had died, so I couldn't make calls.

In the distance, I saw a blue-lit emergency phone booth connected to campus law enforcement.

I ran toward the beacon of blue light, my lungs burning from exertion.

When I touched the phone booth, magic surged from my center like a thousand exposed electrical wires and poured from my hands, killing the electricity. I gaped at my hands as they buzzed with the remnants of the current. My magic was no better than whatever dark energy was sharing the quad space.

Unfortunately, this wasn't the first time something like this had happened today. I was an electrical hazard from the moment I woke up. I had shattered four light bulbs in my apartment by merely touching the light switch. The same happened at my lecture hall when I was setting up before class. My touch had killed all lights in the lecture hall, and I had to teach my class in darkness, with the projector as the only source of light, which I had to have a student help me set up.

With the loss of the blue light, darkness blanketed the quad, and I froze in fear like I did so many times as a child. I guided myself down to the ground, brought back to the memories of sitting in the closet, frightened, tears streaming down my face. I squeezed my eyes shut and covered my ears. My inner child reminded me that nowhere was safe.

As I tried to muffle my breathing, the sound of my heartbeat filled my ears. I curled into myself, making myself as small as possible in case the dark energy decided to attack people.

I could feel smoke surround me, and it began to morph into a solid, living, breathing thing. It enveloped me, sniffing, circling, and pushing into me as if trying to identify what I was. Its presence was like a heavy velvet veil.

I wrapped my arms tighter around myself and squeezed my eyes shut.

"Renna..." the darkness whispered.

My heart dropped into my stomach, and I wanted to scream. "Don't hurt me," I pleaded. "*Please.*"

In the distance, students and faculty began to call out for each other in the dark.

"Call out if you need help!" a female called out.

Fear kept me silent. If I screamed for help, would the darkness hurt me?

"Renna..." The darkness continued as it circled me.

"Does anyone else need help?" a male nearby called out.

I wanted to cry out, but instead, I whimpered in fear as the darkness continued to hover over me.

"Why are you doing this?" I asked the darkness.

At my question, the darkness shifted away from my body.

"Is there anyone there?" a second male nearby called out.

Suddenly, the darkness lifted from the ground and violently dissipated into the sky like a dark cloud, quickly spiriting away. The quad was now full of medical care teams escorting people away.

A nearby male student approached me, extending his hand to help me stand.

"Are you alright?" he asked.

I nodded and remained on the ground, my hand on my chest, feeling my heart gallop. "I need a minute."

"Take your time," he said, crouching down to my level and roaming his eyes over me. "Your bicep is cut and bleeding and looks bruised. It's a surface cut, nothing serious. Do you need me to help you stand?"

I looked down at my bicep, and seeing the blood running down to my elbow, I became queasy. It brought to mind another injury—when I had hurt my legs while training with magic. I still had scars.

"You don't look so well," the student said. "Let me go get someone to help."

Left alone, I looked around at the remaining chaos. A cleaning crew had already descended, and I could hear sirens slowly approaching in the distance.

The back of my neck prickled as if a hundred needles poked my skin, and I gasped. The only other time I'd felt that was when someone with magical powers watched me. I turned to find the offender, and Aramis's gaze met mine from across the quad.

He stood with his arms crossed and brows gathered, looking at me while he spoke with law enforcement. His look dripped with judgment, and I flinched under his gaze.

When more law enforcement approached him and he broke his stare, I pushed myself to stand, my body still protesting from shock and the cut on my arm. Without waiting another second, I made my way to my apartment.

~

AFTER CLEANING my cut with shaking hands and applying bandages on my arm as best as I could, I curled up in bed, my body shivering from shock. The darkness, or something in it, had spoken to me, and I was terrified.

Unbidden, my mind recalled when I first remembered accessing and using my magic. My foster mother had brought the usual company to our temporary apartment: drunk men who yelled and threw bottles when angry. I hated their presence as it added more chaos to my turbulent life. When my foster mother had company over, I would try to dilute her guests' drinks with water to lessen the effects of the alcohol. Sometimes they wouldn't notice, but other times . . . it wasn't good to get caught. The bruises on my arms were evidence of their cruelty. My foster mother would remain mute toward the abuse hurled at me. I despised her.

One day, my mother was being yelled at by a man in our apartment over some goods she had failed to distribute. My six-year-old brain couldn't fully understand their conversation, but I knew my foster mother had upset the man in our living room. I closed my eyes as he came toward her, open hand in the air, and my shoulders shook when he slapped her. Despite her cruelty toward me, I hated the violence around me. I curled my small hand into fists, my nails digging into my already sweaty palms. Bottles broke, and my shoulders shook again.

"Go away, go away, go away," I whispered, rocking my body under the dining room table.

It was too late to run to my room.

"What did you say, little shit?" the man suddenly asked, and I willed my eyes open.

The man was staring at me, broken glass in hand.

When I repeated my words, he charged at me.

He was going to hit me with the broken glass.

My foster mother paled when the man swung at me.

In that moment, I realized no one was coming to save me. I was alone in the world. Anger and resentment took over, and mustering all the strength I had in my small body, I took in a deep breath and screamed.

My scream started something inside me, a small spark of what felt like electricity, and within seconds, energy began to furiously spew from my body, tunneling my vision so I could only see the man in front of me.

The broken bottle in his hand shattered, and the lightbulbs in our apartment exploded, shrouding us in darkness. Curses filled the room, and my mother yelled as people tripped over furniture.

And then stillness.

Had I caused all of that?

I had woken sometime later in my bed with a strange man looking down at me. He was sitting at my bedside dressed in a heavy black coat and a black felt fedora. He looked wealthy and lacked the dingy look and smell of my foster mother's usual companions. A gold ring adorned his pinkie finger, engraved with a serpent.

I was ashamed of my dirty appearance—we had run out of body soap last week—and my clothes were too big for my body. His appraisal of me was indifferent, as if my state was inconsequential. I shrunk onto my bed in shame.

The first thing he had said to me was how proud he was that I caused pain to my foster mother's visitor. I had caused the man's eardrums to explode with the *energy* I created. I thought the man in black was a hero—was I being saved after all?

When I flung my arms around him, clinging to the notion of being rescued, the man shoved me off like a dirty dog. He pointed at me, admonishing me for thinking he was good. He informed me no one was coming to save me. I was to remain at my foster mother's home until he deemed it necessary. He told me suffering, anger, and hatred were necessary to create magic and become the person I was meant to be. What that future was, he never shared. I had never heard of energy or magic.

And so began my daily torment by the man in black. The man had no name and preferred to be called my mentor. He would spend the next twelve years trying to force magic from me by any means necessary. I quickly learned he meant to train me to wield energy to hurt others.

As I grew from child to teenager, I would fight back with words and occasionally try to hit him in return. My bouts of rage would simply amuse my mentor. He relished in my anger, and I hated myself for what I was becoming and the dark magic he forced from me.

His torment escalated to physical abuse, which was evidenced by the long scars I had on my legs. They resulted from my mentor wanting to provoke my anger and magic by dropping me from a two-story building. The exercise was meant to force me to brace my landing with magic, but fear overtook me, and I was unable to call forth any magic. My mentor must have taken pity on me because he braced my fall, but I still cut my legs on shattered glass.

One time, he stalked me in my foster mother's apartment, trying to push me into corners, his large face looming over mine, provoking me to fight back. When I told him to leave, he slapped me in the face, and I fell back onto a couch. He was on top of me in a second, hands at my neck, screaming that without him, I was nothing.

I learned very quickly to never speak back to him. It never ended well for me.

One of my mentor's goals was to teach me to summon light with my palms. He would lock me in a dark closet and demand I figure out a way to create light. I knew anger and hatred would aid me in harnessing the energy inside me, but the fear would overtake me every time. I was young and scared. The closet exercises did nothing but traumatize me. I would beg to be let out, but no matter how much I kicked the door and pounded with my fists, my cries meant nothing to him.

I never managed to create light from my palms. At times I believed he pushed me because he cared for me and wanted me to be protected. Other times I knew he got sick satisfaction from seeing me suffer. So, in those moments of total darkness, I learned to freeze and internalize my emotions. If I didn't move, if I went inside myself, the dark would eventually pass, and he would leave the house, screaming about me being useless.

CLASSES WERE CANCELED for the next two days as law enforcement and representatives of the Council swarmed our campus to investigate the quad incident. Students were on edge, and more than once, *magic* and *supernatural* were whispered by students and faculty.

I didn't leave my apartment, and I kept every light on and closet door open. Every noise startled me, and my paranoia grew by the hour. Helena called my CommsPad asking to see me, but I made the excuse that I needed to pack for my trip. I couldn't let her see the mess I had turned into. I had gotten little sleep in the last few days since I didn't feel safe closing my eyes.

I knew I would inevitably need to leave my apartment to teach my last week of classes before summer break, but I dreaded going back because my classes were in the evening, and campus streets were emptier then. Would I experience another attack? Would the darkness seek me again?

As dusk settled outside my window, I sighed at what would likely be another long night.

5

RENNA

At some point, I had fallen asleep, but stillness woke me up.

My studio was located on a busy street, and the sounds of traffic always filled the night. The unnatural quiet was unsettling and began to create pressure in my ears, as if my head would explode.

I shot up in bed, and the room was pitch black.

And then . . . stars.

As if a supernova had ripped off the roof of my apartment, millions of stars hovered above me, all dancing in the cosmos, their beautiful colors a majesty to behold, casting away the darkness. My skin was bathed in millions of luminescent colors, shimmering like the stars themselves.

I covered my mouth in awe. Reaching up a hand, I moved it through glittering clouds of stardust.

And then, I saw *him*—a figure draped in a cloak made of stars. He stood on the left side of my bed, his back to the windows lining the street. From the figure's stature and posture, I could tell it was a male. His body was angled to my bed, as if he looked at me silently.

Although his hood hid his face, I could unequivocally feel that, somehow, every fiber in my body knew who he was. I didn't feel any fear.

"Do you like it?" the figure said, gesturing to the heavens.

His voice was deep, sending shivers of recognition down my spine. He moved from me and stopped at the foot of my bed.

I turned my eyes up to the skies as a beautiful meteor shower descended into the room, the stars softly twinkling and disappearing in a glittering mist before touching my skin. I reached out, turning my hand this way and that to try and catch some of the falling stars.

"Yes," I breathed.

How could anyone not like such beauty?

Although I couldn't see his face, I could almost feel the figure smile at my response as if pleased with himself.

"You brought me the stars," I heard myself say.

"I promised you I would," he responded. "Are you happy to see me?" he asked, his tone unsure.

My mind tingled with the vibration of his voice, rolling off my body in delicious shivers. My heart felt as if I was seeing a close friend or relative who had passed away and was visiting me in a dream, filling me with warm melancholy. Silent tears I didn't understand began to spill down my cheeks.

My body was not my own for the moment as another foreign part of me took over. My vocal cords responded to him on their own.

"I will always be happy to see you," I said, and my lips curved into a smile.

"Come back to me," he whispered, his voice almost a silent plea.

My arm reached for him, as if something ancient within me recognized I would go anywhere with him.

And just as I was about to ask him to take me away, my

CommsPad went off. I looked at my nightstand where it sat, and Helena's face appeared on the screen, requesting a call.

At the reminder of reality, the events of the last two days crashed into me, and the scene before me began to disappear into a black vortex. Everything was gone in the blink of an eye—the stars, the cosmos, everything—as if it had never happened. The only evidence of his existence was faint emerald sparks where he had stood.

At his departure, a feeling of mourning hit my body, and overwhelming grief consumed me. I began to sob uncontrollably, gasping for air as I struggled to breathe. Stabbing pain shot through my heart, and I writhed, feeling like something I loved and cherished was ripped from me, leaving me empty.

Seconds later, I rushed to the bathroom, slamming the door behind me, and proceeded to empty the contents of my stomach.

My mind was numb following my visitor's appearance. He had a life-altering impact on my psyche and emotions as my body felt a deep sense of loss, which I couldn't understand. I searched every corner of my small studio and stood on a chair to touch the roof, wondering how I could have envisioned what I had seen. Endlessly, I stared at the place where he had disappeared as hours passed. I couldn't eat. I couldn't sleep. The dream felt too real for me to simply forget . . . much like the dream at the tattoo parlor. Both dreams and the attack on the quad challenged my reality, and I was left with a gaping hole of uncertainty in my chest as I tried to find an explanation for what I was experiencing.

"Have you eaten today?" Helena asked.

She had visited my lecture class and was now waiting for me

as I packed up. Students were trickling into the hall while I gathered final student exams.

I looked toward my second cup of coffee sitting on my desk.

"I haven't had time," I said, trying to brush her off while my eyes burned from lack of sleep.

Some sleep theories hypothesized that people dreamed things they saw in everyday life or that they manifested subconscious themes that caused a big impact. I could not have possibly dreamed up an entire galaxy in my apartment with a meteor shower and a hooded man asking me if it was okay to visit me out of thin air. I hadn't read any books or seen any films with a remotely similar scenario to inspire that. I also knew that during the dream, some part of me took over, a deeply buried part of me that recognized the figure as someone familiar and dear to me, someone I deeply loved . . . and lost.

Helena stood in front of me as I gathered the papers and stuffed them in my bag.

"Something is going on, and I don't like it," she said, hands on her hips. "Ever since we got tattoos, it's like your mind has been off somewhere—"

My hands froze, and I dropped the papers I was holding. She was right. After I got my tattoo, nothing seemed the same.

Helena cursed and bent down to help me. She sighed. "Ren, you are my friend, and I love you, but I can't force you to tell me what's going on. I just ask that you please not make yourself sick," she pleaded. "Your trip to Xhor is coming up, and you look tired and malnourished."

"I've just had a lot on my mind."

Footsteps sounded just outside the lecture hall's exit.

"Miss Strongborn?" A familiar male voice called my name.

It was Aramis.

6
RENNA

My stomach dove as I heard Aramis's voice, and I closed my eyes for a brief second to collect myself. I knew he wanted to speak with me about the quad incident. How could he not? The judgment on his face that night was clear.

I turned to find him leaning against the doorframe of my classroom, arms crossed and brows furrowed like they had been that night on the quad.

"Yes, Mr. Aramis?" I responded, slinging my portfolio bag around my shoulder.

"I'd like a word." He moved to the side and gestured for me to follow him out to the hallway. When Helena began to follow as well, he looked to her. "I'd like a word with Miss Strongborn, *alone.*"

Helena groaned in annoyance under her breath and grabbed my hand. "I'll call you later today?"

I nodded. "Yeah, that's fine."

"Please eat something," she warned quietly. "I'm going to keep bugging you until you look like you have some color in your cheeks."

I grumbled a yes as Helena left the lecture hall.

I looked to Aramis. "What can I help you with, Mr. Aramis?"

"We need to speak in my office."

I nodded and followed him into the hallway.

"Did you have a good semester?" he asked as we walked toward the stairs that led up to the faculty offices.

"I did . . ."

I hated when people drew out conversations, taking the long way to get to the actual point.

"Great." His voice was clipped, and a long, awkward silence stretched between us as we walked. "And your arm?" He cocked his head to my bandage, and I touched it on instinct.

"Arm is fine. More bruised than anything."

"A souvenir from the quad?"

"Yes."

"Other students were not so lucky. A faculty member just returned from a two-night stay in hospital to recover from a broken leg."

"Oh."

Anger began to course within me at my inability to use magic effectively to prevent some of the chaos. I balled my hand into a fist, my nails digging into my palm as I clenched my jaw to hold my composure.

When we got to his office, Aramis closed the door behind us. "Please take a seat, Miss Strongborn."

"Renna is fine," I said, sitting.

"Renna, then." He sighed as he sat behind his desk.

He leaned back in his chair and simply gazed at me.

Growing uncomfortable, I shifted a few times until I had enough. "What do you wish to discuss?"

"What happened that night?" he asked.

I shrugged. "I was on the quad like any other person. I was coming back from the library and—"

"I thought the incident in my office the first day I met you was inconsequential. It reeked of a person inexperienced with magic. It was erratic."

He knew. I swallowed hard and played with my bag's strap.

"Well? Did you have anything to do with what happened on the quad?"

My mouth popped open with the accusation. "No!"

"And the magic you used?"

"My magic responds to anger and is difficult to control in any other emotional state."

"Miss Strongborn—*Renna*, you have put me in a difficult position. You caught the attention of several people." My eyes widened, and he cleared his throat. "A few students and faculty who were present on the quad reported a young woman likely used magic to cause the chaos that night. I have tried to convince the Council the incident was a mere electrical outage, but they won't budge."

I began to sweat, and my heart sped up. "I was only trying to help. The lampposts were exploding, people were getting hurt, and I tried to keep one of the lampposts on—"

"Do you know what happens to people who use magic on Andora, Renna?"

My pulse pounded in my ears. "Yes." I dried my sweaty palms on my pants. "They . . . they get reprogrammed."

"And why is that?" He cocked his head.

I took a breath. "Andora believes science should be the only truth. Magic and supernatural can tempt people into spiritual beliefs."

Aramis nodded. "And you know spirituality is banned." He lowered his nose to look up at me. "The Council has made it clear spirituality would lead to religions, *yes*?"

I hated the way he spoke to me like I was stupid.

"Yes." I nodded. "The Council has banned religions. *I know*."

My emotions spilled from me then like a snowball. "What was I supposed to do—"

"*Nothing!* It's too risky." He sat back and began massaging his temples. "Representatives from the Council are currently going through student bio photos to match the description. Your face has been selected as one of the candidates to interview."

I wanted to sink to the floor and be devoured by the floor tiles. "This can't be happening."

"Renna." He crossed his arms. "I won't lie to you. The Council already has their eyes on campus after an incident at a tattoo parlor on the outskirts of town. A few people reported strange occurrences—lights shattering, a strong force-like wind entering the shop, a frenzy of people leaving in fear. I tried to quash the reports as much as I could because the media likes me. This situation on the quad, however, is too big to contain. There were way more witnesses to what happened two nights ago."

I thought about the voice in the darkness and how it called out my name. "Did witnesses name anyone specifically?"

"No," he said. "They only gave general descriptions. An average height female, medium-tone skin, brunette, wavy hair." He then stopped and narrowed his eyes at me. "Why? Did you see anyone you know or tell anyone you used magic?"

"No."

"Then you have nothing to worry—"

"The darkness spoke to me."

Aramis froze and lowered his chin as if to process what I was saying. "What do you mean it *spoke to you*?"

"When the quad was encased in darkness, something in the dark spoke to me."

"Like a person—"

"No. Whatever magic attacked the campus took a physical form of some kind and approached me. It spoke to me."

"Fuck!" Aramis stood and began to pace. "This is not good. What did it say? What did it want?"

I shook my head as tears welled in my eyes. "I-I don't know what it wanted. It kept calling my name specifically. Like it was searching for me. I could feel its body hover against mine." I shivered. "I froze, I couldn't move, I-I—"

Aramis came to my side and sat in the chair next to me. "Renna," he spoke quickly. "Listen to me very carefully." He handed me a handkerchief.

Looking up, I took his handkerchief and wiped my eyes.

"I wanted to help," I whispered. "I swear to you!"

He nodded and leaned in, lowering his voice. "The last two days I have been in contact with a colleague who lives near Xhor to discuss the situation with the Council. He practices magic and understands the gravity of this situation. He wants to help. We agreed that I cannot protect you from the Council's jurisdiction here. Now, with this latest news"—he shook his head—"that the darkness *spoke* to you . . ." He shifted in his seat uncomfortably. "Renna, I have to be honest. It's not normal for an attack of that magnitude to focus on a sole person."

Blood drained from my face. "What do you mean?"

He straightened in his seat. "I need to make a phone call. Can you please wait here while I go into the other room?" He pointed to the rear den portion of his office with a couch and a small library.

I nodded and watched as Aramis left.

My CommsPad vibrated inside my bag on my lap. I pulled it out and found a message from Helena asking if I was all right after she left me with Aramis. As I began to type out a reply, Aramis walked back. His face was pale, and he looked at me as if he had seen a ghost.

"Mr. Aramis?" I asked, rising from my seat and taking a step toward him.

He put a finger up to silence me, with a furrowed brow and large pupils. Before I could ask any other questions, he shifted his eyes to the office door.

The door handle moved, and when the door swung open, a man stood in the middle of the doorway. A long black cape was pushed back behind him and extended to the floor. A black shirt draped his torso, and leather pants with knee-high boots adorned his lower body. A silver dagger sat sheathed at his waist. His clothing resembled what some of the elders of the Council wore, except that this man wore all black, unlike the all-white attire the Council fashioned themselves with. His closely shaved hair accentuated his sharp jaw, and his unusual amber eyes contrasted beautifully with his dark honey-colored skin.

He was gorgeous, and I couldn't look away as he closed the door behind him. My face grew hot, and I inhaled sharply.

The stranger turned his attention to me. His mouth opened slightly as he searched my face, moving from my eyes, nose, lips, and then his assessment moved to my hair draped over one shoulder. His eyes lingered there for a moment before roaming the rest of my body.

"Renna," the man said breathlessly.

I looked to Aramis, confused. "Uh—"

Aramis nodded and stuttered as he tried to find words. "Khel," Aramis said, stepping toward the man with an outstretched hand, but Khel still had his gaze locked on me.

I shifted my weight between my feet as Aramis continued. "I had not expected you to arrive so quickly—"

"Introduce me," Khel said to Aramis, his eyes never leaving mine.

"Ah, yes!" Aramis shook his head. "Pardon my manners." He turned to me. "Miss Strongborn," he said, gesturing to me. "Please meet Khellios. He is the colleague I spoke about." He turned his face toward his friend. "Khel, meet Miss Strongborn."

Khellios stepped toward me, his brows furrowed. "Apologies." He bowed his head once in greeting. The gesture was very old fashioned. "Aramis had mentioned your first name on the phone twice. I should have addressed you as Miss Strongborn."

"Renna is fine . . ." I said carefully and looked to both men. "Can someone explain to me what is going on?"

"As we were discussing a few minutes ago, I cannot effectively shelter you from the reach of the Council while you remain on this campus. Now"—Aramis looked to Khellios and back to me—"with this latest development—"

"It spoke to you?" Khellios asked.

I nodded. "It said my name several times as if it was seeking me. I could feel it take physical form." My body shivered.

Khellios turned to Aramis. "She cannot stay here."

Aramis laughed nervously. "Yes, I was beginning to explain that to her before you arrived—"

"Put her studies on hold," he ordered sharply.

"*What*?!" I yelled to Khellios. The anger within me began to rise, and my magic reacted, as if it was peeking its head up, curious. "Excuse me. Do not speak about me as if I am not here."

Aramis opened his mouth to speak, but I sharply cut him off. My attention was still on Khellios. "I've never met you before, and you barge in and decide to take control of my life? I don't think so."

"Miss Strongborn, Khel is only trying to help," Aramis tried to interfere again.

I put my finger up to silence him. "One of you better explain what is going on because I am losing patience *very* quickly."

Khellios crossed his arms. "You are in danger—"

"I gathered as much, *thanks*," I snapped. "The Council seems like a *great* group of men, and whatever was on the quad with me didn't seem friendly either."

"Fuck the Council," Khellios growled. "They can be dealt

with. The real danger here is the entity that attacked campus. That is why I am here." He crossed his arms. "You cannot stay on campus. The entity *will* attack again."

My heart stopped. "Do you know what it is?"

"Suffice it to say that for now, the entity is a god, as old as the universe itself. None say his name for doing so is like speaking a curse."

"Why is it after me, and how would it know my name?"

"The entity is weak and is looking to strengthen its power by using whoever wields his brand of magic. Aramis mentioned you used magic recently?"

Pressure began to build in my chest, and I had to remember to breathe. "It wasn't intentional! And my magic is minimal at best. I avoid it at all costs. Whenever I try to use it for something good when I'm not angry, my magic feels like it's trapped within me. It will not respond effectively, and it either becomes volatile as I fight to try and use it for something good, or it does not respond at all and remains mute inside me."

Aramis turned to Khellios with a curious look before speaking. "Renna, when we first met in my office, the magic you used was a result of your anger at the college changes, correct?"

"Yes. My magic only responds to anger," I reminded him.

Khellios stepped up closer to me and lowered his voice. "The god who attacked campus and the outskirts of town wields a unique type of magic," Khellios began. "His magic is some of the darkest magic known to exist. It's also only activated through anger." Khellios did not miss when I flinched, but he continued, his eyes quietly assessing me. "It is rare for magic to *only* respond to anger."

"Why is it rare?"

"Well, one can either be born with magic or learn magic. If you are born with magic, it flows from you without thinking and is as easy to wield as breathing. If you are born with magic and later learn it, you usually learn a set of skills, like spells, to wield it. It is unusual for a person to be born with magic and for it to be dormant in the body until strong emotions activate it."

Dormant. That was the perfect way to describe what my magic did when feelings of anger vanished. I could not find it or call it unless I was angry. When I tried to force it from my body like moments on the quad, it became chaotic and painful. I could not command it to do what I wanted it to do.

"What does he want with me?" I thought of my mentor. His magic had also only responded to anger. "I can't be unique. There must be other people whose magic is also only linked to anger."

"Your recent use of magic likely tracked him to you. He must have learned everything about you—including your name." Khellios averted his eyes from me. "The uniqueness of your magic and his links you to him. You are not safe. He wants your magic. His attack is him hunting for you. Attacking you and calling you by name is a direct provocation."

I buried my head in my hands as I processed everything. My fingers and the rest of my body were frigid as my heart began to beat irregularly, my breaths sawing in and out of me. I was going into shock.

"Renna," Aramis said, sitting next to me. "As head of your college, I want to see you complete your studies, but not at the expense of your safety. The Council investigations and now this latest development puts you and the rest of the students and faculty on this campus at risk."

I looked up. "What are you saying?"

"The colleague I was speaking to you about earlier who lives near Xhor is Khel." He gestured to his friend. "He lives in a secure location that is a safe haven for people with magical abilities. The location, known as *Taria*, is shielded by magic in a dimension of its own to protect people from the Council and beings who wield dark magic—like this entity."

The idea of being around many people who practiced magic triggered my flight-or-fight response. "I want nothing to do with magic. I refuse to go to a place where I will be surrounded by it every waking moment. Look at what it's brought me." I spread my arms, indicating the events that have unfolded.

Khellios tried to cut in, but I didn't let him. "I walked away from everything that represents magic in my life. Before Aramis arrived on campus, I hadn't used magic for *seven years*. It was a conscious effort to quell it within me *every time* I felt triggered."

"You cannot stay here," Khellios said, crossing his arms.

"That's fine." I lifted my chin and crossed my arms. "I will go to Xhor. The entity won't find me on our satellite campus there."

He shook his head. "It doesn't matter *where* in this galaxy you are, he *will* find you. He would not have called you by name if he was not interested in you. For that reason alone, you need to stay in Taria where we can protect you."

When my mentor died, I thought his presence in my life would eventually become a small blip in my memory. But the skills he had taught me now put me in direct danger.

I felt like I was rapidly losing control of the direction of a life I had very intentionally crafted for myself.

Aramis spoke. "Renna, I realize how sudden this is, but we are only looking out for your safety. You should take Khellios's offer of shelter." When I didn't respond, he asked, "What is going through your mind?"

I looked to Khellios, who stood with a sour expression, plainly judging me, like I was an ungrateful child for not taking his help. "I'm not ungrateful for what you're offering."

"Then take my help," he snapped.

"It's not that simple to leave everything I've known for the past seven years and just go off *with you*!" I scoffed. "I just learned that who I am is a hazard. Not to mention, I also just met you."

Khellios pinched the bridge of his nose. "Take my help."

"Can you not see how difficult this is to process? It's too much," I snapped.

"Why are you being so difficult?" he yelled and looked up to the heavens. He shook his head. "It doesn't matter either way. You are coming with me."

"Then why make it seem like I have a choice?" I yelled back.

"*Because,*" he gritted out, "I am trying to be polite. I want you to go willingly."

"This is your definition of polite?"

"You are making it *very difficult* to be polite."

"And you cannot see how this situation is affecting me right now?"

Khellios cursed and turned from me.

"Renna," Aramis said gently. "Sometimes we cannot control the circumstances set before us. You know that going to Taria is the right choice. I sense this hesitation may be about losing control of this rapidly spiraling situation."

And there it was. The theme of my life: control. I could not control the things that happened to me as a child, so I strived to control everything around me as an adult.

He continued. "It may seem like we are taking control of a very scary and unprecedented situation, but that is far from it. By making the conscious choice to accept help, you are not relinquishing control. In fact, you are taking it."

"Thank you for saying that," I said quietly. When Khellios muttered under his breath and rolled his eyes, I added, "Thank you, Aramis, for saying that *politely.*"

Khellios wound around to look at me and put his hands on his hips. He chuckled bitterly. "You are not what I expected."

"What's that supposed to mean?"

Khellios paused before answering. "It doesn't matter."

"Excuse me?" I fired back. "If you are going to insult me, at least be honest about it."

"I thought PhD students had some intelligence. It's like you refuse to take the path that clearly leads you to safety to spite me."

My jaw dropped, and I saw red. "To spite *you*?" I laughed. "Because this situation clearly is about you, right? I may have issues with control, but what about you?"

"What about me?" he snapped.

"Renna, Khellios," Aramis said suddenly. "There is no need for personal attacks. Let us all take a few moments to look at the bigger picture. *Renna*," he said, "you need to get to a place of safety. Khellios is offering you that. And *Khellios*." He turned to his friend. "I understand your need to protect Renna," he added and then very quickly said, "because you do not want to see anyone hurt, but she needs time to process all of this. Renna is a very smart woman and knows the risks."

Khellios glared at me, and I rolled my eyes.

Aramis spoke once more. "Renna, Khellios will remain on campus tonight on watch. While he may be able to offer some protection to our campus tonight because this entity is weak, Khellios cannot ensure our safety on a long-term basis. I encourage you to go home, rest, and think about what Khellios is offering. He does not want to take you with him to Taria against your will, and I would not allow you to be removed from here in that matter."

I bit my cheek and nodded.

Khellios stood with arms crossed as Aramis walked me to his office door and escorted me out.

"I hope to hear from you tomorrow, Renna," Aramis said. "We only want what is best for you."

I smiled politely and walked back to my apartment. My

thoughts were chaotic, and I couldn't make sense of everything I'd just learned.

I didn't even notice I had arrived at my building until I walked into the lobby. Inside my studio, I sank down in bed and closed my eyes, begging for sleep to quiet my mind. It was the afternoon, and my brain was still running a mile a minute from my conversation with Aramis and Khellios. I forced my mind to think about something pleasant, and my mind drifted to the man I had dreamed of the night before. Recalling his presence brought me comfort.

I KNEW I was no longer in my apartment when I shifted in sleep because a soft wind blew against my skin. While my studio had floor-to-ceiling windows, they didn't open.

I kept my eyes closed to assess where I was . . . and I felt warm sand under my fingers. You weren't supposed to feel in dreams, right? Wasn't that one universal rule or something— that no matter what you dreamed, they weren't supposed to elicit feelings of physical touch?

I ran my hand through the sand again.

This felt *real*.

My eyes shot open, and a vast night sky stretched out before me.

I sat up immediately, disoriented.

I was at a riverbank among tall, beautiful reeds that swayed gently in a night breeze. The water before me, crystalline, moved in ripples, reflecting the majestic starlit sky in all its glory. The sky was reminiscent of my previous dream, and my heart sped up as my eyes searched for *him*.

"These stars have long ceased to exist. They are a memory," a familiar, deep voice said into the night.

It was *him*. The man from my dream.

My heart thundered in my chest, and I was afraid he could hear the effect he had on me. Hearing his voice meant this was another dream, and I was disappointed it wasn't reality.

A black cloak shrouded his body once more, but this time I could see his figure outlined more clearly. He had to be about six feet tall, and although he faced the water, keeping me from seeing his face, I could only imagine what he truly looked like given how beautiful his voice was.

"Where am I?" I asked, not wanting to move for fear of waking up.

I wanted to stay in his presence as long as I could to ask him who he was and why I was dreaming of him twice in a row. I never remembered my dreams, but now I was paying attention.

Dreaming about someone twice in a row meant something, right?

"You are asleep in your apartment. This is a dream. You are safe," he said, looking up at the stars.

I sighed in relief. His mention of safety made my throat close up with emotions, and tears threatened to spill as I recalled my conversation with Aramis. "Safety has been a big topic for me today."

"I'm sorry. Please believe me when I say you are safe here."

I hugged my arms around myself. "Why am I dreaming about you? Have we met before?"

"Do you think we have met before?" he said, his voice lilting with amusement.

I thought about my first dream with him. There was something deeply familiar about him that I couldn't pinpoint. "I'm not sure. Part of me thinks I know you in a way, but I can't remember from where or when."

When he didn't respond, I probed further. "Who are you?"

"I am the soul created for you from the beginning of time—"

"So like a . . . spirit guide?" I furrowed my brows.

He cocked his head and paused. "All souls have a . . . comple-ment. And those souls who are *designed* for each other guard each other in every lifetime."

With how slowly he spoke, it was as though he was picking his words carefully, intentionally.

"I am your soul's guardian, sworn to keep you safe."

"Are you an angel?" I asked.

I had never encountered one before, but I knew they guarded humans.

He turned from me and walked to the body of water. "I am not an angel because angels do not practice magic."

He began to hover his palms above the water, and soft green electricity emerged from his palms, the electrical bolts moving in slow motion as he controlled the energy in his palms.

"Does everyone have a guardian?"

As the water responded to the energy emanating from his hands, my own palms began to tingle, and shocks of electric energy began to course down my arms.

"Every soul has another who watches over them. However, I am not privy to the lives of others."

"How are you in my dream?"

"Our bond allows me to visit you via dreams." As he spoke, he moved his hands clockwise once, and the water responded, rippling outward.

I felt no fear from his magic, which was . . . refreshing. I had only ever been exposed to my mentor's magic, and he had trau-matized me, and then more recently in Aramis's office from Galene, which had only angered me as she had no right to use magic so invasively against me.

I inched a bit closer to get a better look at how he was manipulating the energy.

"How do I know you do not mean to harm me?" I asked as colors flashed in the water.

"If I wanted to harm you, I would have done so the first night I came to you."

The water began to rapidly spiral down into a blackened vortex. Swirls of red and deep green shimmered in the water. It was frightening and mesmerizing at the same time.

"You could harm me now." I crossed my arms.

I recalled the first night I had met my mentor and the relief I felt thinking a savior had come to take me from the abusive clutches of my foster mother, only to endure more abuse and harm. Trusting new people was difficult, but at least I knew his magic did not instill fear in me . . . yet.

"I could." He nodded. "That would defeat the purpose of my role as your soul's guardian."

Living under my mentor's shadow made me wary of someone claiming to give enough fucks to protect me.

I stepped up to him. "If you are my guardian, where have you been?"

His hands stopped, and he turned to fully face me. The water that had been active seconds ago was now still and clear.

I put my hands up and shrugged. "Where have you been all these years?"

"Renna—"

I shook my head. "I have needed someone by my side to protect me so many times."

My mind flashed to my mentor slamming my face against a wall because I spoke back to him.

I flinched at the memory.

"You decide to come into my life *now*?"

"I never meant—"

"You never meant *what*?" I lifted my chin. "The word guardian represents someone who *guards* and *protects*. I was on my own for so many years. *Now* is a good time for you to finally show up?"

"I never meant to leave you unprotected."

"Where were you?"

"Trying to find you."

His words made no sense. "If our souls have been bound from the beginning of time, you would have known where I was from the day I was born. I was left outside of an orphanage." My voice was bitter. Angry. The magic inside me began to swirl. I hated feeling like I was at someone's mercy. "I was then transferred into the foster system. I was alone. *For years.*" I blinked back angry tears. "So don't ask me to trust someone who claims it is their duty to protect me when *you failed* to do so." I turned from him before a traitorous tear escaped from my eyes.

"Renna," he began. "I searched for you. For years. It is your mentor who kept me from you. His magic shielded you from me."

My heartbeat slowed, and my blood pumped loudly in my ears. "*What?*" My voice broke, and I faced him.

There was no way anyone could know about my past. My foster mother, the only person who knew, had died shortly after my mentor.

"What did you say?" I stepped up to him.

"Your mentor," he gritted out, his fists curled. "I know what he did to you. His magic prevented me from getting close to you."

"He died seven years ago."

"I know."

"*You know?*" I laughed bitterly. "Where have you been since?"

"I guarded you for the last seven years from a distance. I've made sure you stayed safe."

I crossed my arms. "How?" I narrowed my eyes. "I have not felt your presence."

"Lotus flowers."

Bringing one hand to my mouth, I tried to stifle the gasp that escaped. My other hand immediately went to the lotus flower tattoo by my breast. Only Helena knew about it and its significance. The gravity of the truth in his claim left me speechless.

He stepped toward me, and I was frozen to the spot as tears built in my eyes.

"I have watched you and protected you and have sent you signs to help guide you for the last seven years. Every time you felt uncertain or needed guidance, I have been there. As is my duty."

As though sensing I needed further proof, he continued. "Two years ago, you were contemplating pursuing a doctorate in gender studies."

I drew in a sharp breath.

"You were unsure if the topic would be fulfilling though. One day, you saw an article about the ruins of Xhor posted on a bulletin board as you walked out of your archaeology class."

Blood began to pump loudly in my ears as my heart anticipated what he would say next.

"A lotus flower picture was pinned next to the article, and you declared your field of study the next morning. Then, the woman in the college office had a pen with a lotus flower glued to it."

I smiled through glassy eyes. "She said she glued it there because people tended to steal her pens."

He nodded.

"Why . . ." I wiped the silent tears falling on my cheeks. "Why have you not made yourself known until now?"

He was silent. "Because your need of me has changed. I am no longer merely providing guidance as to what field of study to choose from."

I covered my face with my hands and began to cry. I cried for the little girl inside me who was unprotected for so many years and feared for her life every day. I cried for a young woman who ventured off to university feeling alone even when she was with her best friend because she would never be able to be truthful about magic and the burden she carried. Lotus flowers were the one sign that was my anchor. Whenever I saw one, I felt like I was less alone in the world. Like maybe someone out there was truly watching over me.

It had been him all along. He had been the one guarding over me.

"Show me your face," I said quickly. "I have a right to see it. I have learned to have little trust in the dark and shadows."

"As you wish."

He brought his fingers up to his hood, and I took a deep breath as he pulled it back. Silver hair that almost seemed to glow was pulled back halfway in different braids. My eyes were next pulled to his slightly pointed ears, which were beautiful. But his gray-blue eyes captivated me as a strange magic lurked in them, making them glow dimly. He was young but seemed older than me.

As his eyes searched mine, my heart sped up and my face heated.

"Better?" he said, lifting his chin in challenge.

I nodded and pushed my hair behind my ear.

His eyes tracked the movement, and then he seemed to follow the blush spreading over my neck and face. He furrowed his brows and shook his head, clearing his throat.

"How do you feel?" he asked.

"In shock." My tears had stopped, but my breathing and heartbeat were still erratic, and my body tingled from the rush of emotions.

"You should sit down," he said gently.

My nod was jittery, and my body was tense as I lowered myself to the ground.

"It will be a while until your body regulates itself. You'll be okay."

Words were difficult.

"You have to know how sorry I am that I was unable to be by your side all those years." He shook his head. "You called me a failure, and that's how I feel. I failed you."

I tried to form words, but nothing was coming out. My diaphragm burned as I let in small, erratic breaths.

"Renna, you have to breathe deeply." He moved closer and kneeled in front of me, bringing his face level with mine. He looked into my eyes, his brows gathered. "Can you breathe with me?"

Returning his gaze, I was captivated by the icy magic dwelling there. As he walked me through a breathing exercise, I took in my first deep breath and was hit with his scent, which was a unique mix of sandalwood, bergamot, a soft warm vanilla, and fresh air during a clear night sky. It was wonderful, and I gasped at the surprise of it. After several breaths, I felt as if his scent enveloped my body and lulled me into a state of calm. My body sagged and grew sluggish as the aftermath of the shock settled deep into my bones.

"You must rest. You must leave this dreamtime place and sleep."

Panic rushed through me, and I shook my head. My chest painfully protested from the emotional whiplash of revelations tonight. I had so many questions for him about my magic and the attack on campus.

"No—" I scrambled to my knees. "Where will you go?"

"You will always have me in dreamtime."

I was crashing from the adrenaline rush, and exhaustion barreled into me.

"For now you must sleep," he whispered and waved a hand in front of my face.

Faint glimmers of emerald and black magic emerged from his palms, and before I knew it, I felt a cool pillow underneath me. In my subconscious, I questioned whether I had made it all up.

7

RENNA

My guardian appeared to me again, proving I hadn't made it all up. This time I found him sitting along a cliff edge, his profile outlining his sharp jaw and nose. He wore black leather trousers and a long-sleeved top, his cloak noticeably absent. His hair reached the middle of his back, and it glowed in the night as if his hair was made of the stars itself. He looked majestic, like a prince of the night, and I couldn't look away.

He didn't turn when I approached but simply stared off into the horizon.

"You're here" was the only thing I could come up with.

His lips curved to a smile. "Where else would I be?" He turned to me and looked up, his ice-blue-gray eyes sending my heartbeat into overdrive. He grinned lazily. "You've been staring at me for a few minutes without saying anything. It's quite rude."

My face reddened.

He cocked his head to the side and lifted an eyebrow. "Are you going to sit down?"

"Is this what you do for a living?" I brought my hands to my hips.

There was a familiarity and ease in being in his presence that I couldn't shake. I attributed the feeling to his explanation that he was assigned to guard my soul. Perhaps my soul recognized his role in my life.

"What?"

"Stalk people in their dreams and boss them around?"

He smirked and turned to face forward. "I could never boss you around." He grabbed a small rock and threw it off the cliff to an inconceivable distance. "You're too stubborn to boss around."

His words were refreshing after my confrontation with Khellios and his accusations I was difficult.

I sat down next to my guide. "I could be the most easygoing person you've ever met, and you wouldn't even know it."

He chuckled. "Well, are you?"

"I guess you'll have to find out." I shrugged. "I may kick you out of my dream, you know."

"Easygoing, huh?"

I narrowed my eyes to keep from smiling. "So, what now?"

He turned to face me and lifted an eyebrow.

"You're just going to hang around my subconscious until I need something?"

"Evidently." He shrugged and smirked.

Something about his expression had my stomach flipping.

I took a deep breath, shaking off the feeling, and grabbed a rock. I lobbed it to mimic his throw, but mine only traveled a few feet before free-falling. "What if I don't need anything tonight?"

He shrugged. "You could leave?"

"But this is my dream." I crossed my arms. "You leave."

I uncrossed my arms and threw another rock. My second attempt was just as pathetic as my first.

He leaned in and whispered exaggeratedly, "You have to use magic."

"I don't need magic."

"That's how I was able to throw my rock that far."

"Is this a rock-throwing contest?"

"No, it isn't a contest," he said, leaning back on his palms to survey the horizon with a smug look. "Because for it to be a contest, there would have to be competition."

My jaw dropped. *Oh, he had jokes.* "You would insult me in my own dream?" I bit my lip to keep from smiling.

"It's your call." He threw another rock. "I can't force you to use magic."

"Show off." I scoffed.

He chuckled. "Oh, you're *definitely* the most *easygoing* person I've ever met."

"Well, that's a relief to hear." I rolled my eyes, still keeping my smile at bay.

After a few seconds, I asked, "So, how does one's soul become bound to another? Seems like your job as a guardian is a pretty boring occupation. You just hang around waiting for people to fall asleep?"

He laughed. "That's top-secret information. And you don't have to call me a 'guardian' every time."

My eyebrows shot up. "Oh, you have a name?"

"Why is that surprising?"

"I don't know." I shrugged. "Do angels have names?"

"Yes."

"What do I call *you*?"

"Sethos."

"Sethos." Testing his name on my tongue felt like I was uttering an ancient spell, sending waves throughout my body. The energy felt ancient, like it was waking up all the cells of my body at once. It was exhilarating.

I shivered and turned to him. "What was that?"

He looked at me intently. "What did you feel?"

"When I said your name, I felt like something traveled and

spread through my body. That's never happened to me before."

"Was it a bad feeling, or did it make you uncomfortable?"

"No . . ." It was interesting that although the energy was powerful, I felt no danger. It felt devoid of the ominous and darker qualities I was used to from my training or even from the moments in the tattoo parlor and quad. "What was it?"

He looked to the horizon. "Hard to say," he answered. "Sometimes souls recognize each other when one speaks the other's name for the first time."

Before I had a chance to ask another question, Sethos stood and looked down to me, holding out his hand.

"Are we going someplace?"

"You alluded to this *occupation* being boring. I'd like to show you around."

"This is an interesting spot." I gestured to the cliff. "With the forest behind us and then this cliff. Where are we? How is my subconscious able to dream this if I have never been here? I thought it was a universal rule of dreaming that you only dream what you have experienced."

"We are in Daya. It's a faerie realm. We are here because I am the best soul guardian and know how to bend a few rules of reality. To answer your second question, a person's body always remains asleep in the last place they fell asleep, but with the right magic, that person's subconscious can travel anywhere in dreamtime. It's called astral projection."

"And why are we here?" I took his hand and felt my magic rise to the surface, excited by our touch.

Once I stood and our hands dropped, my magic protested like we had lost something that belonged to us. It was an odd feeling I could not understand, and I made a mental note to revisit my magic's reaction to Sethos later.

"Daya is ruled by the faerie, but it's one of the last wild fauna habitats left. The land is untouched by construction and is peaceful. I like to come here to think."

"Moments of quiet solitude and stalking people's dreams." I laughed. "Wow, you really *do* have an exciting life."

"You have no idea." He smirked. "Come," he said, grabbing my hand and leading me into the forest.

I sucked in a breath as my stomach fluttered again.

I hadn't known what to expect inside a faerie forest, and my face lit up at the wonder. My mentor had taught me the different types of magical beings, but I had never encountered any or imagined what their lands would look like.

"There's so much light." My voice came out like a whisper as we walked under thousands of butterflies with fluorescent wings flying below the tall tree canopy. Their wings created an enchanting but haunting melody, eliciting a feeling of sacredness as we walked. "It's beautiful. And peaceful. It's so different from anything on Andora."

Sethos nodded. "Faerie realms have different infrastructures, much like human ones. They can be modern like Andora, full of skyscrapers, sky cars for everyday travel, or constructed with ancient castles and woodland homes. Daya is untouched. It's wild."

At the mention of Andora, my decision of whether to accept refuge in Taria came to the forefront of my mind. I chewed my lip as my mind struggled with what to do.

"What is on your mind?" he asked.

"My university and town were attacked."

He immediately stepped in front of me and looked down at me. "By what?"

"A god." I shook my head. "That is what Aramis, my college's director, and his colleague Khellios called it."

"What makes them say that?"

I shrugged. "Khellios didn't explain. They just said it was a god."

"Were you hurt?"

I paused before answering. "Yes—"

"*Show me*," he cut in, his tone fierce.

I gestured to my injury, covered by my long-sleeve shirt. "The god attacked the lampposts on the quad, and glass exploded everywhere. When some of the glass from the lampposts shattered, it cut my arm, but it was a surface cut. I've never experienced magic of that magnitude."

"Where you hurt anywhere else?" His jaw ticked, and he balled his hands into fists.

"No."

"What did this being want?"

A chill settled in my bones. "Khellios says the god is weak and wants to reinforce his power through my magic."

"Why your magic?"

"Khellios says my magic is the same type, and he wants me to leave campus." I began walking again, and Sethos followed.

"Where would you go?"

"Khellios has offered me a secure location to stay outside of Xhor."

"When do you leave?"

I grew silent.

"Why do you hesitate?" He raised his eyebrows. "Renna, if this man is offering you protection—"

"I know. The unexpected makes me shut down because my brain struggles to process the unknown. I enter this mental loop of fear and anxiety and panic, and I can't escape my thoughts. They stab me like knives until I can't breathe. I don't like feeling like I'm not in control. As a child, I couldn't control my environment—"

"So, you try to control things around you as an adult as much as possible."

I nodded. "I don't know what to expect when I arrive at that location—who I will meet, will I be happy when I'm there? The location is a haven for people who practice magic, but I've avoided magic for as long as possible. Will I be expected to use magic while there? There are too many unknowns. Nothing will stay the same." I turned to him. "Will you remain my guardian?"

He angled his body toward me and searched my face. "Being your guardian has nothing to do with where you are physically located. I have been sworn to provide you with guidance and protection—should you wish it. I have made it clear that the choice is yours."

Sethos had a calming energy around him, and it soothed me that his presence would be a constant, providing me with some stability while living in a strange place.

"When do you have to make a decision?" he asked.

"It's not about making a decision. I know in my heart I should go. My brain is having difficulty catching up to logic."

"Accept Aramis's offer of protection. I think you know that is the best course of action. However, you need to speak with Aramis and share your concerns."

After a few minutes, I nodded. "I'll speak to Aramis tomorrow and accept Khellios's offer."

Sethos inclined his head.

"Thank you." I smiled as warmth spread throughout me.

"For what?"

"For being a constant in my life even when I haven't known it."

He searched my eyes and smiled. "That's what I'm here for."

8

RENNA

I met Aramis at his office the next day, but Khellios was nowhere in sight.

"Have you come to a decision?" he asked from behind his desk.

"I will go to Taria," I began. "However, I need to understand what to expect. Who I'll be staying with, who will be my point of contact if I need to speak with someone about any concerns, will I be expected to use magic?"

"Lots of questions." He nodded. "I understand. As head of your college, I will be your point of contact. However, you will be staying in Khellios's home, so he will also be a person you can turn to for questions and concerns."

I bit my tongue to hold back a snarky comment about how well Khellios and I had gotten along the day before.

"Taria originally was an afterlife dimension created by the gods for the priests and priestesses who served them. Over time, as the Council gained traction in their cruel punishment of people using magic, Taria became a safe haven for all people who practice magic. People living in Taria are there by choice, and only those invited to live there know of its exact location. As

I shared before, people in Taria use magic, but you do not need it to live there. I know you are hesitant to exercise your magic, and you would never be forced."

I breathed a little easier at his last sentence. "What does Taria look like?"

"Taria is best described as an island. There are quaint homes that dot seaside mountains, smaller floating islands where people also live, and a metropolitan city that looks more like Andora with tall steel columns and glass buildings. Like on Andora, you will find sky cars that transport people to various places."

"Why would they need sky cars to move around if magic exists?"

"Convenience." He shrugged. "Using magic to move around is draining on the body. Teleporting is not a skill everyone has. Typically, only gods or beings with equal power can teleport successfully, or if you happen to travel with a god or being with that skill to help shift some of the traveling strain off your body."

I nodded, hiding the fact I knew the information he shared firsthand. "Can you do it?" I asked.

Aramis chuckled. "I wish." He shook his head. "Sadly, that is not a gift I possess. The magic running through my family's lineage did not pass down that level of power."

I nodded. My mentor had tried to teach me to teleport using magic, but I never mastered the skill. The most I could travel was across a small room, and afterward I couldn't move for a full two days. Teleporting was hard on the bones.

"Have you?" he asked, cocking a brow.

Before I could shake my head in a lie, Khellios spoke behind me.

"There is always a first time."

I spun around, and he nodded in greeting, his lips curving into a polite smile.

"Ah, Khel!" Aramis said, standing to greet his friend. "Renna here just shared the news that she will accept your offer of help and come to stay in Taria."

Khel's gaze told me that he would have never accepted a no. "Excellent." His tone dripped with sarcasm.

I put my palms up, about to ask him what his problem was, but Aramis cut in, perhaps anticipating another argument between us. "So, my friend, when are you planning on leaving with Renna?"

"Now," Khellios.

That was the only notice I got before he grabbed my hand and pulled me to his chest, and then we blinked out of Aramis's office.

9

RENNA

I had only teleported three times in my life, and each time was much the same. My vision filled with an explosion of colors, and the atoms of my body were pushed and pulled apart as I was catapulted through a fast-moving tunnel, sucking me through a wormhole. Even though I had no physical body as I moved through time, I could somehow hear my subconscious scream in terror.

In the next instant, I materialized onto a marble floor, the bits and pieces of my body put back together, and I was able to take my first breath. Belatedly, I realized I was holding onto Khellios for dear life. We both looked at how our limbs were tangled, and I yanked my body from him, only to stumble and fall back.

But Khellios reached for me, and I never hit the ground.

"Are you alright?" he asked, looking me over to inspect for obvious injuries.

I pushed him away and straightened. "Am I alright?" I screamed. "What the fuck was that?"

"Are you hurt?"

I paused and realized that the usual pain I felt in my joints and muscles when teleporting was missing. Aramis's words about teleporting with someone with enough power to shield the pain echoed in my mind. But admitting that to Khellios felt like allowing him a victory I didn't want to give him.

"No." I glared at him. "But you should have warned me."

"Would you have let me use teleportation if I had asked you?" He cocked his head.

I crossed my arms and huffed. "Not likely. But a warning would have still been nice!"

He rolled his eyes and opened his mouth to speak, but the voice of a female cut in. "I thought that was you!"

We both turned, and a beautiful, tall woman with black hair styled in a pixie cut, dressed in all-black leathers, stood in the middle of a luxurious home I just now began to take in. It looked like it was carved out of precious white stone that resembled opal.

"Nera." Khellios acknowledged her and walked from where we were standing toward a beverage cart.

Standing in the middle of the home, I felt out of place. I hugged my middle and cast Nera a polite smile.

"Rude," Nera called after Khellios, who was now across the room pouring himself a glass of amber liquid. "You should have introduced me."

"Nera, that's Renna. Renna, that is Nera," he said, bored. "Renna hates me."

My jaw dropped. "That is *not* true!"

Khellios raised his glass in my direction in mocking cheers.

Nera rolled her eyes and walked toward me with a warm smile and outstretched hand. "Please ignore the idiot across the room"—she gestured to Khellios—"who has suddenly turned into a beast. I'm Nera."

The dimmest of silver light outlined her hand, and upon looking at her up close, I could see her whole body was outlined in silver. She looked like a divine being, and I began to think through the different supernatural beings my mentor had taught me who might emit a glow. Gods and angels came to mind. My mentor deeply despised both groups.

"I'm Renna." I shook her hand, and warmth flooded my body at the contact, the kind of warmth associated with fond thoughts and memories—not that I had a lot of those.

"Renna, nice to meet you. I heard what happened on your campus, and I am very sorry. Please know you are safe in Taria."

"Thank you," I said, taking my hand back. "It has been an interesting few weeks, to say the least."

"You must be exhausted. Would you like to sit?" She gestured to the white leather couches where Khellios was sitting.

I nodded and followed Nera's lead as she walked toward Khellios.

"Khellios recently renovated his home." Nera motioned to the space around her as we walked. "He could have gone with a more creative color than all-white furniture and walls and art." She shook her head and chuckled. "But he is very set in his ways."

"If you hate my decor, you could always leave." Khellios shrugged.

"For goodness' sake, Khel!" Nera said, punching his arm as she sat next to him. "Do you want Renna to think you are a bully? What is with you today?" Nera crossed her arms and curled her small body on the couch, her black leather clothing a sharp contrast to the neutral hues of the home. "I'm sorry. Please sit." She waved her hand over the sofa.

Before I could accept, an electrical current bolted through the room, making me duck to the floor. Bright light lit up the space, the crystalized walls shining like millions of stars. I shielded my eyes with my arm.

"She has arrived at last," a female said bitterly.

I lowered my arm from my eyes. As my vision adjusted, I lifted my gaze to find an older woman with long white hair in a beautiful royal navy robe surrounded by mist, making it look like she was levitating. The woman stood with her hands folded at her center and her chin raised as she looked down toward the sunken living room area.

Khellios and Nera moved to protectively flank me on either side, and my heart beat rapidly.

Nera spoke. "*Madera,* lovely to see you." Her tone was clipped. "Welcome." The word was dragged out in a quiet warning.

"This is not your home, Nera," the woman pointed out, gesturing to the room around her.

She walked toward us, and Khellios stepped in front of me. I peeked over his shoulder to observe the woman.

Her eyes found mine, and she smiled wickedly before turning her attention to Nera. "This is the home of my son. No need for the warning tone, little goddess."

I looked at Nera's silver glow. *So she was a goddess.*

"Mother," Khellios said, his voice monotone. "Behave."

"Anything for you." Madera smiled at him before turning a bitter stare toward me. "Although I wonder if in indulging my son, I failed him. He doesn't seem to know what is best for him."

"That is enough!" Khellios yelled, his voice echoing throughout the room. "State your business."

Madera crossed her arms. "I've come to ask you to reconsider making the same mistake again."

Khellios fisted his hands. "You will leave."

"I will leave," she spat. "But remember this." She stepped closer. "Xhor's destruction could have been prevented." She swung her eyes to me, fury rolling within them, before she looked to Khellios again. "*She* should not be here. Do not cast us to the same fate."

Nera gasped and stepped forward. "Madera, you cannot say something like that."

"I will say what I please," Madera sneered. "You would do well to remember your place, goddess, before speaking to me again." She looked at her son. "You are making a mistake."

Khellios became deadly still. "Mother," he said, the single word full of hatred. "You are dismissed."

Madera wagged her finger at me and was about to speak when Khellios again cut her off. "Enough!"

A string of expletives flew from Madera before a gust of wind tore through the room, and lightning flashed so brightly that I was forced to cover my eyes with my forearm again.

A crack reverberated throughout the air, and then there was stillness.

I lowered my hand to find Madera gone, with only golden electrical fibers lingering where she had stood seconds ago.

Khellios stepped in front of me, his brows furrowed in anger. "I'm sorry." He shook his head. "That was unacceptable. My mother lends herself to theatrics. That will not happen again."

"Why did she say those things?" I asked. "What would me being here have to do with Xhor?"

Khellios sighed and ran a hand down his face before answering. "Xhor was destroyed two millennia ago when Andora was a young planet. The current Xhor is atop the ruins of the original city."

I nodded. "I know about the ruins. I'm studying the weapons found in the excavation."

"The original city was destroyed by the same god who attacked your campus and town."

My world stopped, and the blood drained from my face.

There was no recorded history as to why the ancient city was destroyed.

"News of the recent attacks is known in Taria, so my mother is hesitant to have you here. She thinks you will lead the god to Taria."

Guilt numbed my body. I put myself in Madera's shoes and could understand her fierceness in protecting Taria. "I don't blame her at all."

Khellios shook his head. "It doesn't matter what my mother thinks. She should have never spoken in that manner."

"I'm intruding on her home—"

"This is *my* home," Khellios growled. "She cannot dictate what goes on under my roof."

I wrapped my arms around my torso, and my face grew hot with shame. "My presence brings you all danger. Why would you even want me here?"

Khellios ran a hand through his closely shaved hair. "I was one of the gods who established Taria," he began.

My eyes fell to his body, and no glow illuminated his skin like Nera's. *Odd.*

"Taria is a safe haven for people with magical gifts, and you need protection. The god who is behind the attacks does not know Taria's location."

I looked down at my hands and picked at my nails, a nervous habit. "How is it possible that after so many years, he doesn't know where Taria is?"

"The shield," Nera chimed in with a smile. "A shield surrounds Taria that was created by combining the power of many gods. A witch made sure to bind the powers in an unbreakable bond. She is the only one who would know how to undo the shield, and she resides in Taria. That god knows Taria exists but has never been able to locate it. We have lived in peace for many years."

The more they shared, the more questions I had, a form of self-preservation ingrained from childhood. "Can the witch undo the spell?"

Nera and Khellios looked uneasy at the question.

I shook my head and apologized. "This is all so new to me."

Khellios nodded. "You are going to have questions because you are in a new place, and we expect that."

His patience and understanding were slightly unexpected given our first interaction. But I appreciated his willingness to try to ease some of my concerns.

He turned to Nera, who nodded encouragingly at him to continue. "It's unlikely the witch would undo the spell because she was offered immortality in exchange for her services."

My eyes widened. I had never heard of immortality being granted. "That seems like a fair trade?"

"It was." Nera nodded. "She was pregnant at the time, and her babe was not expected to live past birth. Khellios granted her immortality to secure her services and ensure her child lived. Her child also became immortal. They both live happily in Taria." She smiled sadly at Khellios, and he looked away from her gaze.

I furrowed my brow. It felt like there was more to the story based on Khellios's reaction.

"That was very generous and kind," I said to him.

Khellios looked up at me with a look that could only be described as haunted. "Someone I knew was killed while expecting a babe of her own."

Dread unexpectedly filled my body then, and on instinct, I placed a hand on my abdomen, imagining losing a child who was wanted. Khellios's sharp eyes followed the movement.

"Don't be fooled by Khel's cranky moods," Nera said with a small smile. "He's soft underneath that hard exterior."

I smiled at Khellios, but he looked away and walked back to

the beverage cart. After pouring another glass of amber liquid, he chugged it and poured himself a refill.

I looked at Nera, and she smiled uneasily at Khellios's display. "So what do you think of Khel's home?" she said, trying to change the topic.

"It's unique." I looked around. "I feel like I'm inside a glowing white geode cavern. Are all homes in Taria like this?"

"No," Nera chuckled. "Come." She beckoned me to follow her to a large balcony carved into the wall on the far side of the room.

We were on the side of a lush mountain, and other homes dotted the landscape just like Aramis had described. Each home was constructed in a different style. One of the homes looked like a castle with turrets. What amazed me most of all was the rolling lilac-colored sea on the horizon.

My face lit up. "I've never seen a body of water this large," I said. Andora was a desert planet and didn't have seas or oceans like other planets in Andromeda. "I've always longed to have enough money to travel to the sea. For some reason it's always called to me."

"Sadly, the sea around Taria is merely an illusion." Nera gazed wistfully at it. "If you were to go in, it would simply feel like smoke."

"How long will I remain in Taria?" I asked and looked up to find Khellios's gaze on me. I hadn't even heard him follow us onto the balcony.

"Too early to tell." Khellios shook his head.

"So much for trying to graduate this year," I lamented as disappointment spread through my body. "I'm not going to be able to afford another year."

"We will work something out with Aramis. You should not be penalized for something outside of your control."

I nodded, but realizing I had none of my clothes for my stay in Taria, I groaned.

"What's the matter?" Nera asked.

"I don't have any clothing for tomorrow or any day thereafter."

Nera lifted her eyebrow at Khellios. "Really?" She chastised him. "You forgot her things?"

He put his hands up in surrender. "I apologize," he said to me. "I admit that I should have given more consideration for things you may need. Nera can take you into town tomorrow."

I turned bright red as I recalled leaving my purse in Aramis's office. "I don't have any money with me . . ."

Nera crossed her arms and narrowed her eyes at Khellios. "You fucked up. How are you going to fix this, dear cousin?"

Khellios threw an unamused look toward Nera. "You have just been the biggest help today, you know that?" he said sarcastically.

"Deal with it. You need someone to call you out on your shit."

My eyes darted back and forth. Nera seemed like a younger sister to him, and the dynamic was amusing.

Khellios turned to me. "Nera is right. I owe you new clothes. I was going to suggest that before she inserted herself in the conversation." He frowned at her, and she rolled her eyes. "Don't worry about the money. You are a guest here."

I felt uneasy taking his money, but I did need new clothes. Even if Khellios went back to my studio to get my clothes, he wouldn't know what to pack. "Thank you." I smiled politely. "I won't spend more than I need."

Nera laughed and leaned in. "Considering he was an asshole to you, he owes you big time."

Unsure how to respond, I looked anywhere but at both gods, and they continued going back and forth with snarky comments. It had been an extremely trying day, and I felt out of place.

"Aramis mentioned the episode in his office when you first met," Khellios said gently. "He said your energy was impulsive and chaotic." When I failed to respond, he added, "Did you ever receive training?"

"No," I lied.

Bringing up my past would only lead to more questions. How could I explain to someone that my mentor enjoyed beating me and emotionally abusing me until I would burst from anger, and then he would demand I train?

Khel studied my face for a long time as if he was trying to figure me out. After a few minutes he nodded and said, "That explains the impulsivity . . ."

I shrugged and turned to look at the seaside landscape. "I want nothing to do with magic."

"Good," he answered, and I turned to look at him.

Khel's gaze was sincere, and his answer surprised me. I was expecting him to pressure me.

"No one will force you to do anything you do not want. This is a safe space. If you never want to speak of or create magic, you will never have to. You do not need magic to live because you have managed well on your own by avoiding it altogether. You also do not need it to stay safe. You have me for that."

I appreciated Khellios's sincerity. Perhaps we had gotten off on the wrong foot, and Nera was right: he is soft underneath his stony exterior.

His words calmed me some, but I was still on edge. No matter his reassurance, something was actively hunting for me.

Khel stepped up to me. "Renna." He clasped his hands behind his back. "Please consider this your home while you are in Taria. I ask that you come to me for anything. You will want for nothing while you are here. Let me take care of whatever you need."

"Thank you." I knew he was being polite, but his words filled me with warmth, and I blushed.

Khel tilted his head as his eyes roved over my face, probably noting the flush on my skin. He cleared his throat and walked back to the beverage cart.

Between sips, Khellios asked Nera to give me a tour and show me to my rooms. Nera agreed.

Before we left the room, Khel called out, "Renna?"

I turned.

"I hope, in time, you can trust me. We all carry heavy burdens."

Nera and I walked silently to reach the room where I would stay. It wasn't for lack of having things to say that I stayed silent but because the cavernous walls and long winding hallways, lacking any windows, made the space feel desolate. The beauty of the white walls with encrusted crystals that emitted light didn't provide warmth to the home.

"How does Khellios get natural sunlight inside his home?" We were walking past what looked like a grotto with a sunken pool. The grotto's walls were devoid of any crystals, and instead, the water itself, a brilliant aquamarine, lit up the room. Several sconces on the walls also provided some light.

"He has some windows . . ." Nera answered, looking at the grotto. "He barely spends time at home, so I don't think sunlight is an issue for him."

"I never thought I would live in a cave," I admitted as we turned onto another long hallway.

I ran a hand against the wall and pulled it back quickly when a crystal pricked my skin. Blood began to well on a small cut on my finger, and I brought it to my mouth, sucking on it.

Nera noticed the cut and locked eyes with me briefly before looking away.

Pricking your finger was bad luck, and I shivered. It wasn't a great way to start my stay in Taria.

"You won't spend all your time here," Nera said suddenly. "There is so much to do in Taria."

The cut, although small and painless, would not stop bleeding. I grabbed the edge of my shirt and applied pressure. "Aramis mentioned there are floating islands."

"Yes! Taria is a haven for many people from different planets and galaxies, so they try to recreate their homes here. People in the Sirius galaxy live on floating islands, so when they come here, they create the same structures for nostalgia."

We arrived at two massive wooden doors. They protested by creaking loudly when Nera pushed them open as if no one had used them in a long while.

"Here we are!" She gestured to the space that looked exactly like the rest of the house. "There are two rooms. This living space area, and the second room beyond is the bedroom." She pointed to another set of thick wooden doors.

A glass dining table sat in the middle of the room, and it felt out of place. I was used to seeing tables in the middle of homes, not individual bedroom spaces.

"Am I going to eat my meals here alone?" I asked, walking to the dining table.

The table was immaculate, and I resisted touching it for fear of leaving fingerprints. I felt like I was inside a museum. I either couldn't touch things or felt out of place if I wanted to.

"Yes . . ." Nera answered. "I can join if you'd like company?" Her words came out like she was confused.

I turned to her. "Is it not customary in Taria to sit down with people to share a meal?"

Nera's eyes turned soft, and she smiled. "How much do you know about gods?" she asked.

I shook my head. "I learned the names of different supernatural species and overall traits, but it seems like I'm missing some vital information."

She nodded. "We don't need food to sustain ourselves."

"At all?"

She shook her head. "Our energy comes directly from Source, or the creator lifeforce that fuels the universe."

Now I was curious. "Have you ever eaten food?"

She nodded. "Yes, I've had mortal food before, but it tastes bland to me. I avoid it. However, I would be happy to join you for your meals to keep you company."

I nodded. "I would like that."

"When we go into town, there are a few restaurants and taverns we can visit for you to try different foods. The diverse population in Taria makes for a delicious mixture of foods, or so I hear."

Nera continued to give me a tour of my space. "I know the lack of windows in this home may seem odd since Andora is made up of glass skyscrapers, but there is one thing you'll enjoy." She smiled and pushed the doors into my bedroom.

Sunlight streamed in through floor-to-ceiling glass walls that led out to a massive balcony overlooking the sea on the west wall.

A smile lit my face, and I ran to the balcony door, which covered the entire wall. I slid it open and stepped out to the balcony. Leaning over the railing, I relished in the sound and salty smell of the sea.

"This magic is incredible." I marveled at the water below.

Magic had only ever brought trouble into my life, and I saw no good in it. However, being in Taria made me question whether I could hate all magic. They had created a refuge for people to live in peace away from persecution, complete with the illusion of water on an arid planet. It was beautiful and *good*.

"Khellios wanted you to have these rooms because of the balcony," Nera said quietly. "He thought you'd like the sea."

I turned. "This is definitely more than I expected," I confessed. "Especially from him. We didn't get off to a great start."

"I meant what I said earlier." Nera walked back into the bedroom, and I followed her. "Khellios is soft hearted despite how tough he seems. He really just wants to keep everyone safe. When he heard about the attacks on your campus, he nearly lost his mind."

"Why?" I walked up to a low-standing bed atop a pink quartz base and sat down.

Nera sighed. "May I?" she asked, referring to the bed. I nodded, and she sat. "Khellios lost the love of his life and his sister when Xhor fell."

"What?"

Nera nodded. "The woman he loved was pregnant when she was killed, and his sister, Khiserys, died defending Khellios's partner and unborn child."

My heart stopped, and I felt as if ice-cold water had been poured over me. I shivered and stood, my body breaking out in goose bumps. An ominous feeling spread throughout my body.

"No wonder Madera hates me," I whispered. "I remind her of the loss she suffered."

Nera stood and grasped my hands gently. "Madera has her own problems. Yes, she suffered, but it is no excuse to treat others with disrespect. I shared the story so you can understand why Khel sometimes acts like a hard-ass. People being threatened, especially by the god who killed people he loved, is very triggering for him."

I nodded, recalling our interaction in Aramis's office. Khellios was rude and even borderline offensive, but it was good to know underneath it all, there was a reason. "Thank you for sharing that."

"I'm sorry to have ruined the mood as you adjust to your new space."

"No." I shook my head. "It helps me understand him a bit more. I am staying in his home, after all. It helps give me more perspective."

Besides, since arriving in Taria, his roughness seemed to have smoothed out some.

Nera nodded. "It still doesn't excuse his rudeness, but I am glad to provide insight." Nera dropped my hands and gestured around us. "Onto happier topics, what do you think of your new room?" She smiled.

I looked around, taking it all in. A spacious armoire and vanity with perfumes and various trinkets lined one wall, and a large gold oblong mirror encrusted with round polished emeralds stood in one corner. "I feel like I'm in a dream. I was on scholarship and worked three jobs to afford living on campus, so this kind of luxury is beyond my wildest dreams. I have never seen jewels like this up close." I walked to the full-length mirror and saw the room reflected behind me. "I look so out of place with my linen garbs and combat boots," I joked.

Nera stepped up next to me. Her leathers and the knife sheathed at her waist were a stark contrast to the room's white palette. "We'll go shopping tomorrow." She waved her hand down her body. "Although you may not want to dress in all leather like me." She laughed. "I wear this because it's easier to move around for what I do on a daily basis."

I cocked my head in a silent question for Nera to elaborate, and she responded, "Khel and I are lunar deities."

"You are the gods of the moon?" I asked in shock, my voice raising several octaves.

She chuckled. "Yes." She paused. "Well, Khel is also a god of stars. He is one of the oldest deities of the enclave. The night sky is his realm. Khel and I work together to patrol the heavens. He, the moons and stars, and I just focus on the moons. Wearing this"—she motioned to her clothes—"allows me to move around up there." She pointed to the sky.

The planets in Andromeda could have one to several moons. Andora had two moons, one close to our orbit and another several thousand kilometers away.

"How are you able to patrol so many moons across so many galaxies?"

"Well . . ." She laughed and scratched the back of her head. "Another fact about gods I can teach you is that we don't sleep, *er*, let me rephrase that." She shook her head. "We choose *not* to sleep. We don't need to sleep to replenish our energy. Some gods sleep because they enjoy it. For Khel and me, we avoid it because we are nocturnal deities. We are the ones who are awake when everyone else is asleep.

"To answer your question as to *how* we are able to patrol the skies." She continued. "There is a platform suspended in the heavens called The Watch. Khel and I are there almost nightly with a few other minor sky deities sailing across galaxies."

"Is that why you mentioned Khellios is never home?" I thought back to her earlier statement.

"Yes and no." She shrugged. "The Watch keeps us busy, but we do have lots of help up there. Khel tends to disappear from time to time. He retreats into himself, and we go several days without hearing from him. It's just the way he is."

I nodded, making a mental note that my host could likely be absent for most of my time here. While Nera had given me some insight into Khellios, I seemed to have more questions the more I learned about him.

11

RENNA

I was late for class. Or at least I thought I was when I jumped up in bed in a hurry, nearly toppling off. My head began to pound from the rush of blood, and my body went into a panic when my foot touched a stone floor instead of the plush rug that was next to my bed in my studio apartment.

I peeked one eye open, and the rush of the previous day came back to me. I looked to the foot of my bed to see the balcony wall I had left open the night before. The sound of the sea calmed me, and I was sad that most in Andora would never experience the sound of the waves, even if by magic. As I stretched in bed, I realized I had slept more soundly than I had in a long time and had a dreamless sleep.

Sethos's face came to mind with his mischievous smirk and sharp eyes that looked like they never missed a thing. My body warmed, recalling how my hand had felt in his as he pulled me into the forest in Daya.

I missed him.

Sometime later, I was wandering the hallways, trying to find a way to the front door. The place was like a labyrinth, as if designed to keep one indoors.

As I turned onto another windowless and endless corridor, Nera spoke behind me. "Renna."

I jumped at the unexpected sound and turned to face her. "I almost gave up trying to find the exit," I joked, gesturing to the long hallway that wound around in a circle. "At least there's light." I pointed to the luminescent walls. "Is the light source coming solely from the walls? What is this stone?"

"The stone is called *Shira*," Nera said. She hovered her hand above the crystals, and they seemed to respond to her, brightening under her hand and illuminating the hallway even more. "Come, I will guide you out." I followed as she continued to speak. "Khellios acquired the material to build this home a very long time ago," she said, canting her head and still hovering her hand over the stone as if recalling a memory. "After the attack on Xhor, he became a bit of a world traveler, traveling to different lands as a mercenary. A kingdom gifted him the stones as a thank-you. The stones were meant as a symbol to help light his way in times of uncertainty."

We now stood outside at the front of the home, and I tilted my face up to the bright sunlight that had been missing inside the cavernous home. The sea greeted us, and a private beach led to the water. I resisted the urge to run down there.

"This place is amazing," I said, looking toward the horizon. "I don't think I could have ever imagined anything like it."

Nera turned toward the waters. "Do you know I've seen the sea a million nights and have never stopped to take in its wonder?"

"Sometimes we don't see the blessings we have in front of us," I said quietly, recalling how calm my life was before the attacks.

Nera smiled sadly, looking out into the horizon. "Having lived as long as I have, it's hard to remember to think like that.

Life is so fragile and ever changing that after a while, for me, it becomes a blur, and I go through the motions day by day."

I tried to put myself in Nera's shoes and found it hard to relate. She was a goddess with unlimited power surrounded by her family, living in a beautiful dimension free from persecution from the Council, where magic was embraced.

A sky car pulled up on the driveway, and Nera spoke. "I took the liberty to ask for a sky car today. I know arriving to Taria was a bit . . . chaotic." Her face turned crimson, and she walked to the car and held the rear door open.

"*That* is an understatement. I was given no warning by your cousin." I nodded in thanks and got into the vehicle, with her following me.

"Khel can be an idiot." She sighed. "I'm really embarrassed how that happened."

I furrowed my brows and shook my head. "Don't apologize for him acting like a brute. You've been nothing but nice and welcoming, so I don't hold anything against you."

She smiled. "Thanks. At least your consolation is spending his money today."

"About that." I squirmed in my seat. "Is there any way I can pay him back? I know he is to blame for my clothes not being here, but I still feel uncomfortable using his money."

Nera shook her head. "Khel would never let you. Plus, you are his guest, and he considers himself responsible for all in Taria as the second god in command in our enclave."

I scoured my memory for everything I'd learned about magic and magical beings but couldn't remember learning about "enclaves." "What's an enclave?" I asked.

Nera's eyes widened with excitement, and she clapped. "Oh! I get to tell you. I keep forgetting how unfamiliar you are with this world." She shifted to face me. "There are three enclaves. An enclave is a fancy term for a group, and I don't exactly know how the term came to be part of the three god group names." She shrugged. "But I digress."

I laughed at how animated she became to tell me all about her world.

"The story goes that when there was nothing, when Source had just been created itself, Source sought a way to experience all that could be possible."

"Who created Source?" I cut in, my researcher mind going a mile a minute.

"Good question!" Nera smiled mischievously and folded her hands. "You will laugh, but no one actually knows who created Source. I certainly have my own hypothesis, but that's a conversation for another day. I've spent quite a bit of time doing my own investigations, which you will appreciate as a researcher."

"Okay," I laughed and nodded. "I look forward to discussing your findings."

Nera smiled. "I will hold you to that conversation. So anyway, Source created life, and within that creation, three god enclaves were formed to oversee all of creation. There is the Celestial Enclave, the Spiritual Enclave, and the Elemental Enclave. Gods who have to do with celestial bodies, like planets, the cosmos, stars, *the moon*"—she pointed to herself—"the sun, etcetera, are all part of the Celestial Enclave. In Taria, you will mostly find celestial deities, which is what we are referred to as."

"Where do the other enclaves live?"

"The elementals live on Moringa, a lush rainforest planet in the next galaxy, and the Spiritual Enclave lives in a star cluster known as Camu."

The enclaves sounded fascinating compared to the restrictive life found on Andora. "Does the Council's reach extend outside of Andromeda?" I asked, referring to my galaxy.

Nera shook her head. "No. Andromeda is the only human-inhabited galaxy after the abandonment of the Milky Way galaxy during the Great Migration."

I'd learned about the mass exodus of humans from the Milky Way galaxy some three thousand years prior. The humans from there trekked to new frontiers on Andromeda after their original galaxy was unable to sustain life.

"What luck that we got stuck with the Council." I crossed my arms and looked out the window.

The landscape had changed from a seaside drive with palatial homes dotting the mountainside to a town with two- and three-story buildings made of glittering limestone and red roofs. Cobblestone lined the roads and sidewalks.

"I do not condone their persecution of people who follow religion and those who have magic abilities, but you have to understand the circumstances that led humans to abandon the Milky Way."

I turned to her. "People are hunted by the Council," I said, my anger rising. "There will never be a good excuse for what they do."

Nera nodded sadly. "I know." When I turned from her to look out the window again, she hesitated before resuming. "Religion and magic, which were openly used back then, became divisive in the previous galaxy. Humans turned against each other. Brothers against brothers. People with magical gifts had to go underground as religious extremism made them fear for their lives. Wars broke out for differing religious and magical views. Much suffering happened during the time preceding the Great Migration."

I had heard it all before from history books while in school. "Yes, and the Council decided to do away with differing spiritual ideologies once they arrived in Andromeda and have a pure science-based society." I spun to face her, my anger and magic now slithering as one to the surface of my skin. It wove through my bones until it got to my hands, where it began concentrating. "That does not excuse what they do with people they find guilty. Some are never heard from again! We don't know where they're taken."

"I know." Nera looked at my hands as if she could see the power building there. Then she looked up at my eyes as if trying to see if I would lose control. "Renna . . . I need you to breathe."

I shook my head. "Is there nothing you can do? You are all gods. You must have the divine power to do away with the Council and allow humans to live the lives they want."

"No." Nera hung her head, answering my question.

The sky car had now stopped, and the driver exited to open our doors.

"There are things Source prohibits even gods from doing. One of the things we cannot do is interfere in human politics. One god from each enclave interfered early on when the Council was first formed, and Source stripped them of their powers. One god went mad from being stripped of her magic and killed herself. The other went into exile, and the third was never heard from again."

"Why would Source do that?"

"Because humans have free will." She sighed. "I have seen civilizations rise and fall, Renna. Humans have the power to demand better futures for their kind. To interfere with free will violates a universal law. The story of humankind is not over. There will be good days to come."

"So we suffer in the interim? Is that what we must do?" My head pounded as the magic thrashed within me, demanding I release it.

I squeezed my palms shut to contain it.

Nera was now sitting up, alert, watching as I began to sweat. "You need to sit back and breathe, Renna. Khel mentioned in private that your magic is activated by anger."

I sat back in my seat, knowing I couldn't add anything else to the conversation or argue. I simply let the anger within me simmer and wrap itself around my body until my diaphragm struggled to take full breaths and my stomach swelled and contracted painfully. I had to subdue it, or I would lash out.

"Breathe," Nera said, scooting closer to my side. "I know you are angry. I know you are fighting to control it. You must breathe." She put her hands up and hovered them over my skin. "May I?" she asked. I looked down at her hands, and her palms glowed brightly with her silver aura. "My magic will help stabilize you."

I nodded and closed my eyes. When Nera's hands made contact with my body, it felt like the warmth of a cool morning spring sun. Her magic traveled across the surface of my skin like small waves, cooling the angry magic that had risen from the center of my soul.

I imagined Sethos then looking into my eyes and telling me to breathe. Seeing his face made my anger withdraw, and when it was manageable, I opened my eyes and took a deep breath.

"I'm so sorry my words caused this," she said once I opened my eyes.

"It isn't your fault. I struggle with my anger. It doesn't help that my magic is entangled with it." I sighed, massaging my temples as my headache was now a dull pain.

She placed her hands on my temples, and more magic surged from her, quieting the pain.

"Thank you," I whispered when my anger had fully receded.

"You are passionate about justice, and that is a good quality to have." Nera smiled. "Aramis told Khel how you barged into his office demanding changes to your college. Khel was impressed you stood up for yourself and others." She chuckled.

I rolled my eyes. "I'm still upset about the changes. He dismissed great people from their jobs."

Nera squeezed my hands. "Never lose that heart. We need more mortals to advocate for those who need it most."

Lively music could be heard in the distance, and Nera and I turned in the direction it came from.

"That would be the equinox preparations underway," Nera explained. "Taria is getting ready for our yearly equinox celebration. It should make for a lively shopping experience as the town will be busier than usual." Nera turned to me and smiled. "We should exit. We have arrived at the heart of Taria."

12

RENNA

The heart of Taria was a mixture of live exotic music, colorful banners decorating shops, flowers adorning lampposts, and street vendors loudly advertising their wares. People gathered in groups, laughing as someone told a funny story while others walked arm in arm toward various shops. The vibrancy of the place was palpable and contagious. I couldn't help but smile.

"I don't think I've ever heard this many languages spoken in one place," I commented as we wove through the busy sidewalks.

"The diversity found in Taria makes this place unique and culturally rich," Nera said, elevating her voice so I could hear her above the throng. "Every planet in Andromeda has different languages, so we get a broad mixture of peoples."

As we walked, I couldn't help but feel out of place in my white linen clothing and worn combat boots as the women we walked past wore colorful sets and dresses.

"I feel underdressed," I said, embarrassed.

Nera shook her head as we stopped outside the doorway of our first store. "Andora is a hot planet with barely any bodies of water. It never rains. I cannot blame you for wearing clothing to shield your skin from the sun and hot sand."

A young man stepped from the store and loudly greeted Nera so that all on the street would hear that a Celestial had graced his shop with their presence.

I couldn't help but chuckle, which won me the disapproving stare of the shop owner.

"Are you lost?" he asked me in a thick foreign accent, looking me up and down like I was a wild animal. "We usually don't get desert rangers in my shop."

I laughed at his assessment because I knew I resembled a ranger or dweller with my layers of clothing.

"Atila." Nera chastised the man. "Renna is a mortal from one of the hottest districts of Andora. She is a guest of Khellios. He asks that Renna be fashioned in the dress of Taria."

Atila pursed his lips at me, unsure.

Nera leaned into him and said, "Khellios is paying."

At her words, Atila's eyes widened with glee as if coins were erupting from his visage, and he embraced me. "Welcome, welcome!" He ushered us inside. "I will be most glad to rid you of this"—he clasped his hands together—"*lovely* attire." He lifted the hood of my half cape, which was meant to shield me from the sun. "The material, it's like it's dead, *no*?"

"Atila," Nera grumbled, shaking her head. "Be nice."

"*Right*," he said, eyeing my clothing like he wanted to incinerate it. "Go sit, and I will bring out color swatches to match your skin. It's lovely, beautiful undertones."

I looked to Nera, who nodded encouragingly, and we both moved farther inside the shop. Atila's assistants surrounded us and guided us to couches and a coffee table in a fitting room with a large floor-length mirror. Nera and I were immediately offered drinks, and after a few minutes, the attendants began inundating me with silks and fabric I had never seen before, covering my skin to find out what colors and fabrics worked best.

"I cannot wait to tell the other shops that I dressed Khellios's *guest*." Atila winked, carrying a tray of refreshments. "Khellios is usually one of the more quiet Celestials. No scandals, no love affairs. I usually just send him clothing for himself. This is the first time he's sent over a woman. How exciting!" He wagged his eyebrows suggestively.

I blushed a deep red, and my eyes grew. "Oh!" I shook my head. "I truly am *just* his guest. No funny business."

Atila set the refreshments on the coffee table and crossed his arms. "That god is too good looking for you to be a mere guest."

I looked to Nera for intervention, but she just laughed.

"You do think he's good looking, do you not?" Atila asked, tilting his head. When I laughed awkwardly, he added, "Have you seen him, or has the hot sun on Andora blinded you?"

"*Atila*," Nera warned again, but he just rolled his eyes and grumbled about the ignorance of youth and relationships.

As Atila fussed about colors and silhouettes for my body type, I thought about his pointed question. Khellios *was* an extremely attractive man. I could stare at his dark tawny skin, amber eyes, and tall stature all day. I wondered what he looked like without a shirt and blushed at the thought.

About two hours later, Nera and I walked out of the shop with several bags. Atila promised to drop off several more bags and boxes to Khellios's home later that day once he and his assistant literally worked their magic and sewed the clothing.

We stopped by two other stores afterward to buy shoes and undergarments, and the last store was a crystal shop. Nera shared that the shop was owned by a witch who enchanted the crystals to help people heal from maladies such as lost love, health concerns, and other things. The shop was so successful that the witch had opened three other locations around Taria.

Gemstones, sold by color, filled large bins situated in each corner of the open floorplan. A few customers were browsing and filling baskets with purchases.

While perusing stones by the entrance, I felt a tingling on the back of my neck. I inconspicuously lifted my gaze to take in my surroundings and find out if I was being watched. Sure enough, through the shop door, I saw a woman in the street, head tilted and eyes narrowed at me. She wore a long black gauze dress, and cascading brown curls spread around her shoulders. Her blue eyes, lined in black kohl, examined me up and down with more curiosity than malice. I tilted my head when my eyes snagged on a serpent cuff around her arm.

Perhaps I looked similar to someone she was seeking?

Feeling uncomfortable under her stare, I shifted to look at other stones but still felt her eyes on me. I let a few seconds pass by, and when I looked up to confront her, she was gone.

I walked outside and looked down the street, but I couldn't locate her among the souls strolling up and down. There was something odd about her, but I couldn't pinpoint what it was.

"Is everything alright?" Nera asked behind me, making me jump.

"Yes. I think so," I replied, scratching the back of my neck discreetly. "I thought I saw something," I lied, shaking my head.

Nera shrugged, and we moved back inside the shop to purchase our goods.

We eventually made our way back to the plaza, and I couldn't wait to collapse into the car waiting for us. As Nera excitedly talked about our day and the other places we had yet to visit, an invisible force hit my body, and I was suspended in midair. I screamed from the impact and covered my face but realized my physical body was still on the ground. I had somehow become detached and was rapidly propelling through the air.

I FELL in a heap onto polished golden floors. Looking down at my limbs, I noticed they were translucent, as if I was a shadow of myself. I lifted my gaze, and a woman stood in front of me, dressed in a shimmering black robe, arms folded, her expression blank.

"What is this?" I asked, scrambling to stand.

Stretching my arms out, I inspected them, but I seemed to have lost feeling in my body. My fall should have killed me.

"Apologies," the woman said, her tone sincere. "There is never a good way to prepare someone for these sorts of things." She gestured to where I stood.

"*What* sorts of things? This is the second time I have been taken from someplace with no warning!" I yelled, trying to feel comfortable in the shadow body I stood in. This couldn't be teleportation because my body wasn't solid. "I have been dragged *out of my body.*" I paused, panic gripping my center, and I attempted to clutch my chest. "*Am I dead?*" I screamed and began gliding across the room. "I died. *I died,*" I kept saying despite the woman's loud assurances that I was very much alive and murmurings that nothing was going according to plan.

"I am Livina," the woman said over my panicked speech. "And I know why you are here."

I paused midway and spun to face her, my mind taking a minute to adjust to my movements. I quickly hovered toward her.

Livina regarded me calmly as we stood nose to nose. "I know who you are and where you come from," she said.

"You don't know anything," I spat and turned around to continue pacing. I spun and pointed a finger. "Return me to my body this instant!"

"I know you have been trained by the most unorthodox of

mentors," she called out. "I know you used to hide in that closet, hoping he would leave you alone. You are not like him. You are inherently good, Renna."

I froze.

This woman listed off personal details of my life that no one but me, my mentor, and my wretched foster mother were privy to.

"You avoided touching magic willingly for over seven years." She stepped closer to me. "You vomited for a week and refused to leave your room when *he* made you use magic to push that woman into oncoming traffic to prove your skills—"

"*Stop!*" I yelled. The memory of that day, the screams of onlookers and the driver who ran out of his car, rolled through me like a wave. "You have *no* right!" I said, rushing toward her, hoping whatever mass I was made of would push her back.

An invisible, energetic wall stopped me, protecting Livina from my fury.

Livina put her hands up sharply, warning me to back down. "I have seen the trajectory of your life, Renna. I am not here to hurt you," she stated. "I am here to help you."

I laughed sarcastically. "Who the fuck are you? I already have a guide to help me." I crossed my arms.

Livina paused, furrowing her brows before answering. "I am Livina, Goddess of Fate and Destiny. Civilizations across this universe have known me by many names. I am here to help you get where you need to be."

"And where exactly am I headed?" I demanded. "A few weeks ago, I was on track to complete my doctorate program, and now I don't know who I am or what I am doing here. I'm in a strange dimension alongside beings I've only ever heard about, waiting for two very real threats to diminish—from the Council and a god who suddenly has taken an interest in me."

"I am forbidden from revealing the future," she said stoically, but I sensed a bit of edge to her voice, as if she was masking frustration. "Doing so would strip me of my power. That is the weakness of gods. What makes us *us* can destroy us. However, I can guide you with information I am authorized to give." Livina stepped closer to me. "You have strayed from your course. You need to access your magic."

"I do not, and I'm tired of telling anyone who will listen that I do not need my magic." I lifted my palms, frustrated. "I'm here in Taria because of my magic. Magic has only ever caused me pain."

"Magic is a part of who you are. It runs in your veins. It envelops you and makes you whole." Her words reminded me of Sethos's.

I crossed my arms. "Khellios seems to be the only one who respects my decision to never touch magic."

"Then he is foolish," she gritted out. "You cannot escape your fate. You must control the magic that boils deep inside you. I can feel glimmers of energy moving within you. Like a fault line, the small tremors keep widening gaps in your soul when you are triggered. If you do not come to terms with what is inside you, your impulsiveness will wreck any hope you have for inner peace. You will become chaos itself. You need inner balance."

"Fate can change." My words were more bitter than I intended.

Livina shook her head. "The end result is the same. How you get there is what you have power over. *Do not* leave your power unchecked."

"Am I in danger?"

Livina folded her arms. "That depends."

"On what?" I wanted to scream.

"On how you define danger." She squinted slightly, betraying her collected demeanor. "Danger is in the eye of the beholder. It could be whispering in your ear. Would you be able to recognize it?"

I rolled my eyes and leaned in. "I'm being forced to reside in Taria because of a god who wants my brand of magic. How about that? Is that *dangerous* enough for you?" I snapped. "I don't need you."

"I am part of your journey, Renna. You *will* need me. And I will help you get home."

My mouth dropped open, and the tension I'd been holding in my body since I arrived in Taria expanded into an anxious bundle. No one had been able to tell me when the danger would abate so I could leave Taria. I was grateful for the shelter, but it was not my world.

"When?" I asked.

"You will journey home before the yearly equinox celebrated in Taria," Livina answered.

"What about the god who is threatening my life?"

"Dangers in this world will always remain. You have the right protector by your side to keep you safe."

My mind immediately thought of Khellios and his role as protector of Taria. Khellios had promised to keep me safe, and Nera and Aramis vouched for my safety in Taria. Hearing I would remain safe from the goddess who could see into my future made me breathe a little easier. She didn't have to help me. I had not sought her out. Like Sethos, she had come to me offering help.

"How will you help me?"

"I will help you when I see you have strayed from your path."

I narrowed my eyes and pointed at her. "You better *not* drag me out of my body again!"

"I apologize. That will not happen again. There was no good time to speak with you."

I shook my head. "What must I do to return home? What can you tell me?"

Livina remained quiet for a few moments as she wrung her hands and closed her eyes as if she was seeing something I could not. "Your strength is in darkness. With the darkness, you will build a home."

None of her words made sense. "*How* do I return home?"

"Home will call you. Its pull will be undeniable. That *force* . . ." She paused and opened her eyes. "The force has already begun calling you back . . . you won't be able to escape its hold."

I shook my head, confused. I had no family except Helena, and she didn't practice magic. She didn't even know I had left campus. "I don't understand. So I am to stay in Taria until the equinox?"

Livina nodded.

"Will something happen that will take me home?"

"Yes. I cannot share anymore."

At her words, I felt my spirit being pulled back, much in the same manner as I had been brought here.

"I will find a way to communicate with you." Livina's words were a mere whisper as I traveled in the wind.

Within seconds, I reunited with my body, rocking forward as if I had been bumped into. Nera caught me quickly and righted me.

"Are you okay?" she asked, clutching my arm.

We were still walking toward the car waiting to return us to Khel's home. No time had passed. If Nera was a goddess and had not detected the power wielded by Livina, then I suspected Livina did not wish me to share what had happened. She would have met me face-to-face in the open if she wanted people to know she was helping me.

I nodded. "I tripped," I blurted out, my face blushing from the lie.

I hoped she thought I was red from embarrassment.

Nera smiled, and we continued to make our way back to the car.

A man with green eyes stepped into our path, bringing us to a stop.

"I would be remiss if I didn't introduce myself to Khel's . . . *guest*," the man said, mischievously grinning down at me.

My time in Taria was certainly eventful today.

"Give it a rest, Cylas," Nera said. She crossed her arms and rolled her eyes with an exasperated sigh.

"Nera," he said with a forced smile. "Forever loyal and forever shortchanged. How *is* Khel?" he asked her with mocking interest.

Like the other gods I had met—with the exception of Khellios—Cylas also had a silver aura surrounding him that signaled his divinity. He differed from Khellios not just in looks, with his wild, full brown-black hair in stark contrast to Khellios's sharp haircut, but also in his relaxed and carefree body language. Cylas wore a black leather motorbike jacket, a white V-neck shirt, necklaces that looked like military dog tags seen in Earth pawn shops, and combat pants.

Catching me staring at him, Cylas ran a hand through his hair, openly smirking.

Nera looked between us and shook her head. "I'll wait for you in the car, Renna," she said with a tight smile. "Don't be long."

"No, *don't leave*," Cylas mockingly pleaded. "Come back . . ." he said in a high-pitched tone with a hand reaching for her retreating form. "Was it something I said?" He turned to me with a shrug. "People can be *very* touchy around here," he said, his tone half teasing.

He stuck his hand out.

"You would be a hit at parties," I said, shaking his hand, which engulfed mine.

"I usually am," He winked, his eyes dancing with mirth. "The name's Cylas," he said, my hand still in his. "My friends call me the god of creation—"

I laughed.

"—the one who listens to dutiful prayers"—he leaned in next to my ear—"and the one who is good with his tongue."

I choked on my spit at the last phrase and began coughing, hitting my chest.

"*Not* the response I usually get." Stepping back, he gave me a self-satisfied smile.

"*Not* the introduction I was expecting." I chuckled.

"I should re-evaluate my one-liners." He pursed his lips.

"Depends on the audience," I said, grinning now.

This was the first time I had smiled freely while in Taria. I could feel Nera's eyes on me, and I turned to find her scowling as she watched us from the car.

Following my lead, Cylas also looked to Nera. He smiled deviously. "I see Nera has been showing you around Taria." He began circling me like I was prey.

I shivered as my skin prickled deliciously down my neck, to my nipples that now stood erect, and down the sides of my ribs. Not understanding my body's response to Cylas's closeness, I clasped my hands below my waist and smiled.

"I wonder how long until you inevitably return home. Perhaps I can convince you to stay." He winked.

"Hard to say." I deflected, thinking about Livina's words.

"Come or go, do as you please," he said close to my neck. "You don't owe these people anything. Don't let anyone rule you."

I shrugged. "Well, at the moment, I am currently staying in

Taria because of threats against me. So I imagine I'll remain here until the threat is defused."

I kept my words vague, unsure how much of my circumstances were public knowledge.

Cylas smiled politely, his grin forced. "Am-Re will never go away. He is a plague."

He knew.

My blood ran cold through my body. "Is that its name? The one who is hunting me?"

Cylas narrowed his eyes and nodded. "That is the name of your enemy." He pursed his lips. "None of the cowardly gods who live here would have told you his name. You should at least know who your foe is."

I looked down at my hands, clutching my shopping bags and slightly trembling. I had a name now for the entity who was hunting me, and it was terrifying. It made the danger all the more real.

Cylas lifted my chin, and I was met with a tight smile. His green eyes searched mine. "I know you are scared. You have every right to be. You do not know me well, but Khel and I will do what we can to keep you safe. Am-Re is our common enemy. He has been a thorn in my side for ages. His chaos threatens all of my creations."

I tilted my head. "Is that what your magic does? Do you create life?"

He nodded and dropped his hand from my chin. "I have been tasked with the creation of planets and all flora and fauna on them."

"I didn't know Am-Re could be capable of destroying planets. Although, I don't know much about him." As the sheer power of Am-Re's magical abilities settled in my mind, I began to panic.

"He's capable of a lot worse."

Livina's warning for me to learn to hone my magic rang in my ears.

"Renna," Cylas said, "I'll be brief and to the point."

"I'm sure you usually are."

"Are you sure about the first part?" He cocked his head.

My skin heated.

"I'd like to get to know you." Cylas smiled, lifting one eyebrow devilishly.

I laughed nervously at his brazenness. "You're already getting to know me."

He replied in a low whisper, "There is more than one way to get to know somebody."

As if his words had reached Nera's ears, she immediately exited the car and held the door open, signaling she was ready to leave.

"I'll see you," I quickly said, my voice a pathetically embarrassing high pitch, and I almost ran to the car.

"Is that a 'yes'?" he called after me. "I'll call on you tomorrow."

I waved him off, trying to hold in my laughter.

"You didn't say no," he was still calling after me.

"Well," Nera said, crossing her arms with a sigh as I got in the car.

She climbed in after me, and we began the drive back to Khellios's home.

"I am sure Khel will have my head for *that*." She huffed.

I turned to see Cylas staring after us with a smile that showed a quiet type of resignation I did not understand. I sat back, facing forward.

"Try not to mention Cylas to Khel," Nera said lightly.

"Why?" I asked, thinking it was an odd request. "I don't owe Khel anything. I barely know him."

I hoped my response wasn't deemed disrespectful, but Cylas,

despite his brazen demeanor, had been pleasant to speak to. And easy on the eyes.

Nera eyed me cautiously, her nose tilting down and eyebrows raising ever so slightly. "They don't get along," Nera explained. "Never have, never will."

"Cylas is *very* attractive," I confessed, feeling my face redden.

Nera groaned. "You can't be serious," she said, horrified.

Nera turned from me, grumbling, but I only caught a few words about how something like this "would" happen "this time around" and that she did not have the mental or emotional capacity to deal with it.

"I'm sorry if my talking to Cylas was a mistake," I said, embarrassed. "I didn't know . . .?"

Nera sighed and rolled her eyes, pinching the bridge of her nose. "Don't bring Cylas or this conversation up with Khel," she began, rubbing her face until her fingertips rested on her cheeks. "Khel has not been doing well lately with the attacks, and Cylas just makes everything complicated."

"Understood." I smiled politely and turned to face my window.

I didn't want to argue. And besides, I wouldn't be in Taria for long.

We remained silent for the rest of the car ride.

KHELLIOS'S HOME seemed empty when we arrived. Nera had mentioned Khellios was seldom home because of his role as Taria's protector and his presence in The Watch, but I had hoped to see him to thank him for replacing my wardrobe.

As Nera and I made our way through the space with my shopping bags, the sound of steel clashing and expletives broke the silence. I looked to Nera in alarm, but she smiled and pointed to a set of open doors in the living room that led outside.

"It's just Khel and Ukara training," Nera explained. "They always train on the beach. Come, let's say hello."

We set our bags down and walked to the open doors. Outside, we stepped onto a beautiful, lush green grassy patio with chairs and tables surrounded by tall trees swaying in the wind. Taking a pathway on the right, we walked down to the private beach I had seen earlier that day. The ocean was a fantastic backdrop, but Khellios's bare torso captivated my attention as he moved inside a fighting ring with a large sword. His skin glistened in the sun, accentuating his tight muscles.

I licked my lips.

A woman in full golden armor was with him, wielding a spear and sword. Her beautiful curly hair bounced as she moved, swiftly deflecting Khellios's attacks. When she unarmed Khellios and shoved him to the sand, she laughed with a brilliant smile and stuck her hand out to help him.

He smirked and took her hand, only to pull her down to the sand and then immediately get up.

"You cheat!" she laughed.

Khellios laughed with her. "You should be more alert, then, Goddess of War."

As we approached, Khellios's back stiffened, and he turned our way, his eyes immediately locking with mine. My stomach flipped.

"Cousin." Nera greeted him with a wave.

"Nera." He pulled his eyes from mine to nod to her in greeting.

Turning to me again, he smiled.

I waved awkwardly. "Hello."

"How was your day?" he asked, walking to the fence.

He grabbed a towel and began wiping the sweat from his body.

My eyes followed that towel over the expanse of skin and muscle.

"Beautiful," I said, staring at him as he ran the towel up and down his abdomen.

Nera snorted.

Immediately realizing I had given the most absurd response, I turned red and looked anywhere but at him. "My day was *great*."

"And beautiful?"

I looked at him to find him smirking.

"Yep." I scratched the back of my neck. "Yours?"

"Beautiful." He smiled lazily.

My heart and stomach dropped, and I wanted to be buried in the sand from embarrassment.

The woman he was sparring with moved toward us, and up close, I could see she had ice-blue eyes, and the side of her head was shaved.

"I heard you were writing a thesis on ancient Xhorian weapons." She inclined her head to the weapons they had used. "I would suggest you study the art of ancient warfare first."

She stepped toward me, her hand out in greeting.

I quickly shook her hand, and she continued. "I'm Ukara. I hope you have found Taria hospitable amid so much sudden change." She squeezed my hand and smiled.

"Thank you." I returned her smile. "I'm Renna. My studies are on hold for the time being," I shared. "I would like to see if I could find some research resources while I am here. Perhaps there is a library with descriptions of weapons from that time. It would be a good way to fill my time here."

"Resources as in *books*?" Ukara exclaimed, her brows knitting. "Books will not truly teach you about weapons."

I turned red, feeling self-conscious. "Books are what I have been using for my thesis. My trip to Xhor would have allowed me to view some of the excavated weapons—"

"We will go to the tombs," she said suddenly.

I shook my head because surely I hadn't heard her correctly. "*Tombs*?" Thinking she was joking, I laughed. "What tombs?"

She nodded. "Some of the weaponry from the time of the old city have been preserved or replicated. They are stored in a few tombs found here in Taria."

"Wow." A huge grin spread across my face. "That would be amazing."

Khellios swung an arm out toward Ukara and smiled at her. "Ukara knows her way around weapons. She is a good resource." He turned to me. "You will be in good hands. The tombs have been meticulously preserved. Your thesis may be on hold, but that doesn't mean you cannot carry on with your research if you wish."

I nodded. "Thank you. It will be good to stay busy."

"Then it's settled," Ukara said as she grabbed her belongings to leave. "I will send word with Nera or Khellios about meeting up in the next several days after you get settled in Taria."

I clasped my hands in front of me and beamed at her. "That sounds great."

"How was your time in the shops?" Khellios asked Nera and me.

"Hopefully you didn't bump into Cylas," Ukara said over her shoulder as she walked past us to the pathway back to the house. "He was in town today."

Nera and I became still, and I glared at Ukara's retreating form, then looked at the ground. Khellios's mood immediately dipped.

"Nera? You saw him?" Khel asked accusingly.

"Who?" she asked nonchalantly.

She was a terrible liar.

"Cut the crap," Khellios deadpanned.

I looked up and was caught in Khel's frosty stare.

"Cylas spoke to you?" he gritted out with a thunderous expression I could only describe as deep hatred.

I looked to Nera for backup, but she looked down to the ground, suddenly very interested in her shoes.

I sighed and faced Khellios again, and he looked down at me like I was a child who needed to be reprimanded. I had spent years being spoken down to by my mentor, and in that time, I lost my will to fight back and demand respect. That a stranger was now doing the same did not sit well with me.

So, I crossed my arms, mimicking Khel's pose, and raised my chin. I had committed no crime. "Cylas spoke to me, *yes*. He welcomed me to Taria," I said defiantly, stepping toward Khel in challenge.

"I see." He pulled his lips into a tight line.

"Is there a problem?" I said, squaring my jaw.

"Khel—" Nera interjected, suddenly finding her voice. She stepped up next to me, and her show of solidarity reinforced my confidence. "Be reasonable. *Please*."

"Go inside," he said, not breaking eye contact with me. "*Now*."

"Khel," Nera argued, her tone rising, albeit with some hesitation. "This is ridiculous."

"This does not concern you," Khel stated in a tone laced with finality. "*Go inside*," he ordered, his eyes still on me.

Nera squeezed my hand and walked inside.

"I gather you dislike Cylas?" I asked, my words clipped.

His shoulders were tense and silence met me, as if he was trying to come up with the right words to say.

13

KHELLIOS

From Renna's tone and body language, she was clearly upset.

I did not blame her. What the fuck was I doing? She did not know anything about our romantic past or the conflict surrounding Cylas trying to win her favor in more ways than one all those years ago. I was acting like a jackass.

"He and I disagree on a great many things." I clenched my jaw.

I was a coward for not telling Renna about our past. Part of me knew it would be easier to come clean and share with her what she meant to me then and how much it meant to me now that she was back in my life. But the other part of me knew that telling her would not bring back all that she had felt for me once. I could not force her to love me.

"Well," Renna said, her tone still defensive, "I'm sorry you and him do not get along."

Renna looked to me to respond, but I found myself mute.

How could I tell her I was frightened she would reject me for another? I had spent an eternity trying to move on with my life, but her memory and the deaths of those who died alongside her replayed in my head almost nightly for centuries. Now that she was here, I was in a never-ending cycle of grief, guilt, and fear, thinking she would be taken from me once more.

"Cylas treated me well," Renna stated in a more neutral tone. But she quickly added more defensively, "He did not speak ill of you. He assured me you would both keep me safe."

"Did he now?" I crossed my arms. "Nice of him to volunteer."

Renna furrowed her brows and shook her head. "All you have said is that Taria is safe. I was never told I should avoid anyone."

I don't know why, but I laughed. Renna may not have been able to remember me, but every one of her nuances and quirks was fresh in my mind. It was a relief to know that her spitfire and hellion energy had remained the same.

"And now you're laughing at me." Renna's tone was deadly, and the air around us shifted as if the atoms in the air itself began to vibrate faster in response to her mood.

After feeling some of Renna's erratic energy in Aramis's office and inside my home when she arrived in Taria, I could understand why Aramis contacted me. Even though he was supernatural himself and had used magic countless times, there was something chaotic and unbridled in Renna's magic. Renna was a daughter of Am-Re, and like her father, her energy came from anger and chaos. The wound of the father had been inherited by the daughter. Without proper training, her magic was unpredictable and made her dangerous. I could understand why Am-Re wanted his daughter and was looking for her. Am-Re most likely wanted to use Renna as a weapon.

"I'm not laughing at you," I admitted to Renna. "I'm laughing at the fact you don't fear me. You fight back."

Now it was Renna's turn to laugh, but her laugh was bitter. "And why should I fear you?"

There was hurt behind Renna's words.

We did not know much about her upbringing besides that she was in the foster system. Her defensiveness likely stemmed from a difficult past. I didn't understand why Am-Re had reincarnated her only to abandon her with strangers.

Nothing surprised me, but I would do everything I could to protect her.

"You should never fear me." I was honest in my statement. "I want to help you and protect you. I have been around for a long time. Many of the gods around here and outside of Taria tend to listen to what I say."

"So, you're an alpha and a bully," she challenged.

Renna remained on edge. The air around us was still heavy with unstable energy. I feared what would happen if she was unable to control it. I also wondered if using her power would somehow link her to her father. Would he be able to sense her exact location? I would be better able to protect her if she stopped using her magic altogether.

"No." I shrugged. A dark thought entered my mind as I recalled how willingly Renna had submitted to commands of a carnal nature all those years ago. "I think it would take very little to convince you to do as I wanted," I said with a smirk and a cocked brow.

Renna's eyes widened, and she blushed.

"You don't need Cylas," I stated.

"I don't?" She lifted her chin defiantly. "And why is that?"

I crossed my arms and shook my head. "I am a protector of Taria. There is no better person to keep you safe than the one who is in charge of everyone's safety."

I wanted to be the only person Renna turned to for anything she needed. That is how it had been before her death. When she sought asylum with the enclave, I became her protector, her lover, her home. That it would not happen again overnight frustrated me to no end.

"And what about having friends? Or is that not good for my safety either?"

I laughed. "Cylas doesn't want to be your friend. He wants more than that."

Renna narrowed her eyes. "And that bothers you." She stepped closer. "Why?"

A braver man would have told her everything then. But that would be the fastest way to alienate her from me.

So, instead, I sighed nonchalantly. "All I can do is warn you that Cylas is very noncommittal with anything he does. He never takes situations seriously. He's unreliable. And he will do anything he can to string you along."

Renna scoffed and looked toward the sea. The wind was blowing her hair everywhere. "He only just met me. Why would he do that?"

I couldn't help myself, and I reached out and captured one of her wayward strands. She gasped as I gently slid it behind her ear, and a beautiful blush spread on her cheeks.

"Because you're beautiful." Renna's face reddened further, and I could feel myself harden just by her mere presence. I needed this woman. I continued. "You're also smart and you're kind and strong."

"You barely know me." Renna was now looking down at the ground.

Fisting my hands behind my back, I resisted the urge to touch her again and bring her chin up so she could face me. I did not want to scare her by coming on too strong. The fear of rejection began to swirl in my chest once more.

"You are at the top of your academic career and working to obtain a doctorate degree, so I know you are smart. And you have been the victim of two attacks in the last month, yet you have shown incredible strength getting through those events and adjusting to Taria. And you have treated Nera, Ukara, and me with kindness, although I certainly don't deserve it." I silently prayed she would look up at me. "That you are beautiful is obvious. Any man would do anything to gain your attention."

Renna looked up then, her hazel eyes poring into mine as if she was hanging onto every compliment I gave her—as if she was starved of affection. Her energy had calmed, and gone was the anger and war within. However, it was my turn to feel anger build within me as I hated myself for not being able to piece together much of her past. Renna had been deeply hurt again in this lifetime, and I felt helpless for having been unable to save her from her demons again.

"You are free to speak to whomever." I could not help the abrasive tone of my words as I thought of Cylas and her together. "What you do with your personal time here is none of my concern."

Renna's face fell then, and her eyes searched mine as if confused.

I was confused as well. I desired her and wanted her all to myself and to keep her from the dangers of the world, but I also wanted her to live her life and not be a prisoner. My brain struggled with the push and pull of how to act around Renna. My cock was hard, and I wanted nothing more than to grab her and pull her to me because of the history I knew we shared, but that was not what she needed at the moment. Renna was not a quick fuck. If she was anything like in the past, she needed to be romanced. I could count on Cylas not knowing anything about romancing a woman. His liaisons were famously short.

I curled my fists as I attempted to ignore the ache pressing against my pants, and I nodded goodbye, willing my body to walk away.

I was disgusted with myself for having let my guard down when she went missing. I stopped searching for her when I should have fought for her return every second and with every breath.

I didn't deserve her. But I wanted her.

I would have to figure out how to make her want me as well.

14

RENNA

Over the next several days, Nera and I ventured to downtown Taria, and each day, more decorations lined the streets to welcome the equinox. Flowers and delicate floral vines I had never seen before hung from window flower boxes, creating lush and fragrant streetscapes. Street vendor stalls were also decorated with flowers and banners as the area transformed into a lively party atmosphere. Nera and I passed by several street performers, and I indulged in various sweet and savory snacks from different bakeries and vendors who were eager for a friend of a Celestial to try their goods.

As we were exploring, we walked past a darkened street. I stopped and craned my neck. Elaborate wood and brick buildings lined the road with black, dark purple, and different shades of dark blue pointed roofs.

I furrowed my brows. "This is odd." I looked overhead at the sunny day and then back at the street. A few people dressed in black and purple cloaks walked within the street. "It's almost like the light is unwelcome there. Do they not celebrate the equinox? There are no decorations."

Nera came to stand next to me. "This is the witch district of Taria."

I cocked my head. "Is this where the witch who helped secure Taria lives?"

"Yes, she runs the most popular potion business in Taria. She has brought many witches, mages, and warlocks to Taria, all seeking shelter from the Council." Nera sighed. "Despite our best efforts to include them in Taria's everyday life, they prefer to be left alone." Nera lowered her voice and chuckled. "I find witches are very low fuss about most things. They keep to themselves and have their own holidays based on the planet Earth's traditions."

I hummed, not really knowing Earth's traditions. I itched to explore the darkened road, but Nera led me away.

THAT EVENING, when I returned to Khellios's home, I found him standing in his living room area facing his terrace. One hand was in his pocket, while the other held a glass of amber liquid.

My eyes roamed the lines of his body, appreciating his broad shoulders and lean, muscular legs.

My skin flushed.

"Hi," I said awkwardly, feeling like I was intruding on a quiet moment.

Khellios took a sip of his drink and turned.

I waved.

His eyes softened, and he smiled. "How was your visit to town?"

"It was nice, everyone is excited about the equinox. The decorations look beautiful."

Khellios tilted his head. "Your smile doesn't reach your eyes. What's wrong?"

I shifted on my feet. "It's all temporary." I shook my head, recalling Livina's words that I would leave this place soon. "I live each day not knowing what to expect."

Khellios frowned. "About that," he said, setting his drink on a nearby table. He then reached to an armchair that faced away from me and produced a black backpack. "I got you this." He walked toward me and handed it to me.

I took the backpack and opened the main zipper. A datapad, notebooks, and pens were inside. "What's this for?"

Khellios scratched his neck and put his hands in his pockets. "Ukara mentioned she'd like to start helping you with your research this week. You don't have anything to take notes with. I thought it would be nice to—"

I grinned.

"Now *that* smile reaches your eyes." He chuckled.

I blushed and looked down. "Thank you."

"Is the backpack a good size? I wasn't sure what you would need. It looks a little small."

"It fits everything I need. I doubt I'll store research books in here. Ukara seems opposed to them." I laughed.

"Do you want to try it on? I could get you a new one if it isn't right."

I shrugged and swung the backpack over one shoulder, looping my arm through one strap. My hair was in a ponytail, and it got trapped under the backpack.

"Allow me," he said, and he was behind me in an instant, helping free my hair.

He settled my hair around one side of my neck, lingering his fingers just above my collarbone. I held in a breath before he removed his fingers, and goose bumps erupted where his touch had been.

I felt Khellios reach for the other backpack strap. "Let me help you."

His voice was low and right above my ear.

I nodded, and he grabbed my hand and gently pulled my arm back to loop it through the strap. When he was done, he rested his fingers on my shoulder.

I gulped and darted my tongue out to lick my lips.

"Turn," he said, his voice now rough.

My breath quickened, and I turned to face him. His eyes were almost dark gold, like molten amber. His eyes had not taken this quality before. The intimacy between us felt old somehow, as if my body was used to the closeness between us. My lips parted as he looked down to my mouth.

"I'm not finished," he purred and reached for my chest with slow movements.

My heart pounded and my eyes widened, but he reached for two small straps on each side. They connected horizontally across the front.

"I want to make sure it fits right." His voice wove its way to my core, and tingling sensations rippled through my body as he clicked the straps in place. His knuckles brushed against my bare skin above my shirt's low neckline.

I squirmed under his touch, my skin growing hyper-sensitive.

Khellios grabbed my biceps and spun me around so my back was to his front, and he grabbed the loose end of my ponytail to place it behind me.

I closed my eyes and exhaled, waiting for what he would do next.

And then nothing. He stepped away from me.

He cleared his throat. "I'm—" He cleared his throat again. "I'm glad the backpack is to your liking."

I felt like I had been slapped in the face with disappointment. I turned my head slightly and forced a smile. The intimacy of a seemingly simple action had taken me by surprise, and the fact that I hadn't felt anything like it in a while had my body thrashing with want and rejection.

"I spoke with Aramis today. We talked about Helena."

My eyes grew wide, and I spun to face him. "Is she okay?" My heart began pounding rapidly in my chest.

I hadn't spoken to her since I left campus. I hoped she was all right.

"She is. I asked Aramis to pass on a message to her that you had to leave unexpectedly for Xhor. The less details we share the better since your campus has been placed under lockdown by the Council—"

"*What!*"

"—and all remaining summer students are undergoing interrogation about any suspicious activity they may have seen."

I covered my face and breathed deeply. "Will she be safe?" I asked through my fingers.

"I made him swear to me that she will be."

I looked up and crossed my arms, narrowing my eyes. "That means nothing to me. She is my friend." I stepped closer. "I have no assurance she will be okay. What does swearing a promise to you accomplish?"

Khellios's expression and voice turned hard. "Swearing a promise to a god binds the person to abide by it. Breaking the promise results in punishment."

"Of what kind?" My voice rose.

"Whatever the god wishes."

I shook my head in disbelief. Our campus had never been placed on lockdown and students had never been subjected to interrogations. Was Helena scared?

"Renna, I will do whatever you ask of me if it comes to that. You name the punishment, but I know Aramis. He will not fail me."

"And why is that?"

"Because her safety is important to you. And because of that, it's also important to me." Khellios stepped closer to me, his eyes softened.

Looking into his eyes suddenly became too much, and I looked away from him. The swirl of intimate emotions from moments ago resurfaced. There was something about my interactions with Khellios that, like being in Sethos's presence, felt . . . *familiar*. I couldn't explain it.

"I'm on your side, Renna." His voice was almost a whisper.

I dared myself to look up at him and found his amber eyes swirling with a molten gold. "Your eyes," I breathed looking between them.

Khellios cleared his throat and blinked. The gold color was gone and his eyes were back to their regular amber hue.

"What was that?"

He ran a hand through his hair. "Er, nothing."

"That's the second time your eyes have done that. Earlier today, when you were putting on my backpack . . ." My skin flushed at the memory.

Khellios stepped back from me. "Right, well." He nodded. "I will let you know if I speak with Aramis again."

A hollow feeling settled in my chest. I blinked. "Thanks." I nodded and began to walk to my rooms, not daring to look back.

With my door shut securely behind me, I ran to the bathroom and quickly disrobed to stand under a cool shower. I braced myself against the tiled wall as I attempted to ignore the ache in between my thighs from my interaction with Khellios.

He had called me beautiful days before, but he was true beauty in the way he held himself with a confident and proud posture and his piercing eyes that never missed anything. His chiseled face and smirk only added to the appeal, while his voice, which was smooth and commanding, made me wish he would . . .

I shook my head. Made me wish he would do what?

I was way in over my head. He was granting me protection as a favor to Aramis. Attraction and action were two separate things. We could flirt and admire each other, but would any of it go anywhere? Maybe it was best I avoid thinking about Khellios that way . . .

My pussy throbbed

Suddenly a pair of ice-gray eyes came to mind.

Sethos.

Khellios.

I trailed my fingers down the tiles in front of me and moved to my aching center, brushing my swollen clit.

I rubbed back and forth, pressing my body against the tiles so I could feel the cold on my skin. My nipples pebbled, and I moaned.

I stepped my feet farther apart and closed my eyes, picturing Khellios behind me, kissing and licking my neck while wrapping one hand under my arm to grab my breast and gently squeeze.

Sethos was suddenly there too, on my other side, nibbling my ear while I imagined him moving one of his hands down and pushing mine away, so he could thrum my clit himself.

I moaned softly, and the idea of Khellios's and Sethos's hands on me sent euphoria spreading through my body in waves as my pussy began to clench.

"This pussy is mine," Sethos would whisper. "Tell me it belongs to me."

I nodded against the tile as I inched closer to the edge.

"Tell me it belongs to me," he would grit out between his teeth.

"Yes," I cried out.

"Yes, what?" he would demand. "I won't let you come until you tell me this pussy is mine," he growled in my ear.

"It's yours," I sobbed.

"Good girl." He kissed my temple. *"Now come."*

I shattered into a million pieces as my orgasm rolled through me, my fingers working me through the wave.

My breaths came out in heavy pants, and I dropped my hand to my side as my forehead thunked against the tile, the water still cascading down my body. As I shifted on my feet and tried to calm my racing pulse, I thought about how I pictured Sethos as the one making me come and not Khellios. I groaned and turned to lean my back against the tile before sliding to the floor.

Pulling my knees up to my chest, I tucked my head into my arms. "Fuck."

15

RENNA

Sethos visited me every night. He became a necessity I craved every time I closed my eyes. He never talked about himself and instead wanted to hear about my upbringing in the foster system and my hopes and dreams for the future. Each night, he took me to a new dream place. I loved when we met among the stars, suspended above the planets. Other times, we would sail in a small rowboat on a vast body of water that reflected the sky above, creating an illusion of a never-ending night sky.

One night, I awoke along a seashore, the soft sound of the waves waking me. I sat up, and Sethos stood a few feet from me. He cut a lone figure, looking out at the vast sea, almost black in its depths. In the distance, bioluminescence dotted the water where reefs came to the surface. It was magical. I would have jumped to run toward the water, but something in Sethos's posture made me pause.

I sat on the sand, watching him as his cape drifted in the wind along with his hair that glowed under the moon. He looked burdened as he gazed at the horizon, and I longed to comfort him just as he was doing for me as my guide.

I stood.

"You are troubled," I shouted over the thundering waves threatening to mute my voice.

Sethos did not turn to me, so I walked over and joined him. I followed his gaze and could see it was trained on caves that rose from the sea far in the distance.

"I'm supposed to be the one asking you questions." He smiled, not turning toward me. "I'm the guide, remember?"

I shrugged. "Something is clearly bothering you. What are you looking at? Where are we?" I looked around but could see nothing but shore as far as the eye could see.

"We are at a distant shoreline, far away from Andora."

I crossed my arms and chuckled. "That's awfully vague."

"This was my mother's birthplace," he said, looking intently at the caves. "She came from the sea. I was thinking of places to take you to tonight, and her calming presence came to mind. I didn't anticipate being this affected."

"Does she live?" I asked gently, thinking perhaps she had passed based on his melancholy state.

"She died long ago."

"I'm sorry." Instinct made me reach for his arm, and I squeezed gently, hoping to provide some comfort. "You know I never knew my parents and that my childhood was chaotic."

"And yet the chaos has not poisoned you." He laughed sadly. "I wish I could say the same."

I stepped in front of him and searched his eyes. Deep sadness settled in their depths. "I wouldn't say I'm unaffected by the chaos around me," I began. "My magic is tied to anger, which is a product of the chaos, and both my anger and magic are difficult to control. It may seem like the chaos did not poison me on the outside, but on the inside, I hate who I am most days because it feels wrong to reject the chaos within me. Sometimes I think it would be easier to give in to the magic and embrace who I am and not have to fight it all the time. But I know giving in to the darker elements that make up my magic would make me like my mentor." I faced the sea again, shoulder to shoulder with Sethos. "Whenever my magic surges within me, he always comes to mind. *Always*. It feels like I can't escape him. The memories of him suffocate me. I can't escape him."

"That is why you refuse to use your magic."

I nodded and hugged my arms around myself as the cool sea breeze made me shiver. Noticing, Sethos took off his black cape and swung it around my shoulders. The cape was made of wool and felt heavy on my shoulders. It smelled like Sethos, of sandalwood and bergamot. I clipped it and gathered the fabric to wrap it tightly around me. It pooled around my feet, highlighting our height difference.

"I'm sorry you're cold. I shouldn't have brought you here," he said, looking down at me.

"The cape significantly helps." I smiled. With my chin, I gestured to the caves as I gripped the fabric. "Would you like to talk about your mother?"

"There isn't much to say." He sighed. "She was a poor fae woman who hailed from a sea fae race. She got into some bad company and left home. She met my father, who was not fae, shortly thereafter, and she followed that man wherever he went, hoping he would one day marry her. I resulted from their union, and he left her shortly after I was born. She died a prostitute trying to make ends meet."

I searched for the right words to comfort him, but I didn't know what to say. "I'm sorry," I simply said. "I think the chaos has not poisoned *you*."

Sethos laughed. "And why is that?"

"You are counseling me during a time when I feel lost. I'm surrounded by strangers far away from home, and you provide me with a space where I can talk freely about things that are on my mind. Talking with you helps ground me."

It was Sethos's turn to step in front of me. "Do you not feel comfortable in Taria?" His voice was hard. "Be honest."

"I am treated kindly." I assured him. "I'm just getting to know everyone. Navigating through the different dynamics and relationships is not easy."

He nodded. "Who are you staying with?"

"Khellios."

He lifted his eyebrows. "You mentioned him before. What does he do?"

"He is part of the Celestial Enclave. He is a lunar and star deity."

Sethos snorted a laugh. "Pretentious. How could anyone be the god of the moon and stars?"

"*Hey!*" I laughed. "Don't make fun of him. He has been somewhat nice to me."

Sethos frowned. "*Somewhat* nice to you? You just told me you are being treated kindly."

I sighed. "He is just . . . *moody*." I shrugged. "And bossy. He takes Taria's security very seriously, and everyone does what he says."

"Should we walk?" Sethos asked, gesturing to the shoreline.

I nodded, and we began to walk along together.

"Tell more about this Khellios so I know if I need to curse him," Sethos asked, folding his hands behind his back.

I laughed. "There aren't many specific details to tell yet. I'm just getting to know him. Nera says he has a lot on his mind as one of the main protectors of Taria."

"So that's an excuse for him to be an ass?" Sethos shook his head. "I hope you don't stand for ill-treatment."

"I speak my mind when needed." I smiled. "As you well know."

Sethos chuckled. "Good girl. Always stand up for yourself."

I blushed and looked sideways at him. "He's not *all* that bad," I stated.

Sethos stopped walking and groaned. "Why do you say that? Are you giving him a pass because of good looks?" He shook his head. "You are not attracted to him, are you?" He wrinkled his nose and curled his lip in disgust.

I laughed. "I mean, he's not bad to look at."

"Not bad to look at?" Sethos exclaimed. "Not bad to look at, she says." He tilted his head back, looking skyward. "Heavens help me with the mortal who is under my watch."

"Dramatic much?" I shoved him playfully, and Sethos grabbed my hands.

He held them together and brought them to his chest. My heart began to beat loudly.

Sethos narrowed his eyes. "I mean it, Renna. I better not hear that he mistreats you. I don't give a flying duck's arse if he has a good excuse for being a tragic hero. You deserve respect."

I swallowed and nodded. I was taken aback by his intensity.

"Do you have to stay with him, or can you go someplace else if your relationship with him goes sour?"

"Nera shared he is seldom home," I said. "He is always at The Watch, sailing across galaxies or patrolling the shield of Taria. If we don't get on, it's not like I would see him that much."

"You're not answering my question. Is there someplace you could stay within Taria if you decide one day you cannot stand the sight of him?"

"I suppose I could stay with Nera. I have yet to go to her home, but she has been *very* kind to me."

Sethos nodded. "Khellios sounds like a very important man. Is there no one to help him patrol the skies or the shield of Taria?" He tucked one of my hands into the crook of his arm and propelled us forward again.

I tagged along happily.

"Yes. Nera and other minor sky deities work with Khellios at The Watch. She explained it's a platform that allows them to move from galaxy to galaxy every night to patrol different celestial bodies."

"Sounds like a dream job," Sethos drawled sarcastically.

"You mean like your job?" I joked. "Waiting on me, hand and foot, when I dream?"

Sethos turned to look at me and searched my eyes. "I'd wait on you anywhere."

"Sure, sure," I said playfully, shoving him again, but my stomach flipped with the implication.

We continued walking along the shore in companionable silence.

"This is nice." I sighed happily.

"I thought you'd enjoy a moonlit walk along the shore." He smirked.

I looked up to the sky. "I wonder if people can see us from The Watch down here since the moon is here."

"Why?" Sethos teased. "Do you miss your moon boy? Should we call him down?" Sethos looked up to the sky and began yelling, wildly flinging his arms around.

I turned red. "Hey!" I wrestled his hand down and hit him on the arm. "Quit it!"

"Why?" he laughed. "There is no one here but us. Plus, your body is not truly here. This is merely an astral projection."

"So no one can see us?"

He shook his head and laughed. "Like I shared the previous night, your body is back where you left it."

"But if my body is not really here, why can I feel in these dreams? Tonight I can feel the sand beneath my toes, and in the second dream I saw you, I felt the rocks I threw down the cliff."

He shrugged. "I don't make up the rules of astral traveling. It just is."

"Well can you warn me about the next place you plan on taking me? I'd like to dress appropriately."

"I happen to think you look perfectly appropriate wearing my cloak." A devilish smile grew on his lips.

"You know what I mean." I rolled my eyes and then stopped when a thought popped into my mind. "Nera shared that the sea in Taria is an illusion. It is not truly there, so it would not feel like water if one stepped into it. Is this shore real?" I pointed to the dark sea.

"Yes." Sethos nodded.

"So if I walk into the sea, I will feel the water?"

"I don't see why not." He crossed his arms and narrowed his eyes. "*Why*?"

The urge to run toward the water was overwhelming. I longed to know what the sea felt like on my skin. I imagined it would feel different from my swims in the rivers in Andora.

I narrowed my eyes at Sethos, who regarded me cautiously, and a grin broke out on my lips. "Race you to the water!" I screamed and took off.

Sethos cursed, and I could feel him following me. I should have known his cloak would weigh me down as I ran through the sand, but I didn't care.

"Renna!" Sethos called. "This is ridiculous. You can barely run in that!"

"You just don't want me to win!" I called back, and when I looked over my shoulder, I saw a very determined Sethos running after me.

I laughed and kept running.

Right as my feet were about to hit the water, Sethos ducked and grabbed me by the waist with one arm, hoisting me up on his shoulder with my head dangling over his back and my feet by his chest. Feeling his hard muscles against my body made my stomach dip, and I couldn't help the smile that split my face.

"You cheated," I yelled.

"Semantics," he said, and with a quick maneuver of his free hand, he unclipped his cloak from my body.

It fell around his legs, and he then stepped into the water.

"Where are we going now?"

"You and I both know you were likely going to excitedly launch yourself in the water wearing my cloak. Do you want to drown? I'd rather you stay alive."

Deep down I knew he was right. I would have likely ran into the water at full speed foolishly. But I still wanted to goad him. "You're just a sore loser."

Sethos playfully pinched the back of my thigh, and I felt it to my core. I squeezed my legs together in response.

"Be nice, or I'll drop you," he warned.

"No, you won't." I laughed. "So what are we doing now?" I said, feigning boredom as we waded deeper into the water.

The water was now at Sethos's perfectly round, muscular backside, and I couldn't pull my eyes away as he continued to carry me.

"Are you cold?" he asked.

"No." His body heat was keeping me warm. I reached down, feeling the water. "The water is pleasant. I thought it would be frigid."

"Good."

I brought up a bent elbow and, placing it on his back, leaned my chin on my wrist. "Where are we going? Am I a hostage now?"

"Will you be patient?" he asked. "Heavens, woman. You are insufferable. I am trying to bring us to a shoal so you can stand up safely."

"I know how to swim." I laughed. "And what is a shoal?"

"Well, from the looks of it, you've never been in the sea, otherwise you would have taken more precaution running into it, especially at night. If you're not an experienced swimmer, the water can be dangerous at night."

"Let me guess," I sighed. "You are?"

"*Very*. Swimming is second nature to me, even if I am only half sea fae. A shoal is a raised portion of land where the water is shallow. We're almost there."

When we reached the shoal, we began to ascend out of the water until just his feet were below the surface. Securing his arms around me, he slid me down his body. I tried to maintain as much contact as possible between us by keeping my hands on him until they rested on his chest and we stood face-to-face.

"There," he said quietly, his gaze soft on my face.

"Thank you," I whispered and lowered my eyes, feeling self-conscious.

Sethos gently tilted my chin up. "Don't lower your eyes from me," he whispered tenderly. "They are much too pretty to not look at."

My eyes dropped down to his lips, and he brought us closer. My pulse whooshed loudly in my ears.

"Ren . . ." He lowered his face to mine.

For some reason, my heart flipped when he called me by my nickname.

My breath hitched, and I licked my lips.

Before Sethos could close the distance between us, a wave crashed onto the shoal, pushing us off and tossing me into the ocean.

I panicked, struggling to find something to hold onto. I swallowed water, and it burned my throat.

Sethos's strong arms hooked under mine, and he pulled me from the water. Adjusting me in his grip, he carried me toward the shore.

"I got you," he said through gritted teeth, holding me close. "I got you."

I nodded against his chest, and as he strode to shore, I could see the water only reached his upper thighs, and I felt pathetic for having struggled.

On land, Sethos gently set me down and sat by me as I coughed up water. Sethos patted my back, and as I struggled to regain control of my breathing, my foot began to feel like it was on fire.

I yelled out and brought my foot toward me to inspect it.

A large gash marred my skin, and blood was quickly trickling out. The salt in the water wasn't helping the pain.

"You must have cut it on the coral," Sethos explained. "May I see?"

I nodded, and Sethos took my foot, applying pressure with his palms. His touch felt like ice on my skin, and it was only when emerald light began to emanate from his hands that I realized it was his magic that felt cold. His magic was unlike Nera's, which felt warm when she helped settle my anger. Sethos's magic on my skin did not feel unpleasant, just different.

When he removed his hand, my foot was no longer bleeding. "Thank you."

Seeing his magic heal my foot and knowing how Nera's magic had also helped me highlighted how much my magic failed me.

"What's wrong?" he asked, tilting to try and catch my eye.

I shook my head. "My magic was created to react to anger and create chaos. I can't heal. I couldn't help the people hurt in the quad during the attacks."

"I can help you. If you let me."

My eyes shot to his.

"It doesn't have to be like this for you," he said. "Let me teach you."

My stomach began to twist with anxiety, and I looked away from him. "No."

Sethos sat back, quietly observing me. "I won't force you, Ren."

"Just stop asking," I snapped.

He nodded and looked out toward the sea.

I was annoyed at my cowardice. I hated being at the mercy of anyone, yet I was relying on Khellios's protection in Taria because I lacked the ability to protect myself. My inner voice reminded me that even if I had learned my magic, I would still likely need protection. The gods hid in Taria from Am-Re.

Was anyone safe from him?

16

RENNA

The next day, a black sky car arrived to pick me up for a meeting with Ukara. When I walked outside of Khellios's home, he stood by the vehicle talking with the driver. As I approached, he turned to me, his eyes lazily drinking me in, and my face heated. I dropped my eyes and adjusted the backpack on my shoulders.

"Sleep well?" Khellios asked. "You look very tired."

How could I explain that I had traveled with my dream guide to a faraway land to stroll on a beach and all that had happened there? I was sure Khellios would lose his mind if he knew I had left my body to travel with someone he didn't know. He would likely think it was a breach of security, so I stayed silent about my dreamtime visitor.

"I had a restless night," I said through a yawn.

"Is everything all right?"

I nodded. "I'll catch up on sleep tonight," I lied, knowing full well I would likely be visited by Sethos again.

"Let me know if I can help. A few witches in town make sleeping potions for all sorts of sleeping maladies." He smiled. "I would be happy to acquire something to help you."

I nodded, remembering the witch district. "I'll keep that in mind, thank you."

Khellios opened the vehicle's door.

"So, what are your plans today after seeing Ukara?" he asked.

"I'm not sure," I answered. Without a looming thesis due date, my days were free. I was glad to meet with Ukara to keep me busy, but other than that, I had no set schedule. "I guess I could explore Taria some more." I shrugged.

"What do you usually do for fun?"

I laughed. "That's an easy one," I said self-deprecatingly. "I am one of the most un-fun people you will ever meet. My fun consists of staying in with books, wine, and sweets."

"What's not fun about that?" He grinned. "What type of books do you usually read?"

"Well," I began and put my hands on my waist, recalling I had none of my books since I had come to Taria so abruptly. "If I had my books with me, I would read romance . . ." I narrowed my eyes at him.

Khellios put his hands up in defeat and chuckled. "I know, I know." He put a hand over his heart. "I'm sorry I brought you here the way I did."

"Now I won't have any fun," I said jokingly.

"I wouldn't be so sure about that," he said, licking his bottom lip and tilting his head.

My stomach did a somersault, and I smiled down at my toes.

"Well, I won't keep you from your trip to see Ukara today," Khellios said.

"Right." I nodded and went into the sky car. "It was nice seeing you this morning, Khellios."

Once inside, I closed the door and nodded to the driver that I was ready.

The driver looked to Khellios for confirmation, and when

Khellios nodded and tapped on the vehicle, the driver pulled away.

Khellios wasn't joking when he said people tended to do everything he told them.

We started down the driveway, but the car came to a stop. I looked to the driver, furrowing my brows, but his eyes were trained on Khellios, who was once again standing outside the car on my side, gesturing for the driver to lower the window.

I drew my hand to my chest, startled by how quickly he moved.

Khellios leaned in when the window was all the way down. "Have a good day, Renna," Khellios said, his eyes hungry as he took in my face. "And one more thing."

I lifted my eyebrows, motioning for him to continue.

"I would like it if you called me Khel."

My lips formed a lopsided smile as my emotions tangled through me. "I will."

He grinned and stood, nodding to the driver to continue.

As the car drove away, my cheeks were sore from the huge smile that had settled on my face.

THE DRIVE TO see Ukara was longer than expected. We drove through downtown Taria and through the desert. Then, out of nowhere, like a mirage, a fenced-off pen materialized in the distance. A lone figure stood in the middle, hand on their visor, watching the car arrive.

It was Ukara.

She was dressed in dark, fitted cargo pants, as was the style for soldiers in the galaxy, and a black tank top, and her hands were wrapped in leather straps. Like me, she, too, wore combat boots.

I felt wholly inadequate wearing shorts, but I was not in Taria to train.

When the car stopped outside the pen, I wasted no time opening the door and walking toward her. Crates that looked big enough to store human bodies were strewn around her. Stacked against the fence were several spears and lances.

My eyes bulged when I recognized some of the weapons from my research books. Weapons like these were supposed to be two thousand years old.

My researcher brain went off in a frenzy. I had so many questions.

How had Ukara acquired the weapons? Something told me, from the way some of them looked blunted and dusty, that these were not replicas . . .

"Apologies for not taking you to the tombs today," she began, her brows rising in displeasure. "I did not realize I had to clear your presence with the god of the underworld. He is not a Celestial and can be hard to get a hold of. Instead, I thought I'd show you some of my personal weapons. Many of the weapons I currently use have not changed from what I used in the old city. Feel free to take notes and ask questions."

Pen and notebook in hand, I began to inspect the items before me. A jeweled spear caught my eye. It was almost identical to ones I'd seen in my research books. It was intricately crafted with turquoise beading embedded into the hilt and carvings on the metal point. The leather of the spear looked worn, as if it had been used over the years by an experienced hand.

I marveled at the items she had acquired for my study. "This is incredible. I would have never thought it was possible to see any of these up close."

"I'm happy to be showing them to you. You cannot study true ancient Xhorian weapons without experiencing the weapons you claim expertise on," she stressed.

I blushed. "Not everyone has the privilege to study some-thing like this hands on," I politely responded.

"These weapons were created for me by a god of the Elemental Enclave, who is the patron god of blacksmithing. He crafts tools using rare steel found in his home galaxy. The steel is protected by magic and is unbreakable," she explained, grab-bing a sword encrusted with lapis and amethyst, her grin wide. "The god boasted he was better than me in one-to-one combat. I challenged him and bet on brand new weapons." She shrugged and gestured to her weapons with a smirk. "I won more than the fight."

"That was generous of him," I said, marveling at a double-ended golden spear encrusted with emeralds in the handle.

"His enclave has the best resources for weapons. His chief enclave god keeps him busy creating weapons. That is how their enclave stays wealthy. Weapons trade."

"That sounds like a lot of pressure."

"Well, he must answer to his chief god."

"And who do you answer to?" I asked.

"Who do *I* answer to?" Ukara laughed, her tone bitter, the energy around us shifting as if responding to her. "I answer to nobody."

I shifted on my feet, the desert suddenly moving and molding under and around me. "I'm sorry, I did not mean to offend—"

The desert quickly changed to a mirage of blinding, glim-mering specks of gold, lined in hundreds of rows. When I squinted at the changing landscape that was coming into focus, I realized the gold specks were hundreds of warriors standing before us in rows of formation, their armor made of gold, weapons drawn, and eyes trained on the horizon. They stood motionless as if they were a moment in time, a phantom memory.

Ukara walked up to the warriors like a general inspecting her troops.

"I am Ukara, Goddess of War. Born of my father, Arios, King of the Sun. I belong only to myself and am affiliated with no enclave," Ukara said, turning her attention to me. "However, my father thinks he rules me to bolster the strength of his enclave," she added quietly.

I stayed silent as Ukara gazed at the mirage longingly.

She was an impressive woman to behold, and I was intimidated by her strength and sheer power. The woman commanded armies.

"You must think me ridiculous for my approach to research using books."

Ukara shook her head, and with a wave of her hand, the mirage disappeared. "Females cannot judge each other for trying to carve a place in male-dominated spaces. I fought for my place on the battlefield. My title did not come easily. You have been in school for many years, and earning a PhD is not an easy feat. I respect your drive to exist in this male-dominated research space."

I nodded my thanks and sat on the ground, immediately getting to work sketching and describing the artifacts surrounding me.

After a while, Ukara stepped in front of me and closed my notebook.

I looked up, startled, and scrambled to my feet.

"C'mon," Ukara said and grabbed a spear with a sharp, dark tip. "Grab one." Ukara stepped into the center of the fenced-off area.

I scratched my head. "Wait, what?" I laughed in disbelief. "What are you asking me to do?"

When Ukara turned to me with a black spear pointed in my

direction, I began to panic. "Ukara, you don't expect me to fight you . . . right?"

"Pick a spear, Renna." Her face was serious.

"How am I supposed to handle these?"

From the haphazard way the weapons were scattered, I wasn't sure Ukara cared.

I shook my head. "No. I'm—" I hesitated, looking between the spears before me and Ukara. "I'm not going to fight you."

"Suit yourself." She shrugged and lunged at me.

I jumped backward, dropping my notebook and pen and almost tripping on my boots. I grabbed the nearest spear and, ducking to the right, just missed her blow.

"Are you fucking kidding me right now?" I yelled.

I dodged another blow, and this time, I managed to swing my spear in her direction, but she blocked me with hers. My arms burned.

"Keep your feet wide and bend your knees," she yelled. "You can't be stiff when you move—stay agile."

"This is not how I want to research these weapons, Ukara!" I gritted out, backing up as far as I could while Ukara advanced on me with a wicked, catlike grin.

"Then how?" she yelled, swinging at me again.

This time, I anticipated her blow and deflected her attack. She nodded in praise but quickly jabbed again, and I ducked.

She cracked her neck and crouched low, preparing for her next move. "You want to be an expert on weapons without ever handling one? Don't call yourself a true researcher, then."

Like a lioness, Ukara lunged at me again.

Her comment provoked me, and I lunged at her, only to be hit defensively on the shins and thrown off balance. I fell on my back, sand covering my clothes and face. I coughed, fine, gritty dirt coating my mouth, and anger swirled and moved within me like black smoke. I felt like a child again, pushed and pulled to perform.

"Get up," she said sharply as I coughed and tried to control the reaction within me.

I curled my hands into fists. I wanted to hurt her for knocking me down, for making me *remember*.

She stalked around me in a circle. "Up!" she urged me.

I pushed up from the ground, magic burning my forearms, begging to be used against her, to hurt her, to punish her for hurting me. I shook my head. Khel was already wary of my magic. I didn't want to make other people worried.

"What is your problem?" I yelled. "We're not training for war, Ukara!"

Ukara stormed toward me. "Aren't we?" she challenged. "You find yourself in Taria because there is something out *there*"—she pointed with her spear to the distance— "that poses a threat to *you*. You need to learn to defend yourself. Coincidences don't just *happen*," she spat, looking at me up and down. "I heard you refuse to use your magic?" She narrowed her eyes. "Without magic, you'll have *no* chance if I don't train you."

"I don't like who I am with my powers," I admitted, my shoulders dropping. She didn't know how easy it had been all those years ago to simply wish pain upon someone to hurt them. To simply wish for them to walk into traffic . . . "It's not that easy to control it." I shook my head.

Ukara approached me with her spear down, breathing heavily, and pointed to my face. "I don't know what happened to you before you arrived in Taria to make you hate this part of yourself, but you have magic in your veins. It's your right to refuse to use magic, but know this: don't *ever* be at the mercy of another person to defend you. You are a researcher of weapons, and now you find yourself in need of protection. I am giving you a chance to learn."

Dumbfounded, I nodded.

"Shoulders back," she yelled.

She possessed the command and voice of the general she was but with the catlike grace of a dancer. Ukara sounded like she had disciplined a thousand armies.

I pushed my shoulders back and took up the stance she instructed earlier.

"*This*," she said, lunging at me, teaching me a new technique, "is like a dance."

I blocked her, and my arms vibrated with the force of her deflected blow.

"When you strike, you want to make sure every movement is drawn from your legs and core. Do not let your arms be the sole source of power. Draw from your legs." She arced the spear wide toward me. "You do not always have to meet my blow. Move your body around the space. The goal is to tire your opponent."

Ukara and I trained for what seemed like hours. In the end, we sat on the sand, drinking water she had brought. I had taken off my T-shirt and was in my sports bra, winded from exerting myself. I never exercised except for the occasional run when I needed to clear my mind, and today's training had thoroughly exhausted me.

I was about to joke that I would rather go back to book-only research for my thesis when I heard a motorbike in the distance.

I looked to my right and squinted.

A rider clad in black gear sped through the desert, their slick bike hovering over the sand, leaving a trail of dust behind as they rode toward us.

It was Cylas.

17

RENNA

"I would have paid to see this," Cylas spoke, smiling cheekily as he got off his bike.

Ukara rolled her eyes and stood. She began cleaning her spear, giving Cylas her back.

It seemed only I was a fan of Cylas. Interesting.

As if testing the waters of my favor, Cylas slowly raked his eyes down my body and back up. His brazen look felt somehow darker than Khel's and more daring than Sethos's.

Having not put my shirt back on, I heated under his perusal.

Noticing everything, Cylas smirked knowingly. "Renna." He nodded in greeting.

"You're trying to get me in trouble." I smiled back, appreciating what I saw.

Cylas was attractive. I could easily find myself lusting after him like a lovesick fool.

"Do elaborate." He shoved his hands in his pockets and rocked back on his heels.

"I'm supposed to be working on my thesis."

"Evidently." His tone was sarcastic. "If you need war training,

I should have been invited to give a few pointers. I have seen enough warfare on my planets."

"What do you want, Cylas?" Ukara snapped, clearly having overheard.

"Not that I owe you a recount of my comings and goings, but I'm visiting my good friend, Renna. Don't know if you've heard, but she's the shiny new siren in town, and everyone knows I am naturally drawn to shiny new things."

"Typical," Ukara said under her breath and went back to ignoring him.

I perhaps should have considered his comment rude, but Cylas seemed to have a sarcastic type of humor.

"Can I take a break?" I asked Ukara.

When she waved me off, I walked to the fence where he was. Something about Cylas made me feel bold.

"You're such a bad girl, blowing off training," he teased playfully, leaning in close. "I came here because I just acquired a shiny new desert bike." He waved to the black dirt bike behind him. "And I wanted to invite you along to bask in my presence and take her for a spin."

"Really?" I exclaimed and ran around the fence toward the bike, which glimmered in the desert sun.

"I think she likes it," Cylas said to Ukara.

"Well, someone has to," she murmured, rolling her eyes and busying herself with her weapons.

The bike was beautiful. I had never been on a motorbike before, but it was something Helena would tell me to try if she was here.

I tried on one of two helmets that sat on the bike.

"Renna?" Ukara called, gesturing to the black car that had dropped me off and was now approaching to pick me up. She stared intently between Cylas and me. "How will you get home? What do I tell Khel?"

I paused and took off the helmet, replacing it on the bike. I walked back to Ukara. "You don't have to tell him anything," I said, shrugging.

"Hear! Hear!" Cylas echoed and walked back to his bike to wait for me.

Ukara groaned.

"Why is everyone so annoyed by Cylas?" I whispered to Ukara.

Ukara pulled me to the side. "It is not my place to speak on behalf of anyone's experiences," she began, "but *for me . . .*" She stared back at him.

I turned to find him sitting on his bike. He faced forward to give us some privacy.

"He's my ex," she whispered.

"You dated each other?" I was surprised.

Ukara was so independent. Cylas was too carefree.

"He's my ex-husband," she clarified.

"Oh . . . *Oh*," I said, my face flushing in horror.

I didn't know what to say.

"Long story short, when we married *a very long time ago*, on a different planet, we were quite young, and a few of the priests and my father thought a female war general needed to be brought to heel and could not be successful on her own in the long term." She sighed. "A husband was the answer, apparently."

"And he went along with this arrangement?" I furrowed my brow.

Cylas seemed to be many things but cruel was not one of them.

Ukara shrugged. "We were young. We remain friends of sorts. There is nothing more."

"You don't sound like friends today."

"Cylas," she sighed. "He puts this mask up that is hard to

understand. It is not easy to get to know who he truly is. Believe me, I have tried."

"Thank you for sharing that."

"Just make sure you know what you're doing, Renna. Cylas is a nice guy . . . despite everything. Just . . . be careful."

I nodded slowly and gathered my backpack and things before returning to Cylas. He still faced forward, his face stoic. I had a feeling he had overheard everything and was waiting for my rejection.

"Have you been definitively warned to stay away from me?" he said, his lips curling into a wicked smile.

After slinging my backpack over my shoulders, I rolled my eyes and took the extra helmet. After securing it on my head, I plopped down behind him and wrapped my arms around his waist. "I'm here, aren't I?" I challenged.

"Good girl." I could hear the grin in his voice, and suddenly we took off.

We zipped around the sand dunes endlessly, and I screamed as we descended each crest. I had never felt so carefree.

I began to realize how much of my past life still lingered in every action. I craved structure and predictability. Risk taking, such as getting on a bike with a god, who I happened to be very attracted to, was a new development.

Cylas slowed down the bike.

"You okay?" he asked, looking over his shoulder. He smiled slightly, his green eyes piercing mine.

"Yep," I responded, breaking eye contact. "It doesn't matter now," I said, looking off into the horizon.

The sun was beginning its descent.

"Well, that's a shitty answer," he said. "Now I'm intrigued."

"A few words wouldn't even begin to cover it," I joked.

Humor was how I learned to deflect pain. And grief.

"Well." He brought the bike to a stop. "Aren't we lucky we

have come to a little haven to rest and decompress?" He waved his hand, and before us, an oasis materialized in the middle of the desert with strange purple and blue luminescent greenery.

Cylas moved his hands to mold the oasis in front of us, his brows furrowed in concentration and his gaze moving from the ground up to the tops of the large trees that glowed in the rapidly darkening evening.

Cylas and I dismounted his bike, and I took my helmet off to better take in the setting.

As long as I lived, Taria would be imprinted on my soul. No place could ever replicate the magic that existed here. As Cylas situated the bike, I walked into the oasis. Exotic bird noises and sounds of animals I had never heard before filled the air as I walked along cobalt-blue soil that glowed in the dark. Luminescent leaves glowed around me, and a soft breeze blew through the oasis, sending ripples over the large pond in the middle of this haven.

I sat next to the pond and stared at the sky's reflection on the water, constellations dotting the surface.

Cylas lowered himself next to me. He threw a rock in the water, and it splashed me.

"That has to be the worst rock-skipping job I have ever seen." I laughed.

"It's the water's fault." He chuckled.

"This place is incredible," I said, looking around and leaning back on my elbows.

"You're just putting off the inevitable," he teased, eyebrows raised. "I brought you here to hear about your traumatic past."

I turned to him. "Traumatic past?" I laughed, brushing it off.

When Cylas gave me a knowing look, calling my bluff, I knew I had to give him something.

"I mean," I said, pretending to get serious. I even sat up. "There's not that much to share that would interest anybody. My childhood was hard. My foster mother was cruel. She exposed me to things that I . . ." I shook my head. "Now she's dead."

"Orphans. I knew we were kindred spirits," he said bitterly.

"Do you have a 'sob story' as well?" I carefully steered the conversation toward him.

"Oh, you know, the usual, orphan shows up from the void. No known parents. Is exceptionally good looking." He wagged his eyebrows. "Is *great* with his hands and generally has a handful of haters who wonder how in all the galaxies they can get to my level."

I wanted to point out his childhood was likely better than mine as the energy he wielded seemed good and not dark or destructive. I wondered about his powers.

The more I saw people wield magic, the more I became curious about my own. Not that I was ready to explore it. Perhaps I'd never be ready.

"Can I ask you a question?" I probed, not knowing how to ask.

"Ask away."

"I'm not sure if I'm asking this question correctly, but how does your magic create life?"

He chuckled. "What is your favorite animal?"

I thought it was an odd question. Animals in Andora were kept under lock and key in reserves as a way to conserve species. The Council made it clear that the fifty species of fauna that had survived the Great Migration were Andora's greatest treasure and kept them heavily protected.

"I'm not sure," I confessed. "We have limited access to animals on Andora. Visiting them at the reserves is expensive. So it's hard to have a favorite animal."

"Fair enough," Cylas said, scratching his chin. "Here is my favorite animal. Watch my hands."

Cylas extended his palm and concentrated on the center of

it. Within seconds, his palm glowed with white-blue light, and a sphere of stars appeared. The ball began to hover and drifted to the far end of the pond.

Within minutes, the ball expanded and filled the oasis with a brilliant warm hue until it dimmed, revealing a four-legged beast that resembled a horse but was svelte and graceful and had majestic horns. The creature lowered its head to the pond to drink water, casting a beautiful bright reflection on the surface.

"That's beautiful," I breathed. "What animal is that?"

"A red stag," Cylas said proudly. "He is my chosen animal symbol or a *dretani*."

"What is a *dretani*?"

"Every god has an animal, or a *dretani* as we used to call it in our original god language, that they chose to represent their power in places like battle. Many gods choose to adopt the qualities of their *dretani* when fighting, as the *dretani* enhances the god's power. The animal protects as well when it senses a threat against the god and their powers."

The stag looked up then, and although it was far away, I could feel it stare intensely at me, and I shifted uncomfortably. The stag tracked my movement with precision and began to stamp its hooves aggressively as it swung its head from side to side.

I stared back, frozen, blood rapidly pumping through my veins as my heart began to pound.

When it lowered its head ominously and pinned its ears back, the magic inside me awoke and rushed from my soul's center to the surface of my skin, where it began to travel in slow electrical waves to my palms. Fear had overtaken my body, and my palms buzzed with volatile and unfocused energy. Like during the attack on the quad, my magic recognized a threat, but I didn't know how to effectively channel it to protect myself without anger, and I currently felt no anger, just pure, raw fear.

Cylas stood. "I don't understand," he began to say and lifted his palms to the beast.

The *dretani* would not settle and snorted angrily.

"I don't understand why it's reacting like this. It thinks you are a threat." He shook his head in disbelief.

"What do I do?" I whispered, slowly backing away. "Can't you do something? Can't you control it?"

The stag lifted its hooves in the air, stomped them down repeatedly, and began to grunt aggressively.

Cylas cursed under his breath, and his palms began to glow with white-blue light. With his eyes trained on the stag, he began chanting in a language I couldn't understand. When the stag bellowed and charged across the water toward us, Cylas brought his palms together and shot a ball of magic toward the stag. The white-blue light encapsulated the stag, and within moments, it was gone.

I breathed heavily as remnants of Cylas's magic trickled down from where the stag had been into the pond below like falling stars.

Cylas turned to me, his gaze cautious. "Renna, I'm sorry." He shook his head. "My stag has never done that. I don't know why it thought you were a threat." He covered his mouth in disbelief before scrubbing his hand down his face. "I have heard of *dretani* overriding commands if they think protecting their god is in their god's best interests."

"Do *you* think I am a threat?" I stood up, my body trembling with shock from the aftermath of not only the dretani charging toward me but also the reminder that my magic would not protect me in times of fear.

I felt defenseless and weak.

Cylas's eyes widened, and he rushed to my side and grasped my shaking hands. "No!" He squeezed my hands gently. "I do not think you are a threat."

"Your *dretani* thinks you are wrong," I whispered. "Maybe it senses my magic is chaotic like that of Am-Re's and identifies me as a threat."

Cylas grew quiet and dropped my hands.

"You said Am-Re is a threat to your creation because he destroys life. It must have thought I was the same type of threat."

Cylas did not answer me and instead lifted my palms. "I felt magic coming from your palms right before he charged. The air crackled with energy. It felt electric. Did you try and use magic?"

I shook my head and pulled my hands back. "The magic rose in response to the threat. I can never access it when I'm in fear. I need anger to be able to control it. I shared with Khellios and Aramis that it feels like my magic has been bound to anger. I feel like a prisoner in my own body when I cannot wield my magic in times of fear or any other emotion."

"Have you always felt this way? When was the first time you used magic?"

I recalled the episode at my foster mother's home when I first accessed my magic, and Cylas must have noticed the shift in my expression because he stepped closer but stayed quiet, searching my face and nodding encouragingly, as if telling me it was safe to share my experience.

"The first time I used magic was to protect myself as a child in my foster mother's home." I looked down at my feet.

"What did she do?" Cylas's voice held a sharp edge.

"She's dead." I shook my head. "Why does it matter what she did to me?" I shrugged, and when I didn't receive an answer, I looked up.

He was very still, looking off into the distance, a deadly look in his eyes. His jaw was locked, and his hands were in a fist.

"*What* did she do?" he gritted out.

"Cylas." I placed my hand on his arm. "It doesn't matter."

He brought his gaze to mine. "It matters to me. I didn't lie when I said I want to get to know you, Renna. Help me get to know you."

If I gave into the intimacy Cylas was asking for, it would complicate my already convoluted feelings. It wasn't for lack of attraction to Cylas because *I did* feel attracted to him. Cylas represented raw sexuality. I owed it to myself to figure out what to do with my feelings with the other two people on my mind.

With Sethos, there was a natural connection where I felt comfortable sharing *anything* . . . even an almost kiss. Sethos made my heart race, and he made me feel daring. When he tossed me over his shoulder and squeezed my thigh, I thought my heart would leave my body. The problem was he only existed in my dreams.

With Khellios, our most recent flirtations and his attempts to help me acclimate made me reconsider many of my initial impressions. Nera's insights into what made him who he was helped me understand him. He was fiercely loyal to his people and carried memories that haunted him—much like me. I could understand the torment he likely lived in, blaming himself for the past much in the way I blamed myself for not being able to fight back when my mentor abused me. And unlike Sethos, Khellios existed in the here and now.

"Cylas." I smiled sadly and squeezed his shoulder. "This has been a very long day. I'd rather not dive into this tonight."

Cylas nodded, an apologetic look furrowing his brow. "I'm sorry." He bowed his head. "I'm sorry you have gone through all this."

"Thank you for saying that."

I wrapped my arms around myself and turned back to the pond. We stood in silence, staring into the oasis.

After a while, Cylas sighed. "Let's get you home, pretty girl." He gestured to a newly created path.

Back on the bike with Cylas, I looked up at the sky, mesmerized by the stars that were out in full force. As we rode back to Khel's home, Cylas sped through the desert, and my hair whipped wildly in the wind. I couldn't help but grin as Cylas showed off. My stomach dipped, and my heart raced as we sped through turns until, eventually, he and I laughed so hard that tears came out of my eyes. I could feel Cylas's laughter rumble through him as I held onto his abdomen for dear life. As we turned into Khel's long tree-lined driveway, Cylas grabbed one of my hands and held it tightly.

"I'm glad I made you laugh tonight," he said as Khellios's front door came into view. "I had a good time."

I smiled. "Me too."

And it was true. Despite talking about my past and the scare with his stag, I had enjoyed Cylas's company and the oasis he had created.

Cylas's muscles tensed beneath my hands, and I looked up to see Khellios coming outside. He stood with his hands in his pockets, looking none too pleased. His eyes were focused on where Cylas's hand covered mine. I felt like I had been caught doing something wrong, but then I remembered Khellios telling me my personal life was none of his business. His look tonight, however, led me to believe he hadn't meant those words.

Anger stirred within me as I expected Khellios to say something inappropriate, and my jaw tightened at the prospect of having to tell him off.

"Grandpa!" Cylas called to Khellios as the bike rolled to a stop. "You waited for Renna. How nice."

I buried my head against Cylas's back and groaned. Did he have to goad him?

"You guys hate each other that much, huh?" I whispered.

"Hate is a strong word," he whispered back, so low I was sure only I could hear it. "An eternity of living brings out the worst in people. It's a long story."

I dismounted the bike and handed him my helmet.

"Thank you for tonight." I smiled with my back to Khellios.

Cylas flipped up his visor, which only revealed his eyes, but with the way his eyes crinkled, I could tell he was smiling. "Sure thing, beautiful." He winked. "Sorry for keeping you out so late. I hope you're not too tired." He leaned slightly to get a better look at Khellios. "I didn't know she had a bedtime, old man."

I resisted the urge to look back at Khellios.

"She has none. I am not her keeper," Khellios said dryly.

"Oh good." Cylas mocked him. "How magnanimous of you."

"I'm going inside," I said and turned to find Khellios's fierce stare on me, but before I could walk past him to head inside, Cylas grabbed my hand.

I froze, and Khellios furrowed his brow slightly, eyes trained on Cylas's grip on me. Khellios brought his gaze to mine and narrowed his eyes. It was like he was asking if I would turn to face Cylas or pull my hand back and walk inside.

It felt rude not to acknowledge Cylas, so I faced him and smiled politely.

"Can we have a few minutes?" Cylas asked Khellios. "Alone?"

Khellios grunted and walked away, muttering under his breath.

I bit my lip as he walked into the house.

Cylas took his helmet off with a giant smile.

"Why did you do that?" I asked, taking my hand back and crossing my arms.

"I want to take you out again."

My eyebrows shot up to my hairline. "Cylas—"

"Why not?" He tilted his head.

I didn't feel like sharing the inner workings of my confused mind, so I took the cowardly way out and partially lied. "I just arrived in Taria. I'm still getting used to being here, and it's been overwhelming."

"So it's not a no . . ."

I blushed. Cylas's insistence in pursuing me made me feel sexy and wanted in a way Sethos and Khellios hadn't made me feel.

"It's a no for right now." And that was the truth.

He nodded and smirked. "Alright." He licked his bottom lip. "I'll see you around, pretty girl."

I couldn't help but laugh at the endearment, and he laughed with me.

He stared at my lips before putting on his helmet. "Don't dream of me tonight." He winked and sped off.

Oh. He had no idea that a fae with long silver hair already occupied my dreams.

18

RENNA

As I walked through Khellios's house, it seemed as though he wasn't there. Had he left after the encounter with Cylas, or was he in his room?

My palms tingled from the memory of holding onto Cylas on his bike, and my fingers felt electric from having touched his bare abs when his shirt rode up on more than one occasion as we zipped through the desert.

And his laugh.

And eyes. He looked at me like he wanted to disrobe me in plain daylight.

Would I let him?

I almost slammed into my bedroom door, not noticing I had arrived because of my thoughts of Cylas. I shook my head and walked inside. Sighing, I set down my backpack with my notes and sketches from my time with Ukara earlier that day. My muscles protested the movement, and I groaned. A bath sounded glorious, so I headed into the attached bathroom and began to draw the water in the stone grotto-like tub. The tub was almost a pool, large enough for at least three people. Fluorescent blue crystal lined the bottom and glowed like everything else inside Khellios's home.

Once the tub was hot and ready, I disrobed and climbed in.

I closed my eyes and let my mind drift as my muscles relaxed. The water reminded me of my dream with Sethos when we almost kissed on the shoal. Fucking waves. I kept replaying the way he grabbed me and put me over his shoulder. And the way the water splashed on his muscular behind as he walked us into the water . . . his thighs outlined by the water. They were large and defined and . . .

I brought one of my hands to my stomach and trailed it down to my core as I thought about him. My fingers brushed my already aching clit. My pulse sped up, and my breaths were coming faster. I swallowed hard and applied pressure to my clit, rubbing back and forth, back and forth. I brought my other hand to my entrance and eased a finger inside, gliding in and out, keeping time with the fingers rubbing my clit . . .

I moaned.

Fuck. I was fantasizing about him *again*. I had a problem.

"Renna?"

I squealed and popped my eyes open. I ducked under the water, submerging myself up to my ears.

Khellios was outside my bathroom.

I moved my mouth above the water. "Yes?" I called.

"I was looking for you . . . do you have a minute?" he said through the door.

"Is everything all right?"

"I did not see you in the house, so I came looking for you and did not see you in the connecting room, and your bedroom door was open."

"What is it?"

"I want to apologize for earlier tonight. I acted like an over-protective asshole."

I crossed my arms, and they pushed my breasts up into the night air. My nipples hardened.

I cleared my throat. "You were very clear that I could talk with whomever I wanted. That you didn't care."

Khellios sighed. "Can we please speak face-to-face?"

"Uh . . ." I panicked.

"Wait—" Khellios groaned. "Is that water I hear . . . are you in the bath?"

I laughed nervously.

Khellios stayed silent for a few seconds. "I keep fucking up. I'm sorry. I'm leaving."

"Wait!" I called and instantly muttered a curse. What was I doing?

"Renna," he groaned. "I can't have a conversation while you're naked."

"I could be clothed . . . ?" I offered awkwardly.

"Are you?"

I covered my face with my hands. I wanted to die from embarrassment.

"Have you been naked this whole time?" he asked.

"Uh . . ."

"That's my cue to leave," he said, his voice sounding farther away from my door. "We need to talk . . . at some point. Good night."

"Good night."

After I heard my bedroom door close, I let out a huge breath.

With my bath ruined, I quickly washed up and left the bathroom. I changed into my pajamas and settled in bed with my notes and sketches from my backpack. Going over my notes and making more observations on the weapons I had seen would take my mind off the day and all the conflicting emotions.

After sitting in bed for a while, I got up to stretch. Needing fresh air, I stepped onto my balcony, glad for the cool sea breeze, even if it was only an illusion. The tide was high tonight, and I marveled at how the waves crashed on the shore with force, reflecting the multitude of emotions raging inside me. I braced my hands on the railing and breathed in deeply.

As I scanned the beach below, movement a few feet from me caught my eye. Khel stood on the shore, illuminated by the moonlight. He was looking away from me, his face upturned to the sky as he smoked. I would have thought he would be at The Watch, but it appeared he had stayed behind tonight. He looked troubled as he stared up at the dark night.

He was beautiful even though he looked like he had the weight of the universe on his shoulders.

As if I had called to him with a mere gaze, Khel turned in my direction, and I was caught in his stare. His eyes were probing, accusing, and burning heat into mine all at once.

I thought back to how it made me feel when I arrived with Cylas and Khellios had met us outside. On one hand, I was angry that Khellios was sending me mixed signals. His body language and flirty words indicated he was interested in me, but then he told me he didn't care what I did, as if he chose not to act on anything he could potentially feel for me. On the other hand, in instances like now, where he was devouring me with his eyes and looking at me like he wanted to fuck me on my balcony, I wanted to explore the attraction between us because I felt an inexplicable connection to him. Like with Sethos, I felt like I had known Khellios a lot longer than I had.

The thought of Khel taking me on my balcony had my skin pebbling with goose bumps and my dark nipples straining against my white tank top, the friction a delicious torture. Khel trailed his eyes down to my chest, making my skin burn with want. His chest expanded like he was taking a deep breath. I looked down to see what he saw—my nipples in sharp points, begging for attention . . .

I brought my gaze back to Khellios, and he took a drag of his cigarette, the corner of his mouth turning up as if he was reading my thoughts. Would we ever get to a point where I would let him kiss me, touch me . . . *take me*?

My core clenched at the thought of having Khel between my legs, and my face turned crimson.

Keeping his eyes trained on me, Khel threw his cigarette down and sped into the house.

I cursed and ran back inside my room, locking the balcony door. In the distance, I could hear several doors opening and closing and hurried but sure footsteps moving through the house. The steps got louder.

He was coming for me, and my stomach flipped as desire charged through my body.

Instinctively, I locked my bedroom door and then walked backward, debating whether I should unlock it. I stood in the middle of my bedroom, breathing fast with my hands on my stomach.

I wanted him physically, didn't I? What was I expecting him to do? To barge in and take me? I felt there was too much left unsaid between Khellios and I.

Eventually, the door to my study opened and closed quietly.

He was mere feet away. I heard his footsteps still, now muted by the carpet.

And then silence.

I moved toward my bedroom door with soundless steps. I knew he was on the other side. I could feel him. I touched the door as if that could somehow bring me closer to him. I had a choice. I could let him in and release the unsatisfied tension I'd built in the bath. . .

I hovered my hand over the lock, but instead of unlocking the door, the fear of not being enough took over. I grew up being told repeatedly that I was stupid and inadequate. That my magic would never measure up. Would I be enough for someone like Khellios? It was one thing to be wanted—but was I sufficient?

I suddenly felt empty and silly for expecting anything. I felt as undeserving as my mentor had reminded me so often that I was.

As if Khel could read my energy from the other side of the door, I felt more than heard him slowly back away from the door, and my heart sank.

I held my breath as I waited for what he would do next.

Moments later, I heard the door to my antechamber close and the retreating footsteps that followed.

I stood frozen to the spot for many minutes after, wondering when I would be free of the unworthiness ingrained in me.

THE NEXT MORNING, I lay out on a lounge bed on the terrace of Khel's home, soaking in the sunlight, my research notebooks and datapad sprawled around me on the patio table and chairs adjacent to me. I had been unable to fall back asleep last night after my almost encounter with Khellios, and I had contemplated staying in my room all morning to avoid him. Our exchange on the balcony made our attraction for each other clear. He had come inside the house for me. What would have happened if I had been brave enough? Would I have given him anything?

The wicked part of me said *yes.* I would have given him *everything.*

Suddenly, a shadow loomed over me, and a familiar voice spoke up.

"Well, that book seems to be riveting."

I looked up to find electric-green eyes peering down at me. Cylas smirked as usual, and I blushed.

He quirked a brow and continued. "You've read the same line in your book for the last minute." He sat across from me on a patio chair.

"Hello," I laughed. "Fancy seeing you today," I replied.

"I'm just visiting. I'm not here to seduce you," he teased. "I'll be on my best behavior today."

"I'm sure," I said, my face hot. "What can I help you with?"

Cylas sighed dramatically. "Since you will not go on a date with me, I figured I would come to you and see if you'd like some company today. No strings attached." He tilted his face up in challenge with a mischievous smile.

"Well, you might get bored," I said, sitting up. "Ukara sent me word this morning that she received permission from your underworld god for us to visit a tomb today. I'm meeting her at a tomb for a woman named . . ." I flipped through my pages to find the name I had scribbled for citation purposes. "It's a female warrior's tomb . . ."

"Let me guess." He sighed. "It's Khira's tomb," Cylas said dryly.

When I saw her name written down, I looked up, surprised. "How did you know that?"

Cylas rolled his eyes. "Lucky guess." He shrugged. "It is meticulously preserved."

"What makes the tomb so special?"

"That's for Ukara to share. I stopped being involved in that situation a long time ago. She wasn't forthcoming when we were married, which I sure as fuck would have appreciated at the time, and she is *less* forthcoming now." Cylas shook his head.

There seemed to be deep wounds between Ukara and Cylas, and now the knowledge of a mysterious tomb made me curious for more information. Cursed researching mind.

"I brought my bike today. Do you need a ride to see Ukara?"

Cylas asked me, his eyes dancing with mischief. He cocked his head, waiting for my reply.

"She wasn't happy to see you last time. I don't want to cause tension."

Cylas leaned in and lowered his voice. "I would happily trade her ire for moments with you."

I blushed, unsure how to respond.

Cylas leaned back and slowly raked his eyes over me. "Or you can ride in that stuffy town car chauffeuring you around like a *good girl.*"

I almost choked on my spit at the innuendo lacing his words.

"So, what will it be?" he challenged.

Before I could answer, Cylas swung his gaze to something behind me and smiled mockingly. He folded his hands on his stomach and sat back. "Khel, we meet again," he said smartly.

I didn't dare turn around. Memories of the night before burned my skin.

"This is my home," Khel spat.

His voice made me shiver, and I shifted in my seat, pushing images of last night from my mind.

"What are *you* doing here? Again?" Khel asked him.

"Just picking up our girl to take her for a spin," Cylas said smugly. "Last night was not enough."

I coughed.

Khel approached and leaned on the backrest of my lounge seat. He hooked his fingers on the chair, his hands slightly grazing my back. This touch felt intentional. Was it an apology of sorts for not trying harder to follow through with whatever happened between us?

I suppressed a shiver.

"I see you haven't changed, cousin," Khel said, his voice deadly.

"I see nothing wrong with our beautiful guest exploring *all* Taria has to offer." Cylas sat forward, his eyes narrowed at Khel.

I dared not turn to see Khel's expression. I was sure it was murderous.

"You're not her keeper, old chap."

"You're right, actually." Khel's voice took on a mocking, joking tone.

He began to rub the back of his fingers against my back, playing with my hair. From where Cylas was sitting, he couldn't see, and I was frozen in place as I imagined what it would be like to have Khel pull my hair in real life . . .

"I think it's great for Renna to explore Taria. She can learn what she does and does not like about this place." Khel continued as he rubbed my skin ever so slightly.

My nipples reacted to his touch, and I squeezed my thighs.

The subtext of Khel's words was clear; he was referring to me deciding which man I would choose.

Before Cylas could say another word, I jumped up from my chair. "I realize you both have some unresolved issues," I said, putting my hands up, "but I'm leaving. I'm headed to see Ukara." I began to gather my things.

I made the mistake of turning to face Khel, and my stomach dropped—my heartbeat rattling against my ribs. Khel regarded me with his golden eyes, and I recognized the desire swirling in them from last night. To anyone else, his face likely looked upset, but to me, the brush of his fingers told me of the tension building under his skin, the unresolved frustration.

I gulped.

"Renna." He tilted his head and smiled.

I cleared my throat. "Khel," I replied, my voice barely squeaking.

"How was the rest of your night last night?" he said, lifting one eyebrow.

I nodded. "Great." I knew my face was deep red, but I couldn't help asking him that question. "Yours?"

"It was . . . *enlightening*." He nodded, a smirk crawling across his lips. "I learned that baths and white shirts may be my most favorite things." He rubbed his lip with his thumb, and my core clenched in response as I focused on his fingers . . .

"*Ha!*" I coughed, forgetting to swallow.

Cylas came between us, swinging his gaze back and forth, confused at our exchange. "Renna?" he said, annoyed. "I'll take you to Ukara. Let's go." Cylas pulled me gently, and my feet followed him on autopilot.

Khel smirked at me as I walked away like he knew everything I was thinking.

I could have sworn he reached for my fingers as I moved past him. When I looked back, Khel's hands were clenched into fists.

Oh, he wanted me. So why couldn't he tell me?

I was fucked. I was so fucked.

19

RENNA

Khira's tomb was located in the middle of the desert in a valley that was lined with about twenty tombs. Each tomb had elaborate ancient Xhorian motifs and art. Khira's tomb had statues of a lion goddess flanking each side of the entrance. The goddess was seated with a sword across her legs, holding the hilt as if she was ready to strike any who entered uninvited.

"Well, that's an ominous warning," I commented quietly as Cylas's bike came to a rolling stop.

"That's Ukara for you," Cylas said. "She never does anything halfway. And certainly not in *this* tomb," he said, looking at the tomb with a pained expression I couldn't decipher.

"Why is she important?" I asked him as I got off the bike.

Cylas frowned slightly, trying to form a response.

"Her name," Ukara said slowly, emerging from the tomb, clad in armor, much like the statues themselves, "was Khira. She was second-in-command to the ruler's army when Xhor fell."

Female warriors in Xhor were poorly documented, and the more I discovered about their importance, the more I was fascinated. "If she was second-in-command, who led the army?" I asked as I fished a pen and paper from my bag.

"Men led the army that night," Ukara gritted out.

"I'll be leaving, Renna," Cylas said abruptly, kissing my cheek goodbye. "I'll pick you up after your practice." He winked.

"Uh . . . sure," I said, a little taken aback.

Cylas wasn't hiding his feelings for me in front of anyone. Not even in front of his ex-wife. I wanted to kick him for putting me in this position.

Ukara and I watched Cylas ride away.

Ukara's expression was tense as she watched him drive into the desert.

She sighed and turned to me. "Shall we head inside?" she said, motioning to the tomb.

I knew that the history between Ukara and Cylas was complicated, and although curiosity wanted me to push and ask if she was well, I kept my mouth shut and followed her inside. I had seen ancient Xhorian tombs recreated in museums around the planet, but nothing prepared me for Khira's. The outside looked like a relatively small mausoleum, but the inside was full of palpable magic that expanded the tomb into what felt like never-ending space.

The domed ceiling was several feet high with complex frescoes of battle scenes painted on the plaster. The firelight dancing in the enormous fire pit in the center of the room glinted beautifully off the golden walls.

The relics and statues along the tomb were also impressive. Small and medium-sized golden statues lined the walls, and a tomb lay at the far end of the space on a platform made of a rough, dark emerald stone.

"She must have been really special to be buried like this . . ." I commented, my eyes drawn to a wall with rows of weapons spanning floor to ceiling.

I had already seen many of the weapons from Ukara's collection. Others I recognized from history books, while some looked foreign and technologically advanced for the time period.

"She was," Ukara said quietly. She walked to the raised tomb and placed a hand on the smooth black surface. "I come here more often than I'd like to admit," she said, now looking up at the domed ceiling.

I followed her gaze to the scene depicted above.

"I come here when I need to . . . think." She shook her head slowly.

"Can I ask why Khira is not living in Taria?" I asked. "I know some of the souls here are in Taria as an afterlife."

"She did not want to return," Ukara said, her eyes still on the scene above us. She gestured to a woman with a glittering gold breastplate on the fresco. "That is Khira."

Khira approached an army of male warriors with an army of female warriors behind her. She looked like a queen ready for battle.

"Someone can refuse entry to Taria?" I asked as she now focused on the wall of weapons.

I came to stand next to her.

"Taria is a place of free will. When someone who served the gods dies and was honorable and good, they can decide to reside in a place like Taria or let their soul rest. Khira was tired of living in a world that despised her. She was tired of fighting for acceptance." Ukara sighed. "The world can be cruel to people who don't fall in love with the gender society says they are supposed to. Andora was not as accepting then as it is now of people's sexual identities. Khira was tired of fighting bigotry and discrimination. She decided to let her soul rest."

I couldn't imagine the pain and suffocation Khira must have felt at that time. My heart was gutted knowing gender identities were limited and discriminated against back then. We had taken many positive steps toward a more inclusive society, but it wasn't enough.

We stood in silence side by side as if paying homage to her life.

"I'm sorry," I whispered, my voice breaking.

I could have sworn a tear slid down Ukara's cheek, but it was gone before I could blink.

She stepped up to the wall and drew a sword. The steel vibrated in the silence of the tomb.

"Come," Ukara said, gesturing to me to step up.

"Are you okay?" I asked gently, moving toward her.

When Ukara refused to answer and handed me a sword instead, I nodded and took it, only to be surprised by the weight as it destabilized me.

"Did these weapons belong to her?"

Ukara shook her head. "Nearly everything was destroyed when Xhor fell. Everything was pillaged and burned. What you see are replicas of what Khira owned," she said, grabbing another sword. She inspected it and continued. "I commissioned every piece to be remade when we founded Taria."

"That's very beautiful that you would do that." I smiled sadly, looking at the tomb. "If she could see you from wherever people go to their final resting place, I'm sure she would be happy with how you honor her."

"I loved her. I would have married her if I had the chance," Ukara said, her soft voice betraying her strength. She cleared her throat and looked around the tomb. "Khira would hate all of this. She hated drawing attention to herself." Ukara looked up again at the fresco. "I have no other physical way to remember her," she whispered.

"Thank you for showing me how you honor her."

Ukara smiled ruefully and looked to me. "Khira would have told you to fight, you know."

I stood speechless, unsure how to respond as Ukara approached me. She shook her head.

"I know you were reluctant the other day to learn to use weapons, but the threat outside of Taria is not going anywhere. No matter what Khel or anyone tells you, there will come a time when you will have to fight for everything you love. Taria cannot protect you forever. You need to be prepared. Khira would have told you the same."

Why was I so resistant to learn to wield a weapon? All anyone assured me of was that I was safe in Taria. I wanted to believe that. I was exhausted from feeling scared for most of my life. It felt good to have assurance from someone else that they would take care of my needs, like safety. I was tired of being in fight or flight. To me, accepting to train meant I didn't truly believe I was safe.

"Come," Ukara said, walking out of the tomb with a sword in each hand. "Bring yours."

"Ukara, we can't use these." I stayed where I was. "These mean everything to you—"

"We are *absolutely* using these," she said seriously. "They have been sitting lifeless for centuries. I can think of no nobler cause for using these than to teach you to defend yourself. Perhaps she would think that is more of a way to honor her than having a lifeless shrine."

Standing in Khira's tomb and hearing Ukara's second warning to learn self-defense filled me with dread as I saw physical evidence of a life taken by Am-Re. I had seen what he could do on my campus and in town. Perhaps, in part, that is why Ukara chose to show me the tomb. She had her own weapons at her disposal that were true to the time of the old city. She didn't need to bring me here.

I gripped the sword tightly to keep it from dragging on the ground and followed Ukara out of the tomb.

"Ukara," I called after her, and she turned. "Am I not safe in Taria?" My stomach churned with those words, but I felt if anyone would be honest with me, it would be her

Ukara stood silent for a long time, and an ominous feeling spread throughout my body. "We have not heard anything about Am-Re"—she lowered her voice when saying his name—"since you arrived." She shook her head.

"Is that not good?"

She sighed and bit her lip. "I have an overwhelming feeling that he's just biding his time . . ." She shifted the swords in her hands. "Just think: if *he* went through the trouble of specifically seeking you out, it makes *no sense* that he would let you go if you disappeared from campus. He would keep searching. And unfortunately, he knows you are in Taria."

At her words, bile rose from my stomach, and I felt nauseous as fear gripped me. "Why would he know I'm in Taria? I have no connection to Taria. I didn't know any of you for him to assume this is where I would be."

Ukara cursed. She set her swords on the sand and walked to where I was. "The reason *Am-Re*"—she gritted his name out—"would assume you are *here* is because Khellios—"

"Do tell, Ukara." It was Khellios who spoke.

I whipped around to face him. He stood with his arms crossed, an expression of hatred I couldn't explain as he stared at Ukara. I turned back to face Ukara.

She crossed her arms as well, disgust in her eyes.

"*Well*?" he asked her.

Ukara shook her head in disbelief. "I am disappointed in you, Khel. I figured by now she would know."

Khel stared at her, hands on his hips. "You're not in my position, Ukara."

"Is someone going to tell me what's going on?" I asked and threw up a hand, waving it around.

Ukara and Khel faced off for a few more seconds, as if an unspoken conversation passed between them, until Khellios spoke.

"He saw me on your campus," Khellios stated. "*That* is why he would assume you are in Taria." His eyes were cold toward Ukara.

Blood drained from my face. "What?!" I yelled.

"Wow . . ." Ukara said to Khellios, lifting her palms in the air. When he simply glared at her, she came nose to nose with him like the warrior she was. "While I cannot sway you from doing things your way, what I can do is warn you: when your plan backfires, you will have no one to blame but yourself. More than one person will be harmed, and I can tell you from experience that it's not the physical wounds one remembers but the emotional ones inflicted on us by the people we love most."

Khellios stayed silent, his back rigid as Ukara walked away from him. Ukara gathered the swords on the ground and spun to face him. "*Do not* ask me to be a part of *this*."

"I asked that you respect my right to speak with Renna," he told her.

I turned to Khellios. "When were you going to tell me Am-Re knows my exact location?" I yelled.

"Unbelievable," Ukara said. "Renna, we will pick up more research another day. I will send word through Nera."

I nodded, and she walked back into the tomb.

I turned to face Khellios. "I asked you a question."

He stared down at me. "It doesn't matter." He crossed his arms.

"Doesn't matter?" I laughed in shock. "I'm here because this is supposed to be a safe place—"

"It still is."

"And I was comforted by the fact that Am-Re didn't know where Taria is—"

"He does not. He would have attacked otherwise. He has not."

I rubbed my temples in frustration. "But now that he knows I'm in Taria and he has directly targeted me because he needs me specifically, don't you think that's more motivation for him to locate Taria? Ukara told me it wouldn't make sense for Am-Re to just forget about me."

Khellios frowned. "Taria is safe. You are safe. We are all safe," Khel stated as if his words were final.

"That's not answering my question. I'm anxious for my safety."

He sighed. "Why is telling you that you are safe not good enough?"

"Khellios, that's *not* what I'm saying—"

"Trust me." He gripped my forearms. "You will be okay. No harm will ever come to you. I would never allow it. This is the safest place for you to be."

I shrugged his hold off and backed away. I didn't like being touched by someone who was angry. "I can't stay here forever. I have a life to live outside of here."

His mouth formed a tight line, and he looked away. "I know."

I crossed my arms. "What if Am-Re never goes away?"

Khel sighed and turned away from me. He put his hands into his pockets and stared up at the sky through the protective dome. "I don't want to discuss this now."

"Then when is a good time to discuss this?" I rested my hands on my hips.

He turned. "I came to visit today because I had a surprise for you after your time with Ukara."

I paused and crossed my arms again. "I'm not in a mood for surprises at the moment."

He nodded and stepped closer. "Yesterday I asked you what you enjoyed. What you found fun."

I recalled our conversation. "Wine and books outside under the hot sun in a desert landscape is not my idea of fun, Khellios."

He laughed. "I realize that. I had hoped to surprise you tonight down on the beach at home. You have been in Taria for a few days now, and you seem to be taking everything in stride. I know this is not how you wanted to spend your summer. So, I wanted to do something nice. Nera has been helping me by setting up blankets and a reading area. I know you love the sea."

His thoughtfulness had my frustration deflating a little.

I wasn't sure how to respond after our conversation. "So what of our conversation about you not being forthcoming?"

"What of it?"

I groaned. "Can you not see how incredibly frustrating and upsetting it is that others knew about Am-Re knowing where I am but me? This directly concerns me. I should have been the first person you told. Even if I am truly safe here. I should know when something concerning my safety changes."

He averted his gaze from me.

"Are you even going to apologize for lying to me, Khellios?"

"Would you consider omitting information as lying?"

I stared back at him. I thought back to not sharing about my past and how I truly learned magic. Was I lying to him by omitting that aspect of my life? He had asked me before if I had ever trained, and I had denied that anyone ever taught me. Aramis and Khellios attributed my chaotic magic to the impulsiveness of someone who had never formally learned magic.

You opened up about your past with Sethos, my inner voice told me.

"It depends," I responded, tilting my chin up. "I would say that you omitting that an entity who wants to harm me and has forced me into hiding now knows where I am constitutes a lie.

Everybody but me knows. How do you think that makes me feel?"

He rubbed his face and looked up at me. "We're not getting anywhere with this conversation."

I wanted to scream. "You can apologize."

"I'm sorry."

"Don't lie to me."

He stared at me for a long time. "I hope that in time, you can understand that all I want is what is best for you. I am doing the best I can to make sure you come out of this with the least amount of damage."

His statement was odd, and it made it seem like he knew he'd eventually disappoint me again. I pursed my lips as I stared back at him.

"Will you accept my peace offering?" he asked cautiously.

I narrowed my eyes. "You had the surprise prepared before this conversation blew up. It's not a peace offering."

"Can you accept something nice that I have done for you?"

"That *Nera* is doing for me," I corrected him. "You said she is the one setting it up."

"This is not how I pictured this going." He pinched the bridge of his nose.

"You lied to me. You made me upset. Do you want me to just snap a finger and forget about it?" I shook my head. "It's going to take me some time to come down from these feelings, Khel."

A smile grew on his lips.

I rolled my eyes. "What?"

"You called me *Khel*."

I groaned and stared up at the fucking domed sky. "So what? You think me calling you by your nickname means we're friends now?"

"I certainly hope so."

I looked back at him, and he had a smirk on his face.

"People who have spoken to each other while naked are probably friends."

My pulse quickened, and heat began to rise on my cheeks. I crossed my arms. "You barged into my room. And we were not naked."

He stepped closer and raised an eyebrow. "You were."

The moments after my bath while I was on the balcony flashed back into my mind. I wanted Khellios that night. *Badly*. I cleared my throat and frowned.

I pointed to him. "I know what you're doing."

"And what is that?" He licked his bottom lip before biting it, and I followed the movement.

I clenched my fists to suppress a delicious shiver that wanted to travel down my spine.

"You're trying to distract me from how upset I should be with you."

He looked down at my lips and up at my eyes again. "Is it working?"

"No." I turned from him to hide the growing flush on my cheeks.

He leaned down to my ear. "What I would give to go back to that night I saw you on your balcony. You certainly liked me then."

Waves of desire spread through my body, and I shivered, but I persisted. "And to think you were lying to me then about Am-Re knowing where I am."

He cleared his throat and straightened. "Fine. If you won't accept the surprise I had for you, I'll take us back to the house, and you can tell Nera you are not interested." He shrugged. "You might break her heart."

I turned and punched his arm. "You're an asshole."

He shrugged again. "I've been called worse."

"Did Nera really help you set up whatever you had planned?"

"Yes."

I closed my eyes and breathed. Nera had been nice to me from the moment I stepped into Taria. She and I had spent almost every day together since. I opened my eyes and glared back at him. "Fine."

Khellios smiled and extended his hand. "Shall we?"

"Wow." I narrowed my eyes and placed my hand in his. "You actually are giving me a warning about teleport—"

We vanished instantly.

20

RENNA

Khellios led me from the terrace and down the path to the beach, where floating candles cast a soft glow above several blankets and pillows on the sand. Piles of books were on the blankets, and upon closer inspection, the titles were romance books I was familiar with. A spread of food, enough for several people, and a carafe of wine and wine glasses were also set out. The lilac sea rolled softly in the background with a quiet breeze.

The surprise was breathtaking. No one had ever given me something like this.

And Nera was nowhere in sight.

Khellios and I now stood at the foot of the sumptuous spread.

"And your assistant, I take it, left?" I narrowed my eyes at him.

He shrugged, hiding a smile. "Odd, isn't it?"

I crossed my arms.

"Here we go," Khellios said under his breath as he took in my expression. He shook his head. "What is it?"

"You're going to want to stay, aren't you?" I gestured to the food and wine. "This isn't for one person, is it?"

He crossed his arms. "Is it wrong to want to share the fruits of my labor?"

"*Nera's* labor." I reminded him.

"So, can I?"

I sighed. "I thought you wanted to do something nice for me."

He scoffed and placed a hand on his heart, feigning offense. "You wound me."

My stomach protested in hunger at the delicious food in front of me, so I relented and gestured for him to join me on the blankets. I sat and grabbed some cheese to nibble on.

Khellios sat and leaned back on a pile of pillows. He stared out at the sea with a smile. The contrast between this and my night with Sethos along a different shore wasn't lost on me. I found both men equally attractive. The only difference was the intimacy I had developed with Sethos was lacking with Khellios. Part of me knew that the fact that Sethos was my guardian had much to do with our bond and the ease with which our connection was developing. Sethos had been my guiding light for seven years, and now that I knew who he was, I couldn't let him go.

Could I develop a similar intimacy with Khellios?

The balcony scene returned to my mind. I eyed the open portion of Khellios's shirt that revealed his muscular dark chest, and I licked my lips.

Khellios handed me a glass of wine, and I took it meeting his eyes.

"*Thirsty*?" he asked.

Knowing he likely caught me staring at him with a wanton look, I blushed. I took a sip from my glass and looked at the food spread before me. I eyed honey-covered dates, and a grin spread across my face. They were my favorite. It was odd as I had never shared my favorite foods with any of the gods. I shrugged internally and reached greedily for a date and a cracker to eat them together. My eyes rolled back as the flavors exploded in my mouth.

I froze when Khel coughed slightly, and I looked at him. He had a smug look on his face.

"What?" I snapped.

Khellios smirked and busied himself by sorting through the pile of books as if trying to select one to read.

"Nera picked these out," he explained, looking at all the spines and back covers.

"What are you doing?" I chuckled.

He stopped and looked up at me. "We're reading. Are we not? I'm picking out a book."

"You want to read?" My eyebrows shot up, and I grabbed another date and cracker.

He rolled his eyes and resumed looking through the pile. "You said you like to read and drink wine on blankets. I intend to do the same."

I chuckled. "People usually read alone."

He paused and looked at me. "They do?"

I shrugged. "It's terrible to be interrupted in the middle of a good book."

"You won't hear a sound from me," he promised and settled into his pillows with a book in hand. He sighed dramatically.

I chuckled and shook my head. "How did you know I liked honey-covered dates?" I asked, grabbing a third one.

He shrugged without looking at me. "It was a lucky guess. Many people like them."

"A very good guess," I muttered.

I ate some more food and drank some wine before crawling to the pile of books, which was conveniently next to him. I felt his eyes on me and saw him peeking from his open book. He covered his face with the book to hide a smirk.

"You're just hogging all the books over here," I grumbled. "Aren't you sorry you made me crawl across these blankets?"

"Some things are worth crawling for. Don't you think?"

My stomach flipped as he lowered his book to meet my eyes. The intensity of his stare made my heartbeat skip, and I cleared my throat when his eyes fell to my lips.

I quickly grabbed the first book on the pile before scrambling to the other side of the blankets.

I piled a few pillows and made myself comfortable avoiding his gaze.

"Would you like more wine?" he asked from his corner.

I glanced at my near-empty wine glass. "No. I'll get too sleepy."

"Okay."

I had just started my book when he spoke again. "What is your book about?"

I sighed and looked at the cover. "A woman who wanted to read a book but kept being interrupted. The offender dies from said crimes."

"*Ouch.*"

"Mm-hmm." A grin spread across my lips, and I went back to my book.

A few moments of peaceful silence passed before he spoke again. "Aren't you going to ask me what my book is about?"

I groaned and covered my face with my book. "No."

"That's rude," he murmured. "I asked you what your book was about. It's only proper for you to then ask me—"

I sat up and slammed my book down. "Tell me!" I folded my hands. "I am dying to know what your book is about."

He scrunched his nose and ignored me, returning to reading.

"That's what I thought." I snatched my wine glass and

chugged what was left, then lay back down. "Now, *please* let me read."

It wasn't long before Khellios was on my side of the blankets to grab food. I ignored him and kept reading before feeling him settle on the pillows next to me.

"What are you doing?" I asked, setting my book down on my stomach.

He sat up halfway and shrugged, looking shocked. He popped a grape in his mouth. "The food is on this side of the blankets. I'm hungry. No need to be so grumpy."

"Gods don't need to eat," I argued. "Nera told me."

"I still like to eat." He settled back down. "Food can be quite pleasurable, you know."

Although annoyed, his last words made me blush, and I picked up my book again to read. When I realized he didn't have a book, I looked sideways at him.

"How did you learn magic?" he asked.

And there it was. The direct question I was dreading from Khellios.

"It doesn't matter." The irony of repeating Khellios's words from earlier didn't escape me.

He lifted his eyebrows. "It does to me."

I set my book down on my stomach again. The most believable way to answer was to stick with the truth as much as possible. "I learned magic while I was in foster care."

Khel nodded for me to continue.

"My foster mother had many people in and out of the places we lived. I was exposed to magic that way. I don't like it."

Khellios was silent for a long while before he spoke. "If it does not bring you joy or pleasure, do not make it part of your life. I often wonder if you eliminate it completely, if it would cut off your connection to Am-Re. You'd be less valuable to him."

My eyes grew wide. "Is that possible?"

"The witch who helped enchant Taria's wards can answer that better than I. I can ask her if you wish."

I didn't know what to say. I had willed magic away from me for so long. Now I potentially had a way to do away with it—perhaps forever.

"Okay." I stared at the domed sky.

The night sky loomed overhead, and thousands of stars dotted the heavens like crystals.

"You would like me to speak with her?"

"I think it would be good to hear what she has to say . . ."

Silence settled between us.

"Renna," he whispered.

I turned to face him.

"The other night . . . on the balcony . . ."

My breath sped up.

"I went to look for you."

I nodded. "I know."

"You locked your door."

"Yes."

"Why?"

Because I was a fool. Because I was scared to be happy. Because I felt undeserving.

"I'm afraid to feel too much," I whispered.

Khellios looked down at my lips, his eyes golden. "If I went to look for you now, would you let me in?"

I turned on my side to look at him. "Yes," I whispered.

"And if I wanted to kiss you . . . ?"

I nodded, my breath catching in my throat.

Khellios came closer. "I don't think I would be able to stop." His voice was a whisper now, and he was a mere breath from me.

I shifted and pressed my thighs together as heat pooled in my core.

He flicked his eyes to my legs, likely noticing the movement, before locking his eyes with mine. "I want you."

"Yes," I breathed.

That's all it took for Khellios to grab my neck and pull me close.

And then he kissed me.

I saw fireworks.

The kiss moved slowly at first as he peppered his lips over mine, his eyes meeting mine every time he pulled away as if making sure I was okay. When I nodded for him to continue, he tossed my book across the blanket and pushed his body flush against mine to kiss me more fully. He slanted his mouth over mine and brought his arms around my waist.

Kissing Khellios felt like coming home to something familiar, and I relished in the feeling.

I sighed into him and dragged my nails across his short hair. He smiled against my mouth before deepening the kiss and swiping his tongue over my bottom lip. I parted my lips, inviting him in. With his tongue, he explored, caressed, and tasted me. I welcomed it by gripping him more forcefully and draping my leg over his hip. I needed pressure. I needed him to move.

Responding to my body, Khellios thrust his hardened cock against me, kissing me almost frantically.

I trailed my hands down to his shoulders, feeling his muscles flex under my touch, and then I circled my arms around his neck, pressing myself against him.

He moved one of his hands from around my waist up my back until he got to the nape of my neck. Burying his fingers in my hair, he held me to him as he began to nip my neck.

"You were made for me, Renna," Khellios said, bringing me down as he rolled onto his back and hoisted me on top of him. Gripping my ass, he pulled me against him, pressing his hardness against my center. "Can you feel how hard you make me?"

I closed my eyes and nodded as I ground against him, the clothing increasing the pressure on my pussy.

Gods, that feels good. I moaned.

I was lost in the storm of feelings between us that pushed and pulled us in a rhythm that singed my soul.

When my hand dropped to the hem of his shirt to pull it up, Khellios tensed. He tilted his head and looked down to see how entangled we were.

"What's wrong?" I breathed, my heart pounding.

He shook his head and began to sit up. He pressed his hands to his eyes as if he was in pain. "Sorry."

"Is everything okay?"

"Sometimes my mind . . . It gets really loud." Khellios shook his head as if trying to shake off whatever was plaguing his mind.

"You have nothing to be sorry for. We got a little off track anyway. We were supposed to be reading." I squeezed his arm reassuringly.

He dropped his hands and looked at me, his eyes apologetic. He offered me a small smile.

I smirked. "*And* I'm supposed to be mad at you anyways." I joked.

He grinned.

I cupped his face in my hands. "In all seriousness, don't lie to me."

He searched my eyes and gathered me in his arms, holding me close for a moment. He pulled back and pressed a kiss to my forehead.

We resituated ourselves, and he reclined against the pillows while I snuggled in against his side. He reached over and grabbed the book he had tossed. Handing it to me, he smiled before grabbing the book he had been reading.

We resumed actually reading, and I fell asleep in his arms.

I KNEW when I awoke that I was in a dream. I had to be.

It was daylight, and I was lying in a four-poster bed draped in white linen sheets. The bed was next to a balcony that overlooked the sea. The sea in this dream looked real. It was a beautiful, clear light blue, unlike the illusion in Taria.

I looked down at my body and found that I was naked with only a linen sheet covering me. A soft snore next to me made me look to my left, and a very tired and *very* naked Khellios lay face down. His muscular bronze arms hugged the pillow underneath him, and his face was turned to mine as he slept.

A mixture of emotions coursed through me—panic that I was naked with Khellios but also a rapid rush of hunger for the naked god next to me. My body was still on fire with pent-up feelings from the beach. The kisses we had shared on the blankets sent goose bumps down my body.

"This is a dream, this is a dream," I whispered.

"Oh, it is."

Sethos.

I sat up, holding the sheet to me. He was sitting on an armchair in a corner facing the bed, draped in his usual black clothing.

"Sethos?" My face burned with heat. "What is this?" I gestured around me.

"This is your dream," he said, bored.

"But why this?" I looked at Khellios. "You and I are usually—"

"*Alone?*" Sethos asked.

"I don't understand."

"When you go to sleep, your mind tends to be blank," he explained, crossing one leg over the other. "I take that opportunity to take you someplace you may enjoy. *Clearly* you had a lot on your mind tonight. Color me surprised when I paid you a dreamtime visit tonight."

"Oh." My body was now deep shades of red. "I see." My voice came out higher than intended.

"But please." He gestured to the bed, lifting one eyebrow. "Continue."

My mouth dropped open. "You can't be serious."

"You clearly want to fuck him." Sethos's eyes bored into mine. "This is your dream. He's just an illusion. The only real part of this dream is you and me."

I shook my head and shifted from Khellios. "I can't actually—"

I couldn't bring myself to say the word. It was too embarrassing with Sethos in the room.

"*Fuck*?" He tilted his head.

I threw myself down on the bed and covered my face with the sheets.

"Well, that's an unusual position," Sethos drawled.

"Go away," I said through the sheets.

"What's that?"

"Go away!" I said a little louder while also internally freaking out that the fantasy version of Khellios might wake up.

Footsteps approached, and the sheets I was gripping were pulled down to my chin, revealing Sethos's face. "You like him, don't you?"

I squeezed my eyes shut. I couldn't think straight with the two men I was most attracted to in the same room. "Don't ask me that."

"It's just a question, Ren."

I didn't answer.

"You do like him. You more than like him. Otherwise, you would not have imagined *this*."

I groaned.

"It's quite the scene," he said curiously. "I never took you for a white-bedsheet-next-to-the-sea fantasy type of woman. It's very romantic."

I opened my eyes, annoyed. "What *did* you picture?" I snapped.

"*Silk*," he breathed.

Desire instantly rushed to my core.

"I pictured you in black silk sheets. Naked. With nothing covering you. Your hair sprawled on a silk pillow."

He pictured me that way? I shifted as my pussy became wet. My lips parted as he continued.

"And the sheets would be just a bit cold," he whispered, leaning in, his eyes never leaving mine. "So that your nipples could stay erect the whole time as you writhed your body against the bed, *thinking*."

"Thinking?" I panted.

He nodded, his eyes now on my lips. "About a great many things."

I whimpered.

"Such as . . ." Sethos lowered his mouth to my ear, so close that his lips brushed my skin. "The kiss we almost had the other night . . ." He moved his lips to my neck. "How it might feel if I touch you . . ."

"You're already touching me," I breathed, tilting my head to give him more access.

He smiled against my skin. "Would you have let me kiss you that night?"

His question echoed Khellios's question about the balcony.

I nodded.

"Use your words."

"Yes." I pressed my thighs together.

"Hmm," he hummed against my skin. "So what were you doing tonight to result in such a lavish dream?"

"I . . ." I struggled to explain. Telling him I had fallen asleep on Khellios felt mortifying. Especially as Sethos now pressed small kisses on my neck, heightening my arousal.

I moaned.

"Did you fuck him?"

My heart stopped. "No."

"Interesting."

He trailed his lips across my collarbone to the other side of my neck.

"What was the last thing you did before falling asleep? He was clearly on your mind."

"We . . . I." My body tingled as the tip of Sethos's tongue made contact with my skin. "I fell asleep on him."

Sethos froze.

"That's peculiar." His tone was monotone, and I couldn't decipher the emotion behind it. "One doesn't typically fall asleep on people."

"We were lying on blankets reading and—"

Sethos raised his head to look at me. A smirk played on his lips. "*Reading*?"

"Yes, he surprised me with—"

"He was lying next to you to *read*?" His laugh had an edge. He straightened. "He's a fool."

"Well," I sighed, adjusting the sheet over me now that Sethos was no longer at my side, breaking me from the lust-filled haze I was in. I cleared my throat. "We did more than read."

Sethos narrowed his eyes. "Oh, really?" He crossed his arms. "Did he act out his favorite poetry passage?" he spat out.

"We kissed."

Sethos became deathly still. "Well, aren't you both adventurous."

"He touched me," I added.

I didn't know why I wanted to push Sethos to see the

emotions I could provoke in him, but I kept pushing and embellishing. "He grabbed me by the waist and hoisted me on top of him, and I let him. I let him play with my breasts, and when he parted my legs, I felt him har—"

Sethos got in my face in an instant. "What are you doing?" he growled.

I tilted my chin up. "I could ask you the same thing."

"You're trying to provoke me. Why?"

"And *you're* trying to seduce me. *Why*?"

"Isn't it obvious?" he whispered, his eyes searching mine before lowering to my lips. "I want you." He looked up at me.

My eyes widened, and my heart began to race. Hearing him say it was jarring, and I was speechless.

"Nothing to say now?" He smirked.

"*Why* do you want me?" I asked, and I almost kicked myself for breaking the moment with my question.

I desired Sethos. I should have just embraced the moment by nodding and letting him do what he wanted.

He cupped my face and looked deeply into my eyes. "You and I are bound, Ren. From the moment our souls were created, you and I were bound. My need for you has no beginning and no end. I crave you against my judgment. Even when I know you would be better off with someone else." He looked over at dreamtime Khellios.

I followed his gaze. Khellios slept peacefully. My eyes drifted down his body to his perfectly toned ass. I wondered if his body truly did look like this in real life. This was my imagination of what it could look like, after all.

Sethos lowered his lips to my ear as my eyes roamed Khellios's body. "I don't blame you for wanting him," he said darkly. "Gods are beautiful creatures. Did he make you come?"

"What?" I whipped my head back to Sethos.

He had pulled back, but his face was still so close.

"When he touched you," he breathed, reading my face. "Did he make you come?"

"No." I shook my head.

Sethos's eyes danced with mischief. "Touch yourself, Renna."

"Here?"

"You came here to be pleasured, *mejtah*."

"What did you call me?" I whispered.

"*Mejtah*, a sea fae term of endearment."

"Oh." I blushed and felt my body warm.

"Go on," Sethos said. He began to walk backward, and I sat up halfway. "Touch yourself."

Sethos sat back down on the armchair and crossed one leg over the other again.

My eyebrows shot up. "With you in the room?"

"I would like that." His eyes burned into me. "Would you?"

The idea enticed me more than I thought it would. I could barely respond with the shock of it all, but I managed to nod once.

"And him?" I gestured to dreamtime Khellios.

"I couldn't care less. He's not real, but know *this*: I don't share."

I swallowed, unsure of what to do.

"Do you want him to stay?" Sethos asked curiously.

My version of Khellios's body was beautiful, and my skin was on fire. I was so worked up that I needed to be touched. By either dreamtime Khellios or Sethos.

I nodded.

Sethos leaned forward. "Then you should wake him up. But be very careful where he touches you, *mejtah*. I won't share."

Sethos's words of ownership over me reverberated through my body like hot waves of pleasure. He told me he craved me, and I melted at his declaration. Over the weeks, every single night, Sethos had become part of me, slowly etching himself into my soul. I wanted him. And now I realized I craved him as much as he craved me.

I shifted over to dreamtime Khellios, holding my sheet over my body, and shook his shoulder. I didn't know what to expect from a dreamtime person in a fantasy.

Dreamtime Khellios instantly opened his eyes. They were milky white. No pupils. Soulless. It was not Khellios but a robotic body that resembled him.

I stared at the body in front of me, mute.

"Excuse me," Sethos said, snapping his fingers impatiently.

Dreamtime Khellios sat up and looked at Sethos. His expression was vacant.

"Touch her, please," Sethos instructed.

Dreamtime Khellios nodded and, like a robot, turned to me and extended his hands toward my breasts.

I was turned off by the soulless mechanical aspect of his movements and backed away from him until my body hit the headboard.

"Stop," Sethos instructed him.

The body before me paused midair, frozen.

"I don't think this is going to work, *mejtah*." Sethos tsked. "Something tells me whatever you have conjured lacks the heart to be fully present in the moment," he said bitterly.

I ran a hand down my face and groaned.

"I know." Sethos stood. He walked up to the bed until he was next to me. "You," Sethos said to the body in front of me, annoyance lacing his words. "Sit behind Renna and restrain her for me."

I gasped and covered my mouth, feeling my blood furiously pump through my body, heating my skin. I couldn't tell if I was more turned on by the thought of being restrained for Sethos or because of Sethos's commanding tone. My pussy throbbed.

Sethos didn't remove his eyes from me as he spoke. "I want

you to sit behind her and hold her arms in place, hold her legs open. I want you to bare her pussy to me. I want to see it all."

Oh my gods. I had to bite down on my lip to hold back a moan. Knowing that someone like Sethos wanted me completely exposed to him gave me a heady rush.

The body in front of me moved as instructed, and I shifted to allow him to sit with his legs spread behind me.

"Do not," Sethos warned him darkly, "*do not* touch her for any other reason but to restrain her as I have instructed."

The body moved his hands down my arms to my inner thighs and spread my legs open. The sheet atop me created a tent.

Sethos shook his head. "Must I do everything myself?"

He snapped a finger, and the sheet was gone. I wiggled as I sat bared to Sethos, who had walked to the foot of the bed.

His eyes locked onto my pussy, and then he slowly moved his gaze up my body until it met mine.

"Touch yourself, *mejtah.*"

I almost wept from the pent-up ball of want inside me, and my fingers rushed to my bundle of nerves. I was so slick already, my arousal allowing me to easily rub back and forth.

"Does that feel good?" Sethos asked, his voice rough.

I nodded.

"Words," Sethos growled.

"Yes," I panted.

"My dear *mejtah.*" He breathed hard, eyes focused on where I worked my fingers over myself. "This will be the only time another man joins us in the bedroom."

I whimpered, feeling my slick drip from me.

"I fear I wouldn't be able to give in to your demands a second time. But for now, he's not real, so it matters not."

All I could do was moan as my pleasure continued to build.

"Open your legs more," Sethos breathed out. "I want to see everything."

I nodded and pushed my legs open farther, never losing eye contact with him. As I continued to move, silken waves of pleasure began to move inside me as a low pressure slowly built at my core. My folds became swollen, and they pulsed, begging for pressure.

"What do you need, *mejtah*?" Sethos said slowly, taking off his long black vest.

The black tunic shirt underneath was open, revealing a chiseled chest.

I gulped as he brought his fingers to his belt.

"You," I cried.

"Hmm . . ." He smirked. "And here I thought you wanted robot prince behind you." He pointed his chin toward the body behind me.

"Please," I begged, working my hands faster.

Sethos got on the bed and began to crawl toward me. My heart sped up as I watched him approach me, like a predator. His eyes were glued to mine, searching. What he looked for, I didn't know. All I could see in his eyes was pure fire. And I wanted to be consumed.

When Sethos kneeled in front of me, he smiled lazily and began unbuttoning his pants. "There will come a time, *mejtah*, when I will take you fully. Tonight is not that night. It is not my pleasure that needs satiating. You created this dream to be pleasured. And so it will be."

He reached into his pants and groaned. When he brought his hand back out, his large cock was in his palm, more impressive than the dreamtime man behind me. This was real, or more real than what I had fantasized about.

Sethos's cock was . . . I blew out a breath. It was perfect. I wanted to run my tongue along the vein on the underside and then around the round tip. He looked big enough to stretch me but deliciously so. My pussy clenched at the thought of him filling me up, and my mouth watered.

I brought my eyes back to his.

He began to stroke himself, not breaking eye contact. "You're going to leave that pussy to me, *mejtah*. Move your hands to your breasts. Imagine it's me there."

I licked my lips and nodded, skimming my hands over my breasts, imagining he was touching me. I imagined his hands would feel strong, large, and slightly rough. I imagined him squeezing my nipples just so, pulling them toward him and releasing them to watch as they formed aching peaks, begging to be squeezed again.

"Bounce them on your palms for me, *mejtah*."

I moaned and did as he asked. They felt heavy with want as I weighed them in my palms and pushed them up to the air as they slammed down into my palms. Over and over.

"One day, I'm going to come in between those delicious breasts of yours," he promised. "But tonight is about you." He looked down at my pussy.

"What do you want?" he asked.

"Touch me," I begged.

"Do you want me to touch you here?" He moved his fingers over my skin, lazily moving south until he stopped just above my sex.

The anticipation was killing me, and I arched my back into his touch. "Yes."

He bent down to my pussy. "I've wanted to do this so much," he whispered against my folds.

As soon as his fingers made contact with my bundle of nerves, I melted back onto the body behind me, letting sweet electric tremors flow through my body—like magic.

I moaned.

"I wonder how much you can take?" he growled. He pressed a finger into me. "Hmmm."

"*More.*" I tilted my pelvis up as much as I could with the body restraining me.

I bucked when Sethos's second finger entered me. In and out, in and out, pushing into my swollen folds that seemed to want to bury him inside me. A third finger inside me and a thumb on my clit.

I screamed.

The wet sounds of my arousal filled the room, and the air smelled of me and Sethos as his scent of musk and bergamot began to waft off his sweat-damp skin.

Suddenly he moved, stomach down, and nestled his face between my thighs with his mouth at my core. My heart began to beat a mile a minute. No one had ever tasted me down there before. I wasn't chaste, but I lacked a thorough education.

When his fingers left me, I panted out a protest, but he merely hushed me gently and parted my folds, each thumb holding me open like a book. My pussy throbbed.

"This is how *I* would read lying next to you, Renna," Sethos growled, and my body began to tremble, anticipating his mouth. "This . . ." He latched his mouth onto me and sucked hard. I screamed again. He came up for air. "*Is . . . how . . .*" He ducked back down and suckled me. "You read."

He then lifted my hips and wrapped my legs around his neck. He brought his head back down to my pussy, locking me in place. I bucked as much as I could, but between the body restraining me and Sethos against me, it made it impossible to move more than a few inches. Sethos pulled back, his mouth making a large pop as he released my clit, and he looked at me. His mouth and chin were wet with *me*.

"Yes," I cried, thrashing my head back while my hips thrust into the air.

"Just look at you," he groaned. "You're so wet, *mejtah*. And it's all for me." He moaned. "And what's this?" he asked mischievously. He lowered his face again, and I jumped when his nose touched my folds. "You have a little dribble of cum just there . . ." He began lapping my pussy like a tiger lapping milk.

The action sent me over the edge, and my body began to shake.

Sethos lapped faster.

When I screamed, Sethos lowered me down, removed his mouth from my core, and thrust four fingers inside my pussy, pumping hard. He brought his mouth to my lotus tattoo and bit down. A powerful shockwave of blinding energy encased us, and my eyes shot open.

I was sitting on the blankets along the beach with Khellios, who was scrambling up and yelling, running toward the shore.

I looked down, and I was fully clothed.

I clutched my head, disoriented, as I heard screaming.

Nera ran to join Khellios.

I looked to where Khellios and Nera screamed.

In the distance, an explosion could be seen.

"Am-Re." Nera whipped her head toward me. "Am-Re is here."

21

RENNA

"*Am-Re is here.*"

Nera's voice echoed in my brain on a constant loop, sending my body into a spiral of stress. I paced my room endlessly, thinking about the last hour since the attack on the beach and the events that transpired.

Immediately after the attack, I was rushed inside Khellios's home. As Khellios and Nera ran with me to my rooms, Ukara teleported to let us know the attack had happened outside the borders of Taria. What we had seen was an attack on the old city.

Taria was put on lockdown as the gods scrambled to protect Taria's borders and begin damage control in Xhor. Khellios and Nera let me know the damage control was to avoid the Council zeroing in on the attack and spreading further oppression and fear.

I now waited in my room for someone come to deliver some news. My heart was on edge as I thought of any potential casualties at the old city site. Crews of archeologists were there daily making new discoveries. My magic rattled inside me, spazzing like a failed electrical current as I battled with fear and anger.

I looked to where my balcony should be. It was now a solid wall. Khellios had wasted no time enchanting my rooms to eliminate all the windows. I was inside a crystallized bunker.

I wished I could hear the sea. Fictional as it was in Taria, it still brought me some calm.

Mejtah. I smiled sadly at what Sethos had called me. I wondered how he would feel being in a sealed room without a view of or sound from the sea. Would the part of him that was sea fae go mad from confinement?

I would be fine.

Right?

Khellios had let me know only he and Nera would be able to enter and exit as long as the danger was present. I didn't disagree with him as the attack triggered trauma deep within me from my life with my mentor and the attacks on my campus and town.

I paced and paced and paced until my feet hurt. Then I sat on the ground against my stone quartz bed frame, staring at my bedroom door, which I couldn't open.

If I had learned how to use my magic effectively, could I be of any help right now? Nera and the other gods would be able to heal any injured because their magic was good.

Unlike mine.

I could picture my mentor cursing me, perhaps shoving me in disgust, telling me I was good for nothing. That I was a failure. That I was better dead.

Maybe getting rid of my magic for good was the healthiest option.

Khellios wanted what was best for me. Right?

My magic was no good.

Spiral, spiral. My mind began to descend.

I stood and paced despite the pain in my feet. The pain distracted me from the mental anguish.

What I wouldn't give for Sethos to exist outside of my dreams so he could be by my side in these moments. Would Khellios mind Sethos's presence?

I shook the ridiculous thought from my mind.

Khellios was jealous of my connection with Cylas. Knowing how much Sethos had grown to mean to me would likely make him lose his mind . . ..

But *why*?

I sank down on the foot of my bed, wondering why Khellios felt a strong claim over me. Within mere days of meeting me, his possessive attitude toward who I spoke with or what I did was . . . *odd*.

With Sethos, my attachment was different. My soul was entwined with his. Even if he had never told me it was, I couldn't deny a strong gravitational pull toward him. Such a strong pull that I had tattooed the symbol he had sent me as guidance over the years on my skin.

My mentor flashed in my mind, his yellow teeth forming a malevolent smile. At the thought of him, my jaw hardened, my breath became shorter, harder, and my chest began to swell as my breathing became erratic.

I had promised myself that I would never feel vulnerable again. And now? I was locked in a room until people outside of it came up with a solution for how to deal with me. I was an adult woman at the mercy of others. I was sitting in my room like the child who had been too physically weak to fight back.

My vision began to tunnel as rage simmered below the surface, and I struggled to control my emotions. A feeling of fire suddenly blazed down my arms, making me cry out.

Faint glimmers of black and emerald shimmered across my skin *like scales*. My eyes grew like saucers, and I flexed my fingers, turning my hands this way and that, and seconds later, my skin returned to normal.

I rubbed my eyes. *Strange.* In all my years wielding magic with my mentor I had never experienced my energy being transmuted to color. Or *shadows.*

Could being locked away in a room for hours make me hallucinate?

I huffed out a frustrated breath and stood to pace again to try and clear my mind. I smoothed my palms down my thighs, and the friction caused an electric shock.

"*Gah!*" I clasped my hands together, cradling them against my chest, nursing the sharp pain that had zapped through them.

I slowly pulled them away from me and inspected my shaky palms again. This time, I couldn't see anything. My hands looked normal.

I shook my head.

What would Sethos tell me now? He had stressed several times that my magic was a part of me . . .

"Help me, Sethos," I whispered to him wherever he was. "I need you."

I couldn't wait for a dream to ask him. I raced to the door and reached out for the handle.

At that moment, footsteps approached on the other side, and I panicked. I backpedaled and clasped my hands behind my back.

Nera opened the door, her face full of anguish as her eyes inspected me up and down to make sure I was all right. Livina was next to her, and she narrowed her eyes at the room behind me, as if she knew the energy I had just used. She moved her eyes to mine and nodded slightly in approval.

I knew she wanted me to use my magic, and my heart began to race. She had told me she would help me when I needed her, so was that why she was here? I sucked in a breath. I had to remember that, according to Nera, I'd never met Livina. Was

Livina here to take me home? I gulped and moved my eyes to Nera, who hadn't noticed our exchange.

"Renna," Nera began, taking a step toward me as if she was unsure how to begin.

Her actions made me anxious about what she might say. I moved my eyes to Livina, but she looked away from me.

Nera continued. "I'm so sorry you have been here for the last few hours." She looked down and clasped her hands, which were shaky. "Things have been . . ."

"*Chaotic.*" Livina finished for her.

Nera nodded and stood beside Livina. "Renna, I want to introduce you to Livina."

Livina's expression was now blank, and she cast me a polite smile as if this was her first time meeting me.

"Livina is the goddess of fate." There was admiration in Nera's words, and she looked up at Livina, who was a whole foot taller than Nera. "Like Ukara, Livina is also not part of the Celestial Enclave because she serves all three enclaves. Her magic stems from the creation of the universe. She is a primordial goddess."

Livina looked to me and nodded slightly. "A pleasure to meet you, Renna Strongborn."

Hearing her say the last name given to me by the orphanage reminded me she likely knew who my parents were. I could not help but wonder where my parents were at this exact moment. Would they stand by my side like Sethos?

"Nice to meet you." I nodded back in greeting.

"Livina asked to come see you. I imagine she has a few things to discuss with you, given this latest attack. Khel thought it good to authorize her to see you," Nera said

I clenched my jaw at the mention of Khellios authorizing someone to speak with me. My argument with him after my meeting with Ukara came back to the forefront of my mind. I crossed my arms, ready to speak, and Livina looked at me know-ingly, as if she could read my thoughts.

Livina raised an eyebrow and turned her chin to Nera. "No one authorizes me to do anything."

Nera's face flushed, and she shook her head. "Khellios does not mean offense—"

"Then he should reconsider his thought processes and actions."

Nera nodded and apologized once more. She cleared her throat. "Renna, I've also come to give you an update on the attack."

"Is everyone okay? Are there any deaths?"

"The old city is no more," Livina answered ominously. "The footprints of the old temples are gone. It is dust. No one was present for the attack."

"It's a miracle. That place is buzzing with archeologists daily. We have several liaisons who work in the local government, covertly pushing our agenda in Xhor on issues we care about. We are pushing the idea to the Council that the explosion was due to a gas pipeline leak from a dig," Nera added.

"Good," I sighed. "The last thing we need is a swarm of Council members descending on Xhor, with it being so close to Taria."

Nera nodded but reminded me the Council would never know of Taria's existence. Livina made a curious face at that statement, and I decided to stow my observation away for later introspection.

"Khellios asks that you remain indoors for the next few days until we can determine if *he* is still in Xhor or in the vicinity," Nera said. "He wants you to know you are *not* being locked in forever and that this is merely a precaution."

"And where is Khellios?" I asked.

"He left to The Watch to enforce precautions there," Nera said embarrassedly. "He sends his apologies."

Livina crossed her arms. "My," she said to Nera, "aren't you a great helper to Khellios by passing along his messages?"

Nera turned red again.

"Suggest to the god of the moon that he should personally deliver messages that directly affect the recipient." Livina's voice was stern. "It is the polite thing to do."

Nera nodded.

"Nera." Livina clasped her hands. "I need to speak with Renna."

Nera nodded with a smile and gestured toward me as if she was giving Livina the floor to speak.

"I need to speak with her *alone*." Livina smiled politely. "Fate demands that I do."

Nera's eyes widened, and she nodded quickly. She turned to me and gave me a quick hug. "I'll stop by tomorrow to check on you." She squeezed my hand and exited my bedroom.

Once we heard Nera exit my front room, Livina lifted her hands, and a translucent dark veil surrounded us like a dome. "Soundproofing," Livina explained.

"You said you would help me when I needed it most," I began. "I need you now."

Livina waved her hands in front of her, and a stool appeared. She walked around it and sat. "You are deviating from your course," Livina said, folding her hands on her lap. "You need to access your magic. And you need to train with Ukara. You have put it off long enough."

"I'm no match for Am-Re. And you know it."

"I know a lot of things," Livina said, lifting an eyebrow. "And believe me when I tell you, you need your magic. And you need to learn self-defense with Ukara."

I thought about Khellios's offer to help me get rid of my magic. "Khellios has offered to—"

Livina put her hand up to halt me. "Accepting his help to quell your magic will be the worst decision you can make. *Don't do it.*"

I sat down on the bed behind me as the realization of being able to actually get rid of my magic was confirmed. "So it's possible?"

"Renna," Livina said gravely, leaning forward. "Don't play with fate. Your journey will only get more complicated."

I sat in silence.

"You used magic before Nera and I arrived. I can sense it in the air still."

"My magic isn't worth shit," I spat. "It destroys. There is no goodness in it."

Livina smiled knowingly. "It's working *just* like your mentor intended it to. He wanted you to feel worthless. He wanted you to lash out so it's chaotic."

My body reignited with the feeling of hatred, and rivulets of energy flowed from my chest and trickled down my arms, a reminder that with a simple flick of my wrist, I could unleash chaos into the room.

"You are not your mentor." Livina's statement echoed throughout the room.

"I hate myself," I whispered as I withdrew farther inward, holding on to the anger like a ball encrusted in my center, burrowing itself into my body, moving and crushing my bones to nestle there and fester. "I don't want to feel like this." I hated how easily triggered I was now while in Taria.

"And that is why you are not like your mentor. Your self-awareness will never let you fall into what he was." Livina smiled softly.

"You don't know what I've done. What he's made me do. The people he had me hurt . . ."

I tried to push away the memories of me as a child, forced to hurt others to strengthen my magic. He had hoped the exercises would harden me over time and desensitize me.

"You were a child. He took advantage of that." Livina sat straighter as she regarded me. "Would you hurt people now? Would you commit those same acts?"

"No." I shook my head. "Never—"

"Then you are not like him." Livina sighed. "I will not pretend to be ignorant of the things he had you do. One of the burdens of my powers is knowing the life trajectory of every single being in existence. I know their birth and death. I know major life events. I know what your life has been to get you to this place."

I immediately shifted the topic. I didn't want to go down the route of remembering my life in detail. "You said I would go home before the equinox."

Livina nodded.

"Khellios is prohibiting anyone from leaving Taria at the moment." I stood from the bed and began pacing my room. "How will I be able to leave? Are you here to take me home?"

Livina shook her head. "I won't be the one who takes you back home. I'm here to remind you about your magic. You will need your magic for self-defense at home. The gods will not always be by your side to deflect danger once you leave Taria."

I shivered at her ominous warning. Although my campus was now seemingly inundated with supernatural beings thanks to Aramis's arrival, I had lived a quiet life without thinking about or using magic.

"Practice your magic here." Livina gestured to my bedroom.

"Here?"

"Where else?" Livina stood. "Whether you practice it now and begin to learn to control your anger and transmute it into something useful for when you need it, or you find yourself lost to the impulsive nature of your magic at your time of need, *know this:* you will not be able to escape magic, and you need to be ready."

I shook my head in disbelief.

"You have free will." Livina narrowed her eyes at me. "You can choose whether you take this opportunity to practice your magic now, *or* you can stay indoors and stare at the walls. Remember that working with energy is universal to all beings, and many humans don't realize they do it every day. *Magic* is simply intentionally channeling energy for a desired result."

"I can't just call up my magic. It's bound to anger. My anger is tied to my past."

"So then," Livina said, squaring her shoulders, "get angry. Don't suppress it. You have been suppressing grief and pain inside for so long—enough for your body to lose its essence. Think about the anger, let your body feel it, *acknowledge it.* You know your magic will surge at that time. Breathe through it. Associate things that bring you joy to your magic so that you can reframe the power within you. Eventually, you'll be able to call your magic when you are in need."

"You make it sound so simple."

"It's not simple." Livina walked toward me. "It takes time to reframe thought patterns. The magic does not exist in you because of anger. Your magic is a gift your soul possesses. Your mentor weaponized it. You can reclaim ownership of your essence. You don't have to let him win."

I hugged my arms around myself. "If my magic is like Am-Re's, won't I be labeled a danger? I don't know what it will do if I fully call it forth."

"You have lived in fear long enough. Will you let one more

being, like Am-Re, dictate how you will live your life and lay ownership to your identity? Live freely, Renna."

I stood motionless and stared at my feet.

"You are good, Renna. Your body, your essence, and your soul do not belong to your teacher. Reclaim who you are." Livina moved to the door, and I stepped toward her.

"Will I see you again?"

Livina paused without facing me. "You will." Her statement was cautious, and I tried again.

"Will I see you again before I go home?"

"No." She turned to face me.

My brows furrowed and I shook my head. "That doesn't make sense. Does that mean I will see you once I arrive home?"

"Yes. My guidance is not done, Renna. When ravens close in, you will find me, and I will help you."

I knew better than to ask for clarification.

"Take care, Renna. You are not alone on your journey."

Livina left me standing in the middle of my bedroom, staring at my hands, wondering if I could learn to love my body and the magic within.

22

CYLAS

I watched too many worlds burn.

Too many lives lost.

My planets and creations destroyed by greed.

Pride.

It was easier to walk around and pretend like none of it affected me. But the death of creation marked my soul with every passing day. Lesser gods worried about trivial things. *I* worried about life.

I could always feel death when it was near my creations.

And this time, I could feel Andora on the precipice of genocide.

I could not let Am-Re destroy Andora.

I could not idly sit by and watch another planet burn.

And so, I found myself in a great throne room of obsidian stone far from Taria. A pool of black magical water was located in the middle of the room.

I had come to make a deal with chaos himself.

I heard his footsteps before I could see him.

"Behold, the god of life. Welcome to my humble realm." A voice echoed throughout the silent hall.

This voice was different.

It was not Am-Re's.

I turned and clenched my jaw to keep myself from reacting.

Am-Re was nowhere in sight. A lone figure wearing Am-Re's crown of obsidian crystals stepped forth. It was someone I had never seen before.

I cleared my throat. "I don't understand."

The figure folded his hands, and a menacing smile appeared on his lips.

"This is . . . unexpected."

The man lowered his nose and looked up at me, his stare deadly and calculating. "Is it truly unexpected? You were always going to come here, God of Planets. Your heart is soft. You care too much."

"Color me surprised. I didn't know you could tell the future." I lifted my eyebrows and looked down at my hands to straighten the cuffs on my tunic.

The man stayed silent, and a long pause settled between us. I looked up at him and tried to mask my expression with a blank stare.

He crossed his arms and cocked his head. "I grow weary of your shit. State your purpose, Creator God."

Had I made a mistake?

23

KHELLIOS

"The hero of the old city. Oh, wait, that place was blown up," Cylas sneered as he slowly clapped when I entered Arios's palace, where the sun god had called a gathering to address the attack.

Cylas sat among the gods, his face sour. He leaned forward in his seat and continued. "Some moons failed to rise yesterday on my planets, Khellios. I heard you didn't make it to The Watch. Were you preoccupied?"

"Khel," Nera said, coming toward me as I found a seat. She put her hand on my shoulder. "Don't respond to him. Just leave it be."

I could not put up with Cylas any longer. "I had no idea you watched my personal whereabouts so closely," I snapped at him and sat down.

"When it concerns *my* planets, I make it my business," Cylas challenged. "Half of the moons didn't rise. I have the fucking Elemental Enclave up my ass about the havoc caused by the chaotic ocean currents as a result of no moons rising. You act like a hero, yet you only bring about chaos." Cylas continued, listing off how my absence had affected each planet one by one until Arios cut him off, apologizing on my behalf to Cylas.

When I interjected, Arios raised his palms. "Please," he said, trying to keep the peace. "This is not why you were called in today." He turned to me. "You can understand why Cylas is bothered, Khellios?"

"Many things bother Cylas." I crossed my arms. "Luckily for everyone here, my arguments with Cylas should be less of a nuisance because, as of last night, I can confirm my relationship with Renna is progressing, and Cylas will no longer need to try and win her favor, *again*," I said casually, feeling my face prickle with heat. I looked to Cylas, who was now seething. "You can go back to whatever it is you do, create another planet . . . Bring on another species. How about some dinosaurs again?"

Cylas stood. "I can assure you we would have never been in this position if you simply let the girl be when she arrived. She needed protection from her father. She did not come to us to be seduced!"

I rose. "She didn't pick you, Cylas." I cocked my head. "Why don't you just tell the room about your pathetic obsession with Renna once and for all?"

Cylas smiled bitterly. "Still keeping her in the dark about her *origin story*? You certainly are living up to the expectations of a majestic knight with your lies." He tapped his chin mockingly with a finger. "I bet she'll *love* that. Luckily for you, I don't need to bed Renna for her to trust me."

I was in front of him in seconds. "Don't speak about her," I growled.

"Ooh," he mockingly said, "I'm terrified."

I made to push him, but Nera and Ukara were at my side in seconds, holding back my arms.

"You know," Cylas said, getting dangerously close, his voice dipping menacingly low. He smiled. "I'm not so sure you'll end up with her in this lifetime either."

I saw red and charged at Cylas, sending us crashing through a wall of Arios's temple. Amid the rubble, we landed on the ground outside. I rose and sprang toward him to grip him by the neck.

"Don't look at her. Don't touch her. Don't breathe the same air she does or—"

"Or what?" he said, struggling against my hold and gripping my hands with his, which were now turning into molten lava.

I jerked my hands away and cradled my burned hands to my chest, silently cursing his ability to call upon any element with a simple thought.

"I don't know what she ever saw in you," he sneered. "How convenient you were there when things weren't working out with Daddy Am-Re. Codependency at its finest."

"What do you want to hear?" I yelled. "That I'm sorry it wasn't you? That I'm sorry she didn't pick you?"

"You took advantage of a girl who was fragile!" he yelled. "The girl was frightened for her life when she arrived in Old Xhor as a refugee, and you were the *first* thing she could hold onto!" He spit on the ground. "Pity that her life unraveled after meeting you. She should have *never* picked you!"

"How dare you." I shook my head. "You have no idea what Renna needed at that time!"

"And you did?" He shot back. "You were going to take her as your consort three months into meeting her! *Three months!*" He ran his hands through his hair. "Do you not see anything wrong with that?!"

"I'm not arguing with you on this," I said, shaking my head and walking away.

I did not have the mental capacity to process his words.

"It could have been *anyone*," Cylas called after me. "She needed *healing. Space. Time* to process her grief at losing her father and homeland."

"What father?!" I spun around and walked back to him. "What father?" I grabbed him by the collar. "She was broken when she came to me!"

Cylas shoved me off. "She didn't come to *you*."

I could feel an audience gather outside Arios's palace, watching us now.

"She came for refuge. She hadn't come to be romanced," Cylas said, shaking his head. "She was an eighteen-year-old girl, barely a woman. For gods' sake, Khellios!"

"You have no idea what we shared."

"No, I don't," Cylas said in earnest. "But I know that your lack of foresight damned us all." He gestured around us.

Several of the gods did not meet my eyes and instead looked to the ground. Cylas dusted off his clothing and walked back inside the palace. He was followed by everyone except Ukara and Nera.

I stood rooted to the spot for what seemed like hours as I processed Cylas's words. I recalled every moment, every look, smile, laugh, touch, and only saw pure love radiate from her eyes. Cylas was wrong. Renna's love for me wasn't just some coping mechanism. Renna and I shared something Cylas had spent lifetimes searching for. *Love.*

"Are you okay?" Nera said softly, facing me.

"He's bitter," Ukara quipped from behind me. "He doesn't know what he's talking about."

"Renna will love you, you know that." Nera smiled at me, but it looked forced.

"Will she?" I was lost in my thoughts. "She has no idea who I truly am."

"Her soul remains the same," Nera said encouragingly.

Nera was ever the optimist.

Was Cylas right? Would Renna have fallen in love with Cylas if we had traded positions? I hated him for making me doubt what I had shared with Renna . . . and what she and I could have in this lifetime.

24

RENNA

L ivina's visit left me restless. I had never intentionally called my magic in a state of rest, and thinking about accessing it at all filled my body with anxiety. As my body tensed up, I began to feel the magic move within me. Old memories of being yelled at and physically hit rose to the surface, and I shut down, covering my face with my hands.

Reframe.

Reframe. I thought about my almost complete thesis, *my friends*, my time in Taria, sword fighting, *anything* to shutter the painful thoughts. I didn't want to think about my past.

Breathe.

Breathe.

In response, the magic within me fizzled out.

I felt weak. Stupid.

I cursed and sat up from the bed. I was undeserving of this magic.

I threw my blankets on the ground angrily and stalked across my room.

In response to my anger, the magic swirled within me again.

I gripped my hair at the roots and almost screamed in frustration.

I knew my mentor had conditioned my magic to respond to anger, but I had never even considered that had he never entered my life, I could have developed it differently. Knowing he came up with ways to manipulate my childhood mind and body to serve his twisted ambitions was sickening and disgusting.

I stared at the wall, wishing for a glimpse of the sea, the outside sky, anything but these damn stone walls. I felt like a captive, and the power within me surged like it was under pressure, like a valve ready to burst. My arms began to burn with magic, the cells and veins within feeling supercharged with white-hot energy. The magic within me pushed my body to the edge, demanding to be let out. It compelled me to hurt someone, something, *anything*.

I was built for destruction.

Self-destruction.

I let out a groan of frustration.

I hated my body. I hated my inability to control my feelings. I hated that I was so connected to my mentor still, even after trying to run away from the memories.

I pounded my head with my fists.

Stop this.

Stop these thoughts.

Shower.

I would shower.

I walked to the bathroom and turned on the hot water. I needed to not think. Suppressing my feelings was my saving grace every time. I wanted to feel numb. I stripped down and walked into the hot spray, squeezing my eyes shut as the water heated my skin uncomfortably. When I was able to think of nothing but my skin under the water, I jumped back and turned the water to a more reasonable temperature. I slithered down to the floor and hugged my knees to my chest, resting my head on them. I would try again. Just not today.

~

SETHOS WAS GONE or had simply not come to me for the last several days. I was going mad without seeing him and couldn't help but feel angry at his absence. His absence wasn't normal. Without him, my sleep felt like a black hole. I fell asleep and woke up feeling nothing. I felt empty.

I missed him, and his absence only made me feel worse about this whole situation. I needed to talk with somebody about the feelings I had inside. He had said he would be there when I needed him, so where was he?

I tried to get angry or provoke my anger with menial things or tasks, but none were enough to call forth any energy of significance. I knew if I wanted to practice my magic, I had to face the trauma locked within me.

Feeling depleted of energy, I lied to Ukara and Nera and told them I had my cycle to get out of weapons training. Nera and Ukara both apologized, admitting to never having a menstrual cycle as those were only reserved for humans, and they left me alone.

Khellios sent me a note, inquiring about how I was and whether I needed anything.

I needed Sethos, and I wept, calling for him to give me a sign.

~

SOMEONE KISSED my forehead while I slept. When I woke, soft remnants of what felt like my magic mixed with bergamot and sandalwood lingered in the air, and on my pillow was a lone white lotus flower.

Sethos.

I shot up in bed and reached for the flower.

Upon touching it, it dissolved into magic dust and evaporated into the air.

Had he been here?

How?

Sethos could only exist in dreamtime.

Right?

The presence of Sethos reignited something in me. The lotus flower was his reminder to keep going. To move forward. I didn't know why he was unable to come to me in my dreams, but he had been here. He had sent me a sign like he did so many times in the past when I felt lost.

He gave me hope.

And so that morning, I got up. I bathed. I got dressed.

And I tried to work with magic again.

I ignited only a small ember in my palms.

As the days passed, Nera became my sole connection to what was happening around Taria. She began sending me notes with updates that would materialize in my room. She even delivered the romance books she had acquired for my night with Khellios on the beach, which I begrudgingly accepted. Romance was the last thing on my mind as Khellios stopped checking in on me and Sethos was gone.

One night while sitting in bed reading, a note from Nera materialized on my lap.

Her note read that Am-Re was still at large and that I would need to remain in my rooms a little while longer. It was ironic that of all the triggers to ignite my magic, Nera's note did it. I looked around the windowless room I was in and screamed. I crumbled her note and threw it along with the book I had been reading. The book slammed against the nearest wall, and I felt tremors of magic under my skin.

I held in a breath and looked down at my hands and at the book on the ground.

My magic slowly receded.

I looked at the remaining books on the bed.

All stories of people living in peace.

I would have no peace while Am-Re lived.

I grabbed another book and screamed, throwing it across the room.

I was angry. Instead of an escape, the books now served as a reminder of everything my life lacked.

The magic swirled under my skin again, this time stronger.

Unable to sit still, I got out of bed.

Was violence the price to pay to conjure magic and avoid flashbacks?

Instead of pacing, I slammed every drawer and door in my rooms, feeling my magic culminate. Spreading my arms, I gritted out a scream and pushed a protective shield from my body. The invisible shield-like dome covered me, stretching to the far corners of my room and bathroom, completely encasing me. The magic felt like it was squeezing, like tight straps banded around my body.

I breathed heavily and looked around me as my chest constricted. I had never erected a shield so large. I began to doubt my ability to maintain it, and in response, the energy around me faltered and flickered like a candle.

I needed to fuel my anger to maintain my magic.

I closed my eyes.

· · ·

MY MENTOR HAD me by the collar. His heavily ringed fingers were pressed against my chin.

I was thirteen.

"You want to pretend any of those fuckers care about you? You filthy scum?" He released me, and I fell to the ground like a pile of bricks.

It was summer, and I had been ordered to do chores around the apartment by my foster mother. After stepping outside to throw out the bucket with dirty water, some other children had offered me ice cream. But I wasn't allowed to have friends. My mentor forbade it. Sometimes I thought he wanted me to be kept locked indoors, like a wild animal, until I became rabid.

"It was only ice cream," I whispered, not daring to look at him.

He towered over me with balled fists as his magic pressed against my throat.

"You have no friends!" he screamed. "Not one of them would care if you died right now."

I wanted to sob, but his phantom grip constricted around my neck. It was forbidden for me to cry. He always reminded me it showed weakness.

His magic then slammed me against the nearest wall, and his face was suddenly there, imposing, threatening, mad. His eyes were something made of nightmares. They were black with gold rims. They were lifeless. They were terrifying. His canines gleamed, reminding me of the beast he was.

"You have no friends." His voice was low. "You are above all of them," he barked. "They are not deemed worthy for the soles on your fucking feet."

"I thought you said I was filthy scum," I snapped back before I could stop myself.

He was physically on me in seconds. He held my face in place by gripping my hair with a fist and slapped me with his open palm. He

*pulled me by my hair and dragged me to my room, where I was tossed
like the worthless scum I was.*

*"If I see you talking to those children again, there will be conse-
quences for them," he yelled. "Do you want to be at fault?"*

*I couldn't shake my head in disagreement because of the throbbing
pain.*

He kicked me in the ribs.

"No!" I screamed and bit my cheeks to keep from crying.

Crying was for the weak.

*"Good." He straightened up, brushing invisible dust off his black
suit. "Go crawl back into your closet," he sneered. "Be the scared little
daughter of a whore you are. We both know you are worthless."*

I whimpered.

"Go!" he screamed.

I scurried off like a frightened animal.

I SCREAMED in anger at the memory. My body began to shake
with white-hot hatred.

I wanted to hurt something.

Someone.

Anything.

I reached for the floor-length mirror kept next to my armoire
and threw it against a wall.

It shattered into a million pieces.

I breathed in satisfaction.

My protective shield would ensure no one heard.

When the mirror began to piece itself back together, through
what I surmised to be the magic around Taria, I screamed and
pulled my hair.

"Is this what you wanted?" I yelled, thinking of my mentor.
"To make me a monster?"

I pummeled the mirror with my fists into millions of pieces

again and again, the magic inside me shielding my hands. And each time, the mirror repaired itself.

I didn't want to see my reflection. I wanted to see nothing.

My magic rose like a tidal wave, making me feel energized, vicious.

I needed to destroy more.

I looked at the bed. It was beautiful, and the pink quartz reminded me of calm.

I hated everyone at that moment. I wanted them all to burn.

I stood and began to direct my magic into my palms.

Livina wanted me to concentrate on transmuting my energy into a ball so I could reframe it into something good.

I was not good.

I was disgusting.

I was unwanted.

I was filth.

As I concentrated, furious energy rose from my soles to my hands. Like riptide currents crashing into my palms, energy began to build there.

I wanted to destroy the bed. I wondered mockingly if Khellios's magic would repair it.

Something sinister laughed within me as the magic in the room began to swirl into visible gray currents of air.

To destroy the bed, I just had to move my hands toward it and direct my energy there, just like my mentor had taught me.

I hesitated. Livina told me I was nothing like my mentor. I was good. Wasn't I?

The magic flickered.

Anger boiled inside me.

I was too weak to follow through. I was too weak to hurt others. I was useless. It was my fault I had been hit so many times. I could have been better.

The energy inside me burned my body like a million suns.

I needed to let it out.

I looked at the mirror that was now on the ground, crystalline clear.

In a fraction of a second, I directed my hands there and sent my magic to the mirror.

It erupted like a maelstrom, smashing the mirror's surface to dust.

There was no chance the mirror would be repaired.

As I turned away with a self-satisfied smile, I heard the eerie sound of glass reforming behind me.

No.

When I turned around, the mirror was different.

It had turned to obsidian.

25

RENNA

I stared at the black mirror for days until I realized I would have to do something to hide it. I didn't have anything long enough to cover it, and placing a bed sheet over it would raise questions. I opted to hide the mirror under the bed. The mirror was a pain to move because of the thick frame with hundreds of encrusted jewels, which had all turned to obsidian, but after several grunts, a few scrapes, and very tired arm and leg muscles, the mirror was safely under the bed. The quartz bedframe was wide enough and low enough that it cast a dark shadow underneath.

I couldn't see the mirror from any angle unless I crouched down to look for it. Out of sight, out of mind. If anyone were to stop by to see me, they would not be able to see it.

The next morning, Nera stopped by to let me know I could leave my rooms but would need to stay inside Khellios's home until the lockdown was lifted across Taria. When I asked her what I could do to pass the time, she mentioned I could try and explore the geode cave system that made up his home. That sounded incredibly boring, but without any windows to look out from, no research to do, and no desire to touch the romance books that had fueled my rage, I resigned myself to wandering the home.

One day while walking endlessly, I heard yelling come from one of the lower levels.

It was Khellios.

And Ukara.

My heart sped up when I heard Khellios's voice, the sound supercharging a thrill of anticipation through my body like a shockwave. It had been so long since I'd heard his voice or seen him. I raced through the halls, following the sounds, my bare feet slapping the floor as I ran.

I paused when I reached the scene. Both were training.

Khellios had his shirt off, sweat glistening across his abdomen as he wielded a sword in each hand. My palms tingled, recalling how they had felt against him that night on the beach, and my stomach flipped.

The memory of each kiss and each touch and how his hardness had felt pressed against my center crashed through me and made me catch my breath.

Ukara slid her gaze to where I stood before Khellios took the opportunity to push her down. She kicked him as she hoisted herself back up. He faltered and stumbled backward to the ground.

"Fuck!" he yelled and slammed a sword on the ground.

I flinched and I took a step back.

Ukara helped him up and patted him on the shoulder. "Yeah, yeah. Go cry about it."

Khellios muttered something angrily and gathered his sword.

"Renna." Ukara smiled toward me, causing Khellios to spin to face me.

I waved meekly. Khellios's eyes softened.

Ukara rolled her eyes. "He gets angry when I beat him."

"When anyone beats me," he grumbled looking to Ukara. "The whole point is not to lose."

"Well then don't."

Khellios shook his head and walked away toward a table with water. He drank some and then dunked the rest of it on his body.

My jaw dropped as my eyes followed each rivulet of water.

Ukara cleared her throat and folded her hands on her sword, which was pointed to the ground.

"What can we do for you, Renna?" Ukara asked.

I peeled my eyes off Khellios. My mind was conflicted. Part of me was upset that he hadn't made an effort to see me after what we shared on the beach, and another part just wanted to bask in his ridiculous attractiveness and how good it felt to be near him . . . and to touch him . . . and kiss him.

I shook my head. "I was walking, and I heard yelling." I shrugged.

Ukara smiled. "Just training. Per usual."

"Losing, per usual." Khellios shook his head.

His mood was calmer, and my senses relaxed a bit.

"Did you want to try . . .?" Ukara asked, gesturing to the weapons on the other side of the room.

Livina's warning came to the forefront of my mind. My magic wasn't doing what I needed it to do. I could claim back some control by choosing to learn about weapons.

At my silence, Ukara nodded and sighed, turning to walk away.

"Okay," I called to her.

She and Khellios turned, each with a different expression.

Hers with excitement, his with trepidation.

"Grab a sword." She motioned for me to follow her.

"Which one?" I asked, following her and recalling the extremely heavy one she had handed me the day at the tombs.

"Hmmm..."

We stood in front of her array of weapons, each one glimmering under the soft glow from the crystal ceiling. Each hilt was made of a different material—leather, metal, and jewels—and each pommel had the face of a ram with spiral horns and fire embossed in gold.

I picked up a sword with a leather hilt and ran my fingers over the pommel, its surface hard and polished.

"My symbol," Ukara said, coming to stand next to me. "Humans used to summon us by drawing our sigils, but belief in us has died, so we haven't been summoned since long ago," she said, gazing longingly at her symbol.

I looked at Khellios. He had moved on to practicing archery, and his back was to us.

"Do you have a sigil?" I asked him.

At my question, he missed his target. "Yes," he responded, not turning around.

"What is it?" I asked, turning to inspect the other swords.

"It's not important," he said nonchalantly.

"That's not what I asked." I chuckled. "Is it something terrible?" I joked and turned to look at him again.

Khellios drew an arrow and aimed at his target. "Not particularly."

He released and missed again.

He must have still been angry that he lost to Ukara.

"Fine, don't share." I rolled my eyes and decided to ignore him as I went back to picking a sword.

One sword, in particular, caught my eye. Its hilt was made of emerald, obsidian, and black metal. The materials were woven together, creating a swirling pattern, and I couldn't tell where each material ended and the other began. The fuller part of the sword was also black metal. It was missing Ukara's signature pommel.

"Is this one yours?" I asked.

Ukara looked over at where I held the sword. "Khellios gave that to me." She picked it up. "It was a gift to him from one of his travels. I guess he missed me beating him up." She laughed. "Who gave this to you again?" she asked, handing me the sword.

Khellios glanced briefly at it before returning to his bow and arrow. "A fae king." He shrugged.

"I feel like that king gifted you a lot of things, didn't he?" Ukara scratched her neck.

"That was a long time ago, Ukara," Khellios said disinterestedly.

Ukara rolled her eyes. "Well, *I* never use it," Ukara whispered to me. "It's too light for what I'm used to and what I need."

I grabbed the sword, and the hilt tingled against my palms. I jumped and must have made a face because Ukara laughed.

"They're all enchanted, Renna, except for the ones in Khira's tombs. I figured with the latest threat so close to home, I should use something a little more . . . effective. You can use it if you like," she said, grabbing a sword with a brown leather strap and moving to the center of the room.

I moved the sword I'd chosen around from side to side. It felt light in my hands, as if it was a part of my arm, and the magic in the sword felt like it was gripping onto the magic under the surface of my skin, like a magnet melding both tool and limb as one.

I swung the sword around once more, and Ukara laughed.

"Okay, don't hurt yourself, please. I'd rather live and not be killed by Khellios because you got hurt."

Khellios sighed and turned to face me. He narrowed his eyes. "Do you really want to do this?"

I nodded.

"Why?" He crossed his arms.

I looked down at my free palm. "My magic may never do what I need it to—"

"You don't need it," he insisted.

"I'd like to feel like I can protect myself—"

"I will protect you. I told you this many times before."

"Khellios, for fuck's sake, back off." Ukara was annoyed. "Let her speak before you cut her off." She nodded toward me encouragingly.

I gave her a smile of thanks and looked down at the sword. "I know you'll protect me." I looked up at Khellios, who wore a stern expression, then to Ukara. "I know you'll all do what you can to protect me."

She nodded.

"But I want to know that should it ever come to it—"

"Which it won't," Khellios insisted.

Ukara cursed.

"—that I can defend myself."

Before Khellios could protest, Ukara cut him off. She grabbed me by the arm and pulled me to the center of the room. Unlike the first time I sparred with her, where she just told me to fight with no real instruction, she taught me stances and how I should hold my body. She critiqued the width of my legs, the height of my elbows, the way my feet were pointing, and from where I drew power for each swing.

She made me pose without swinging, and she would walk around me, pointing out where to improve.

Khellios watched silently from the edge of the room, arms crossed, expression blank as Ukara instructed me.

I was grateful for his silence. I didn't need the added pressure of his disapproval.

"All right." Ukara nodded. "Now put an arm up toward your cheek and step forward like I taught you and swing in an arc."

Training went on for hours until my body was sweating, and I had to take off my top shirt layer.

Khellios watched as I lifted my tank top's hem to wipe sweat off my face. My body grew hot with awareness as he watched me.

"Aren't you supposed to be training or something?" I asked.

"Something like that. I get distracted easily. I was supposed to be reading the other day, and I got sidetracked."

My insides clenched at the memory . . . and the dream with Sethos that followed after.

"Let's focus," Ukara drawled. "You won't be able to stay alive by flirting with an enemy."

I blushed and focused on Ukara.

WE TRAINED FOR DAYS. Each day, my body got stronger, faster, more agile, my mind sharper.

I tried training with other swords, but the emerald sword called to me and felt best in my hands.

Soon Nera joined us, but she simply sat and cheered us on. Her skills were not in battle but in magic, so she opted to watch instead of participating. Khellios sat with Nera most days.

With each session with Ukara, I could feel his judgment of my training growing. Until I'd had enough.

"Say it!" I yelled, spinning to face him as he sat on the floor with Nera.

I had just finished fighting, and I was sweaty and messy and tired.

Khellios looked surprised. "What?"

"Whatever you're thinking, say it!"

Ukara intervened. "He probably thinks you'd be better off with him as a teacher."

"She would," he said cockily.

Nera's face turned red, and she got up and walked away, anticipating an argument.

I braced for the clash of words.

"Oh, really?" Ukara challenged him. "Why don't you try, then? You're just sitting there sulking every day. I'm glad Renna spoke up. You're suffocating."

Khellios looked at me. "Do you want me to teach you?"

I didn't feel like I could say no. "Couldn't you both teach me?" I asked diplomatically.

Ukara laughed. "Don't you see how uncomfortable you're making her? Stop being so controlling," she told Khellios.

When no one spoke up, Ukara sighed. "Renna, I'm going to take the rest of the day off. Why don't you humor your god over there so he can relax and feed his ego?" She walked to the swords stands and set hers down.

"You don't have to leave," I said.

I liked having her around.

"I'd rather leave," she answered. "I'll start critiquing him." She then turned sharply to Khellios. "I'm the one who taught *him* how to fight."

He crossed his arms. "I've learned a thing or two."

"Yet I win every time." She smirked. She turned her head and turned to me. "Will we continue training tomorrow?" she asked.

I nodded.

"Good. I'll leave you with this one."

When we were alone, Khellios went to the stands and picked up one of Ukara's swords.

He met me in the middle of the room and stood in front of me with a grim expression.

"Uh?" I put a free palm up in the air, waiting for instruction. "What do you want me to do?"

He curled his palm, motioning me to come to him.

"You want me to just strike you?" I was confused.

He nodded like he was bored.

"Uh . . . Okay . . ." I stepped forward cautiously and swung.

Khellios deflected my swing like it was nothing. He didn't even move his feet.

I tried again.

He deflected my sword again.

"Do something!" I said, annoyed. "You're just standing there."

"Then try and fight me."

"I'm trying!" I swung again, and he shoved my sword, sending me stumbling backward. "Asshole."

"If you ever fight, Renna—which I will never allow to happen—you won't have Ukara giving you instructions."

I swung again.

He barely moved as he clashed with my sword and shoved me back.

"You will only truly learn if you experiment. Battle is unexpected."

He swung toward me, and I met him halfway, immediately putting both hands on the hilt, anticipating the blow.

We went on and on like this for hours.

Nera eventually rejoined us and sat excitedly on the floor, cheering me on.

By the end of it, I was lying on the ground, my chest heaving, looking up at the ceiling.

Khellios stood next to me and stuck out his hand. I took it, and he pulled me up like I weighed nothing.

"How do you feel?" he asked, looking at me up and down for any injuries.

"Sore. More than with Ukara."

"Good." His voice was serious. "I'll practice with you every day after you finish with her."

"I'll be properly exhausted," I joked, trying to break the tension in the air.

Khellios's gaze darkened, and I thought he would respond, but then he cleared his expression and nodded, not commenting further.

I thought of our time on the beach. It seemed like anything we had experienced had evaporated after the attack. Part of me could understand that he was too preoccupied with the care of Taria, which was still on lockdown, to think about anything other than the safety of his people.

Still, when he took his shirt off for training, I couldn't help but gawk at his beauty and wonder if we'd ever get to explore what was between us. Even though his proximity reminded me that he was here while Sethos was not, Khellios's aloof demeanor—only interacting with me for trainings and to generally inquire how I was—reminded me that neither man was available. Khellios was here, but emotionally and mentally, he wasn't—at least not for me, anyway.

Not once had I received praise from him for how I was progressing. Unlike Ukara, who gave me positive feedback whenever she could to encourage me to keep going, Khellios had only ever demanded I hit him harder and faster and to pay attention. He was always on edge, as if picturing the worst possible scenario that would land me in a fight.

Ukara would remind him several times that it was just practice and to take a break.

"Sometimes I feel like he just shouldn't come to practice," I told Ukara one day. "He gets this blank look on his face like he's not here as he watches us. His mind goes off somewhere."

Ukara was silent for a while before speaking. "The fall of Xhor plagues him. He saw so much death. Out of all of the gods here who were there that night, he is the one who has been unable to move past it. Sometimes things trigger him, and he just goes quiet. At times it can be hard to shake him from wherever his mind goes." Ukara looked down to the ground. "It's gotten better over the years."

"His intended . . ." I asked, an ominous feeling creeping through my body. "Nera mentioned she was killed and was with child. How—" I couldn't bring myself to ask the question without feeling dread. "How exactly did they die?"

"Am-Re's soldiers stormed our bedroom," Khellios said, returning to the room from a break Ukara made him take.

I gasped, and my face heated from embarrassment at having asked.

"She tried fighting back," he said, walking toward the line of swords, not looking at us. "His soldiers teamed up on her. He didn't even kill her himself."

He picked a sword and began weighing it in his hands. He turned toward us, ready to train again, and walked to the center of the room. He looked at us expectantly.

"She and my child within her died in my arms."

Ukara and I looked at each other, unsure if Khellios should train after sharing such a painful memory.

"Khel," Ukara said. "Why don't you sit—"

"*No.*" He gritted. He spread his legs and held the sword in front of him, ready to fight.

"Khel—" Ukara tried again.

I intervened. "Do you need anything?" I asked gently.

He stared at me. "I need you to stay alive."

His response took me aback, and I nodded. "I will."

"Well, then." He tilted his head. "Let's go." He nodded for me to advance toward him.

~

THE NEXT FEW days were more of the same. I typically trained with Ukara during the evenings, and Khellios would spar with me after. Sometimes he joined in, and we trained together with Ukara. Khellios would leave with Nera when the sun would begin to set so they could go to The Watch.

I was left to wander his home alone until I was too tired to loop around endless windowless corridors. My goal was to tire myself out so I could fall asleep quickly and not think about Sethos and yet another dreamless night. I looked every day for a sign from him, but none came.

I don't know when I stopped trying to practice my magic. Perhaps it was the progress I was making with Ukara that made me comfortable with ignoring that part of me that wouldn't cooperate. I knew Livina and Sethos would be disappointed in my lack of trying. But I gained a sense of pride from being able to control my body while training with Ukara and Khellios, while failing to exercise my magic correctly every time only resulted in endless tears and frustration.

One day after practice, Khellios stayed behind as Nera left for The Watch. He and I were left alone in the room, and I had just removed the bandages on my hands that helped better my grip and was getting ready to walk back to my rooms.

"What?" I asked as he stared at me with an expression that wasn't critical for the first time in days. "Did I un-bandage incorrectly?" My voice had an edge.

That day's practice was particularly grueling. We still had no word of Am-Re, and Khellios was frustrated that he and the gods were unable to track him down.

"You're making good progress," Khellios said, putting his hands in his pockets.

I paused. "Wait," I said, putting a hand on my hip. "Wow, a compliment?" I raised my eyebrows.

He nodded.

"Well . . ." I shifted on my feet, not knowing what else to say. "Thanks. I'll leave you to head to The Watch. Have a good night. Stay safe."

I turned to leave.

"Renna."

I stopped and glanced over my shoulder.

"I'm sorry," he said.

I turned around. "For what?"

"For the distance between us." He crossed his arms and cleared his throat.

"I . . ." I shrugged, unable to find the words to express how I felt. "I understand."

"Do you?"

I nodded. "I think?" I walked toward him. "You haven't been able to locate Am-Re. The attack so close to Taria was triggering. And perhaps you see a bit of your consort in me."

He stayed silent, and I panicked after having said the last part.

"Not that I am her." I blushed. "I would *never* imply I am—"

"Renna—"

"—but I mean, the position I'm in with you having to protect me. Perhaps that's triggering for you. And also, your mind is occupied with the safety of the rest of Taria."

"Renna—" He began to close the distance between us.

"So, I understand." I looked down at my shoes. "I won't lie and say I'm unaffected because I liked what we shared on the beach and how we were slowly getting to know one another but . . ." I shook my head. "It's alright."

Having reached me, he placed his hands on my arms, and I looked up at him.

"My mind can get very loud, and I often feel like I'm stuck in a loop of feelings and memories, so I have to retreat to quiet my mind. I never meant to stay away from you. I just don't know how to feel sometimes. I don't feel safe in my own mind."

I placed my hands on top of his as understanding washed through me. That was definitely something I could relate to. "I'm sorry."

His gaze was soft. "You have done nothing wrong. I'm the one who should be apologizing for the distance."

I moved his hands to mine and squeezed. "You play a lot of roles for many people here, and I appreciate everything you are doing for me. You don't ever need to feel like you have to prove anything to me. I like being around you, and I would like to continue being around you, when possible, if that's okay. *And* I like being your friend," I said with a smile. "*Or*, at least, you reminded me we are friends," I added and couldn't help but chuckle.

He smirked and nodded. "That we are."

I nodded too and tried to keep the smile on my face because what else was I supposed to do? My heart was breaking for him, but I didn't know how I could help. I wanted more with him, but we didn't really see each other outside of training, and given the triggers of grief and constant stress, it didn't feel right to ask for more than he could give me. I would take as much as he would allow.

"But I want more," he said suddenly as if echoing my thoughts.

I leaned in because I thought I misheard him. "I'm sorry, *what*?"

"I want more with you, Renna." He squeezed my arms and searched my eyes. "Let's continue the start of whatever we had on the beach. I can't promise we'll get to that level immediately because the last attack sent me to a dark place I haven't exactly emerged from, but maybe we can start slow."

The emotional whiplash of the events of last week, trying to sort out my feelings for him and Sethos, my magic, and training every day left me exhausted.

"Are you sure—"

"I'm sure," he said, searching my eyes. "We will take it slow."

I nodded, understanding the realistic pace he was offering. We needed to get to know one another before getting back to whatever happened on the beach because even *that* was a little out of the ordinary for people who were still virtual strangers. I blamed his body and good looks. Who would be able to say no to a god?

I smiled. "Slow will be nice."

He returned my smile. "Can I walk you back to your rooms?"

"Uh, sure." I blushed, and my flush deepened even further when he offered me his arm.

I took it, and we walked back together. When we got to my door, I reached to open it and turned to face him, taking my arm back.

"Thanks for walking me back."

"Of course."

"Are you headed off to The Watch?"

He nodded and furrowed his brow. "At times, I wish my nights were my own."

I chuckled. "That would be unrealistic for the god of the moon and stars."

"Still," he sighed. "It would be nice to get to choose what I wanted to do at night."

Even though there was no sexual undertone to his words, I still blushed profusely. Seeing him without a shirt and knowing what his body felt like underneath mine made my mind wander.

"You are beautiful when your skin is flushed," he whispered, leaning into me, brushing his check along my temple.

I shivered. "Thank you," I said awkwardly and rolled my lips together.

"I'll leave you now." He squeezed my hands. "Good night."

I smiled. "Good night."

As I watched him walk away, I couldn't help but wonder what it would have been like to let him kiss me again.

I would have let him had he tried.

26

RENNA

The next few days were better. Eventually Khellios joined in on every practice with Ukara, and the three of us trained together. We all ended up on the ground, backs to the floor, groaning as our muscles protested in pain at the end of every day. Khellios would walk me back to my rooms every evening.

We hadn't heard about Am-Re for weeks, and I was able to enjoy my practices without fear of actually having to use my skills to stay alive. Ukara, Khellios, and I built a good rapport, and practices were fun.

"You need some lights in here," Ukara said one day to Khellios as she looked around with a scrunched nose. "Real sunlight." She pointed with her sword at the ceiling. "Not whatever this fake shit is you have providing light."

"Ukara is right, Khel," Nera added from where she sat. "Renna needs sunlight. I know we don't need it as gods, but she does."

Khellios looked at me with a slight smile. "I suppose you do."

"Looking at the sea would be amazing," I added.

I had been living inside his home under crystal lights for a month. It was miserable.

Khellios nodded and smiled. "Anything for you. Done."

He waved his palms around, and windows appeared in the practice room. The evening sun poured in, and I flinched and shielded my face.

"And lift the lockdown in Taria, please," Ukara asked him. "The threat is gone."

"For now." Khellios sighed and rubbed his face.

"For now." Ukara nodded. "But people need to resume their lives. You can't limit them to timed activities and curfews. That is no way to live."

It felt odd to hear that citizens in Taria had the ability to go outside, even if restricted, compared to my constant lock-in. I knew I ran the most risk and posed the most threat, but it still stung to hear others could experience the outdoors.

I missed the sun's heat on my skin and the sound of the sea outside my window. I wanted to see the clouds, even if they looked odd in a lilac haze through the lilac dome covering Taria.

THE NEXT MORNING, I woke to sunlight pouring through my windows, and I jumped up excitedly. I almost cried after seeing the balcony restored to my bedroom, and I pushed open the door and ran outside.

The wind whipped my hair, the sun shone brightly on my face, and I took in a lungful of the cool sea air. I almost forgot it was just an illusion. I leaned on my balcony for a long while, absorbing the sun and sound of the waves.

A pair of gray eyes came to mind.

Sethos.

I thought about Sethos and our moonlit night along the

seashore. I hadn't seen him in weeks, and the waves below made me long for him. Where had he gone?

A part of me was missing without him, even if I was now trying to pursue something with Khellios. I prayed that he came back to make me feel whole again.

～

ONE DAY KHELLIOS was walking me back to my rooms, and he was unusually quiet. We typically talked nonstop, catching up on our day, which we couldn't do while practicing.

I knew he was trying to build intimacy by asking about my days, but my hours were boring and filled with the same mundane things being locked in his house all day. I began to read again, took extremely long baths, read some more, and then poured all my energy into weapons practice.

His days were more exciting as he patrolled Taria, and I couldn't help but feel a bit jealous that he was able to be outdoors. Each evening, he gave me a chaste kiss on the cheek or forehead. It was sweet, but I longed for *more*. The flirtations from before the attack were gone. It seemed like he held back from deepening our connection more than once, as if he was afraid. However, I didn't want to push him. I knew the weight of what he carried was heavy.

"Have you practiced magic lately, Renna?" he asked me.

Magic hadn't crossed my mind in weeks. Focusing my time and energy on training and what my body could do put magic at the back of my mind.

"No."

"How long has it been?"

"A few weeks, perhaps?" I sighed. "It's a colossal failure. I'd rather not talk about it."

He nodded and reached into his pocket, producing a vial of

black liquid. It shimmered with gold specks as he moved it in his palm. "Do you remember I told you about the witch in Taria who may be able to help quell your magic?"

I felt like ice-cold water had been poured on me. Of course, I remembered our conversation. I had agreed to consider it, but between Livina's warning not to pursue it and Khellios never bringing it back up, I'd forgotten about the conversation for a while.

"Yes . . ." I scratched my neck, not meeting his eyes.

Khellios handed me the vial, and I simply stared at it in my palm.

"That's the potion."

This was so sudden that I was speechless.

"It will quell your magic for a time. Not forever. She'll have to make you more as time goes on."

Livina's warning rang in my head.

"I don't know what to say." I laughed nervously.

"You don't need your magic, Renna."

I looked up at him. He seemed excited by the prospect of me getting rid of it.

"*You know* you don't need it," he reiterated.

"Well . . ." I grimaced. "It would be nice if it did what I wanted it to do—"

"But it's not."

I nodded. He was right. "But it's not."

"Your training is progressing very well, and you can hold your own."

I smiled. "Thank you for saying that."

"Am-Re seeks you for your magic. He has not attacked, and we haven't heard from him in a month."

I searched his eyes. "What are you saying?"

He grabbed my arms gently. "Perhaps by quelling your magic, he will realize he does not need you."

"Do you think he would just stop looking for me? After going through all this trouble to find me?"

"It's worth a shot."

Dread washed over my body.

Sethos had told me my magic was a part of my identity and that he could teach me how to use my magic. I could picture his disapproving face telling me to disengage from the conversation and refuse Khellios's offer.

But Sethos hadn't been around lately to help me if I wanted it.

Livina's words echoed in my head once more.

I looked down at the vial.

Wasn't this what I wanted?

"I'll think about it. Thank you for doing this for me."

Khellios nodded. "All I ever want is to keep you safe."

"I know—"

"And if getting rid of your magic keeps you safe, then we know what must be done." He looked down at me. "I'm glad you agree."

I paused. Something about his words didn't sit right with me, and I was so lost in thought that I didn't even answer when he bid me good night with a kiss on my forehead.

When he walked away, I realized what bothered me so much about his phrasing. He said *we* knew what must be done, as if getting rid of my magic was a decision for him to make as well.

His controlling nature had come out again, and I didn't feel good about it for one minute.

27

RENNA

I was on my way to my rooms after practice when Nera intercepted me. She was dressed up in a skintight leather minidress and fishnet stockings with combat boots. Crescent moon earrings dangled from her ears and shimmered as she moved. She looked beautiful.

"Where are you going?" I asked, walking inside my rooms with her in tow.

"We," she corrected with a grin, "are going out."

"Like, out, *out*?" I clarified as I faced her. I was a sweaty mess. "I can't leave this house." I shook my head and continued walking inside.

Nera put up her palms to stop me. "I spoke with Khellios about you being in this house for weeks. I told him that Am-Re has not attacked again and that you need a night out. Restoring the balconies and windows in this home is not enough. You need to get outside. It's not healthy to be cooped up here."

I said nothing as I continued walking toward my bedroom.

"Don't you want to leave? Stretch your legs?"

I smiled and glanced at her. "It might be nice."

"Well . . . Khellios knows training has been hard, and he

thinks it would be good for you to have a night of fun to get your mind off everything. He thinks it's safe for you to leave. So"—she clapped her hands excitedly—"I am taking you to the metropolitan district of Taria where a new club opened and I'm dying to visit. The bar is owned by Misha, Goddess of Lust."

My mouth formed an O when I heard the goddess's title.

"She's not a goddess in any particular enclave, but she decided she likes us well enough to call Taria home."

"Nera," I said, gesturing to my cargo pants and tank top, "I have nothing to wear that would be remotely appropriate for a night out."

"I can't show up alone," Nera begged.

"You're the goddess of the moon. Nightlife *is* your domain."

Nera laughed. "If only it was that easy," She shook her head. "Being a god of the moon means I am usually never around in the evenings. It is not the best for making friends, which is why you need to go with me."

I laughed. "Are there no other lunar gods at The Watch who will go with you?" I joked, hoping she would give me a clue as to where Khellios was.

She blushed and looked at her nails. "There are some lunar gods I like at The Watch . . . but none that I would dare invite. And Khel is no fun for these types of things." Nera rolled her eyes. "Pickings are slim when you share a job with the same group of people for millennia." Nera put her hands together in supplication. "Please go with me tonight."

I groaned. "Nera, even if I said 'yes,' I have *nothing* to wear that would even match the level of what you are wearing."

Nera grinned. "*So,* because I was hoping you would agree to go with me, I may already have an outfit for you . . ." Nera pointed to my bedroom. "I picked out a surprise for you. It might have magically made its way onto your bed." She winked.

I sighed and stepped into my bedroom. On the bed was an

iridescent silky midi dress—black, emerald, and gold shimmered in the low light. The iridescent emerald reminded me of the color of Sethos's magic, and I tried my best to mask my shiver as I imagined what his magic around my body would feel like. Shaking my head, I focused back on the dress, which was beautiful. A high slit split the side of the material, while the bustier was a low square cut with thin straps. A pair of gold strappy heels sat next to the dress.

I grabbed the dress, and it felt weightless, like silk and mesh woven together to create a fabric of its own. It was exquisite and almost felt liquid to the touch.

I squinted at her. "I'm guessing you have been planning this outing for some time since you have all my sizes down to a T?"

Nera laughed, her eyes beaming. "Can you blame me?" She jumped excitedly. "You're going to be a hit!"

"You do realize that on the few occasions I do go out, I never dress like this?" I chuckled. "This is how rich women dress on a night out in Andora."

"And you'll look beautiful wearing all of it!" She brought her hands together in prayer. "*Please?*"

I hung my head in defeat and smiled. I wondered if I would see Khel tonight. The kiss on the beach was still at the forefront of my mind, and I was growing impatient with the chaste kisses each night he walked me to my room. I also hadn't seen Sethos in . . . weeks, so my body and hormones were frustrated.

Nera looked around the room curiously.

"Didn't you have a floor-length mirror?" She spun around, trying to find it. "I thought you did . . ."

I bit my cheek.

"I dislike mirrors in my room." I shrugged, the lie rolling out seamlessly. "I got rid of it a while ago."

"Huh," she said, hands on her hips. She scratched her head. "I remember when Khellios came home with it after one of his mercenary travels years ago. A fae king gave it to him as a thank-you."

I began to panic. What if Khellios wanted the mirror back?

"Nera, should I get ready?" I gestured to the dress, drawing her attention.

Nera turned to me, a wide smile lighting up her face. She nodded.

I walked into the bathroom with the outfit, and I slipped into the dress. It was even more beautiful on, and it shimmered with the light if I moved from side to side. Admiring my reflection in the bathroom mirror, I ran my hands over the fabric. The dress hugged my body in places I didn't even know I had curves since the clothing I typically wore was shapeless and meant to shield me from the desert sun.

When I came out of the bathroom, Nera whistled and clapped, which made me laugh. Nera then took the liberty to style my hair and, with a bit of magic, do my makeup since I had none with me. Before we left the room, I looked at myself in the bathroom mirror. Black kohl liner lined my eyes, and blush accentuated my cheekbones. Nera also applied shimmering highlighter all over my face, which made me look like I was glowing. Helena would be so proud if she could see me. The most makeup I ever applied was eye liner.

Nera and I left my rooms and made our way to the front of the house, talking about what drinks and music to expect at the club. As we walked to the front door, a deep voice stopped us.

Khel stood in the doorway leading to the terrace off the living room, a half-full scotch glass in hand.

"Nera," he said, his voice stern. He then looked toward me and dragged his eyes slowly up my body.

I shivered under his perusal.

"Cousin?" Nera replied, her voice taking on a polite tone.

"What are you doing?" he asked her.

"We're going out," she said confused. "You said we could."

Khel set his glass down and crossed his arms. "I did." He nodded. "Where exactly are you going?"

"Misha's Palace," Nera answered, tipping her chin down, daring Khel to respond.

Khel laughed. "The fuck you are," Khel said, shaking his head. "That place is full of degenerates."

I shifted uncomfortably as they squared off.

"That's not true!" Nera frowned.

Khellios scoffed. "Misha reigns over lust. What do you think happens at her club, Nera?"

"Have *you* been there?" She narrowed her eyes.

"Have *you*?" He retorted. "If *I* have been there, that's beside the point."

"It's just a dance club, Khel!" Nera rolled her eyes. "You're being dramatic."

"A dance club created by the goddess of lust," he spat.

"So?" Nera crossed her arms. "We are just going dancing. Renna deserves to have a night off. She's been locked in this house for weeks."

"Just go, Nera. I veto this idea. Leave my house," Khel barked at her.

"Wait a minute," I said, my hands in the air. "Hello, *hi*." I waved. "I've been standing here the whole time, not that you've bothered to say hello, but you can't just tell Nera to leave."

"Sure I can," he snapped. "This is my home. And *you're* not going anywhere dressed like that." He stalked toward me, and I quickly took two steps back.

"No, no, no." I shook my head, and Khel halted. "This is not how our relationship is going to work. You can't order me around like that."

He smiled mockingly. "I can think of a few scenarios where you wouldn't have a problem taking orders from me."

Blood rushed to my face, and my pores prickled with anger.

I stepped forward and slapped him.

Once I realized what I had done, I was horrified for striking him but also equally enraged at him.

"Asshole," I spat, my face hot from embarrassment. "Why are you being like this? You are *nobody* to tell me what to do."

Khel held his cheek, rage in his eyes. "Are you sure about that?"

"This is too much." I shook my head and grabbed Nera's hand, leading her out of the house. "We're leaving."

Suddenly Khel was in front of me. He raised his palms, and as if he had woven a silent spell, I was suspended midair in a silver mist. Khel cocked his head in challenge, and I was transported back to my room at the speed of light.

When I arrived in my bedroom, Khel was in front of me. He pushed me up against the now slammed door.

"Put me down!" I yelled, my hair now disheveled.

Khel refused to let me down and instead caged me in with his arms.

"You want to try speaking to me again?" he said, cocking his head as he slid his hand down to my waist.

"Asshole!" I said, pushing against him, but he only came closer.

Khel's lips brushed against my neck, and I broke out in goose bumps, my body responding to his touch. I hated my body's response to him.

"This dress," he growled as he traced my shoulders and collarbone. "You're driving me insane, Renna."

He rubbed my nipple over my dress, and I couldn't help my moan, but I quickly cleared my throat and pushed him gently.

"Khel," I said, breathing to clear my mind as he moved closer to me again, his eyes trained on my waist.

"Mmm?" He reached for me again, his amber eyes now shining like molten liquid gold.

"We are not doing this." I pushed him off. "You cannot repeat what you just did out there. I'm not yours to direct."

Khel blinked and stepped back. He sighed and rubbed his face in frustration, and I was gently brought back down to the ground.

Khel stepped from me and began pacing. "You are free to go about Taria," he said, upset. "But I can't have you go to Misha's. Not dressed like that."

"Because you're jealous?" I crossed my arms.

I knew he was, but I wanted to hear him say it.

"Yes!" he yelled. "Yes, I am jealous. I am jealous that anyone would have the opportunity to see you like this. You belong to me, Renna."

I paused. "Khel." I shook my head and furrowed my eyebrows. "You can't say things like that. It makes me uncomfortable."

"But we are in a relationship—"

"*No*. You asked us to get to know each other and to take it slow. And if we were in a relationship, you *still* would *never* be able to treat me like that and dictate how I dress."

He crossed his arms.

"Or tell me who I talk to. Or what I do. You've done that in the past. I don't like it. Are you afraid I'll be interested in another if I dress a certain way? What does that say about how you view me?"

Khel put his hand up to silence me, and the movement caught me so off guard that I stopped talking. "*Don't ever* doubt what you mean to me," he began, slowly walking toward me. "Yes, I hate thinking you will want another. I can't live without you, Renna."

"Khellios, you know I want you. But you said we would move

slowly, and your words right now scare me. This feels so sudden and too strong. And sometimes the things you say . . . you treat me like you have a claim over me. You asked me the other day if I could feel the connection between us, and I shared that yes, it feels like I've known you for a long time, but we only see each other during and after practices, which is fine because you're very busy and I don't pressure you, but you need to just"—I paused, the magic within me swirling in anger and frustration—"stop being so controlling."

Khel remained silent, looking off into the distance, lost in his thoughts. His mouth was tense, as if he had a lot to say but couldn't form the words.

I waited patiently, hoping he would tell me something—*anything*.

"Well," I said, nodding after he still didn't say anything. "You clearly have an issue with communication," I said gently, opening the bedroom door to leave the room.

Khel searched my eyes, and he looked almost hurt. "The last thing I want is to push you away."

"I know," I whispered.

Khel didn't stop me when I walked out of the house with Nera.

I almost wished he would have.

As the car pulled out of the driveway, Khel stepped onto the balcony nearest the front door, hands gripping the rail. He looked directly at me even though the car had black tinted windows.

I glared straight back at him, feeling like he could see me.

28

RENNA

The drive to Misha's Palace seemed to take forever as Nera and I rode in silence.

"Well this certainly feels more like home," I said in awe as we drove through the metropolitan side of Taria.

The streets were lined with impressive, sleek skyscrapers that colored the streetscape in drab gray and black. Black cars glided past ours, going to various destinations.

"Does anyone live in this part of town?" Unlike in downtown Taria, where groups of people were always walking around, giving the area a friendly and loving neighborhood energy, this part had no pedestrians. The area felt less friendly and more uptight, and the energy here was sterile and empty.

"This part of Taria was built by a handful of gods who longed for more modern environments to keep up with the changing landscapes and technologies outside of Taria. More recent soul arrivals chose to live here as it reflects their last place of living more closely than the more ancient-looking areas of Taria. Cylas lives here." She said Cylas's name like a curse.

I wanted to ask Nera about her clear dislike for Cylas, but I'd wait for her to share her feelings on the matter when she wished. I briefly wondered if her dislike for Cylas ran further than him being Ukara's ex-spouse, but I was still upset about my conversation with Khellios. We all had feelings to sort out.

I continued to silently take in the sights of the city. "This is incredible."

"This area has that effect on most people," Nera agreed, looking out her window. "There is beauty in Taria and its tribute to many different civilizations. If you were to ask me which I would choose, I would tell you neither. I would rather live among the stars any day."

Mention of the stars brought me back to my argument with Khel. It had felt good to assert my boundaries, but I felt like shit for how I had ended the conversation. Our relationship started out purely physical, but I knew deep down there was something undeniable developing between us. There was a tenderness to him that made me yearn for more.

"Nera," I began, embarrassed. "About Khel." I paused. "I don't know how to get through to him."

"I know." Nera sighed, looking out the window. "Sometimes *even I* don't know how to talk to him."

"What happened to make him this way? How does he maintain relationships?"

"He doesn't." Nera turned to look at me. "He keeps to himself. Going to practice with you and Ukara is him going out of his shell. Arios has a difficult time wrangling him to come to enclave meetings. I get to see him the most out of anyone because of The Watch."

Part of me was pacified to know he wasn't avoiding only me, but it still didn't feel good to be showered with intense attention and then suddenly left cold for days. I was emotionally strung out. "I'm trying to get to know him, but he makes it incredibly hard at times. He's hot and then cold. I can't understand him."

"Just give it time," Nera said and squeezed my hand.

"Sometimes I wonder if it's worth trying to push for more of what he gives me to move forward, but then I also remind myself that I'm not here forever."

"If Khellios could keep you forever, he would."

There it was again. Another statement about Khellios's strong feelings toward me with no further explanation. "You sound like him." I shook my head, trying to make sense of it. "Khellios treats me like we're meant to be. Yet when I ask him to elaborate, he can't. He can't make broad statements like that and expect me not to ask questions."

Nera looked down at her hands in silence. After a while, she spoke. "After the death of his beloved when the old city fell, Khel went mad." She shook her head. "He sought to replicate her love so many times. He jumped from relationship to relationship to find a semblance of what was ripped from him. He remarried two other times to human women. He was a good husband. After his last wife died, Khel left suddenly to live as a mercenary for several hundred human years to separate himself from his past. He left me as the sole representative at The Watch." Nera turned back to look out the window again, and she wrapped her arms around herself. "His absence was hard on many in the enclave. Then, just as suddenly as he left, he came back. It was as if he was made anew and had some of the same zest for life again. Then, his mood plummeted unexpectedly. He became paranoid. He has mood swings—as I'm sure you have noticed."

Khel was still plagued by the memory of his would-be consort. Suddenly, any potential relationship with Khel seemed muddled as I couldn't compete with a ghost and the fears he projected onto me.

As if Nera could see the war of thoughts circling in my head, she cleared her throat and breathed deeply before saying, "I won't pretend Khel is perfect. You coming here is the best thing that has happened to him in a long time. Don't give up on him. You can help him; I know you can. The old Khellios is still inside him."

I nodded and turned away to look out the window. His controlling nature was one thing I hated about him, and it was hard to see past it even if I tried to be understanding. At what point did one need to make choices that would lead to more healthy outcomes despite a difficult past? I knew he was in pain, but I didn't feel capable of being on the receiving end of his triggers.

Nera thought I could help him return to who he was before he lost *her*, but helping him heal from grief felt intimidating.

~

"IT'S VERY GLAMOROUS," I said, awestruck, as Nera whisked me through the red velvet hotel lobby where Misha's Palace was located.

The floors were made out of a black stone and polished to a reflective surface, while the mirrored ceilings were high and lined with decadent gold chandeliers. Gold vases were scattered around with strange white flowers that gave off sensual, fragrant aromas.

"What are these flowers?" I asked, unable to step away from a vase.

I noticed several people plucking the petals and nibbling on them. The smell of the flowers drew me more and more in until my head became dizzy with a heady feeling of . . . *sex*. My body became hot, and my dress was suddenly a little too tight, rubbing me in places I wanted to touch.

"They are an aphrodisiac," Nera commented gently, pulling me away. "They're everywhere. I would advise you to stay away from their immediate vicinity unless you plan on having sex with anyone and anything."

When I turned to her with wide eyes, she chuckled. "How can a flower do that?" I whispered to Nera as I followed her to an elevator full of people. Everyone seemed to be paired up in couples. "Nera, wouldn't you rather bring someone you wanted to date here? There must be someone you're interested in."

Nera didn't have a chance to respond as we stepped into the crowded elevator.

I fidgeted with my dress as I looked around. Nera and I were overdressed. It seemed that the people around us had decided to wear as little clothing as possible. The shorter the hems or more translucent the clothing, the better. Even the female elevator attendant was wearing lingerie, and it took everything in me not to openly stare at her in admiration for her boldness.

The elevator came to a stop, and everyone poured out into the middle of a large glass dome rooftop courtyard. The courtyard boasted plush seating and high tables. Low, sensual music drifted through the space while the inside of the bar had a dance floor, a wall-to-wall bar with dancers with even less clothing than the patrons, and dark, private booths overlooking the dance floor.

A beautiful employee wearing a bright pink lingerie set led us to a booth, and I followed silently as she and Nera engaged in an animated conversation. Everywhere I looked, I saw immortal beings, easily identifiable by their silver- or gold-lined auras. As we passed the dance floor, Nera stared at the dancers and the sensual dancing they engaged in. This party scene didn't seem to fit Nera's personality, but she had a curiosity that made me wonder if Nera had any sexual experience. She seemed excited to be present but was out of her element.

Once at the booth, after the bar employee served us drinks

and had left, Nera chugged her drink and flagged down a server, who brought her a refill.

"So this is different." I observed her.

Nera looked longingly at the dance floor and occasionally waved shyly to people who greeted her in the distance. The people who greeted Nera wore varying expressions of shock before quickly turning to those they were with. They appeared to be engaging in hushed conversations, occasionally sneaking glances back her way. This was definitely not Nera's scene, and the people at the bar knew that.

Nera smiled and took a drink, pretending not to notice as people around her openly gossiped.

Wanting to distract her, I reached out and squeezed her arm. "Thank you for inviting me out tonight."

"I'm glad you're here." She smiled. "I can't remember the last time I went *out*."

"What made you decide to come out tonight?"

"It's a bit of a long story," she said, looking down at her glass and raising her eyebrows. "Lately I've been feeling restless."

"Can a god truly feel restless when you have eternity?" I joked.

"Yes," she said quietly, and I shifted in my seat, realizing she was serious. "I have always served the gods in my enclave and the rest of humanity. I have always done what is right. Never a step out of place." Nera shifted uncomfortably in her seat. "As a goddess, there is a certain expectation one carries." Nera looked to me as if she was unsure whether to reveal more.

I nodded for her to continue.

"I was created while Earth was still young to specifically balance my sister's, Ukara's, influence. Ukara was my father's star child. They are one and the same, but where my father lacks brute force and strives for diplomacy, my sister makes up for it tenfold. My sister is a brilliant woman. She has commanded many battles across galaxies. She is fearless, strong, and has a larger-than-life personality.

"During a particularly tumultuous time in Earth's history, humanity's supportive stance on female leaders began to wane. Ukara was vilified for her personality. She was not deemed worthy of womanhood due to her strength and power. That's when I was created. My sister is a lioness, and I was made to be more of a demure cat. My role was to embody the ultimate feminine energy to show human women who worshipped our enclave the *correct* way women should act. Quiet, gentle, complicit." Nera shook her head. "I was newly made; I knew little of the world, so I did whatever they told me."

As Nera shared her story, I struggled to process what she was saying. I could relate to being devalued because of who you were, but to go so far as to *create* another being to make up for it? My heart broke for Nera and Ukara.

I furrowed my brow. "They?" I asked.

"The temple priests," she whispered. "They dictated how I should act, dress, speak, and eat. Ukara was gaining too many female followers, and they were worried she would shatter society's feminine-masculine balance."

In current society, females played major scientific and political roles in Andora. In fact, the Council had more females than males. Andora didn't see gender as a hindrance to living a full life. But that clearly wasn't always the case.

"At first, the priest's demands were small," Nera began lowering her voice. "My father, who thrived on human support to embrace our presence on Earth, turned a blind eye to their demands. He, too, felt threatened by Ukara. Eventually, I was forced to take a blood oath of celibacy, and my powers were directly spellbound to my promise to ensure I would stay *pure*." She took a calming breath before saying, "I still have my powers."

I . . .

I didn't even begin to know how to process that.

I blinked and opened my mouth, only to close it again.

I cursed and almost shot up from my seat, but Nera pulled me down and shook her head.

"Please. I know you're angry, but try not to react," she whispered. "I'm already regretting coming here."

"But Nera, they had no right to demand any of that—it's a violation of your free will. I can't believe anyone could force celibacy onto someone—god or not. You have been living an eternity chained to those monsters!"

"I know, I know." Her voice broke. "Long ago, the enclave gave me the option to break the promise, but no one knows how to restore my powers. Isadora, the witch who helped us enchant Taria's wards, is unfamiliar with the magic used to bind my powers." Nera took my hands. "I don't know what else to be *but* a lunar god. What is my purpose if it's not serving my family and fulfilling the role I was made for?"

I hugged Nera tightly and felt her shrink in my arms. Gone was the strong woman I knew, and in her place was a soul who was afraid and broken.

"Nera," I said, my voice also breaking, "how can I help you? Why are we here?"

She took a large gulp of her drink. "Misha opened this place, and well." She looked around. "I know I don't belong here. Everyone knows I don't belong here. I'm the eternal virgin. But I'm curious." She shrugged.

I nodded. "And that's okay. There is nothing wrong with sexuality. It isn't sinful. It isn't evil. It does not diminish who you are as a person," I said. "And this is coming from a person who has minimal sexual experience." I chuckled.

Nera gave me a tentative smile and squeezed my hand. "Thank you." She sighed. "I guess I came here to feel daring—

for once. I want to dance; I want to pretend like I can love openly. I know I can never experience every facet of a relationship with another person, but I want to pretend like I can, even if it's just for one night."

I took Nera's cue and tried not to dwell on the atrocities of the past that made her who she was. There was no changing it. We could only make the best of our situation.

"Well." I stood, holding out my hand. "Then let's dance and find you someone. I'll be nearby. If they're cute, I might even stay, and we can share a dance partner." I laughed.

Nera smiled and took my hand before downing the rest of her beverage. "I'll need another drink though," she said, holding her empty cup.

I grabbed her glass. "Drink first, then." I smiled. "This would be a good time for a hot knight to swoop in and do our bidding."

"Speak of the devil," Nera grumbled, looking off toward the crowd on the dance floor.

Dancing bodies parted as a familiar set of eyes met mine.

Cylas.

29

RENNA

His emerald orbs glowed with the same liquid gold I had seen in Khel's eyes. As he walked toward me, his chin high and stride sure, like a prince in the night, my heart skipped a beat.

I sucked in a breath and held it, hoping it would calm my racing pulse.

Cylas arrived at our table and bowed with a flourish. "Ladies." He leaned down to my ear and whispered, "Breathe, Renna."

I blushed profusely and let out my breath slowly, which only called his attention to my lips.

He smiled lazily, watching my lips before trailing his eyes up my face until he met my gaze. His look held raw sexuality, like he wanted to eat me alive.

"Fancy meeting you here," he said, his eyes dancing with mine.

"I tagged along." I motioned toward Nera.

"Little Nera," he said to her with no emotion. "I heard you were here. I had to come see it for myself."

Nera blushed but quickly masked her reaction with sarcasm. "Master of the Universe, *welcome*."

Cylas smirked. "Finally, some respect around here," he said, focusing back on me and sticking a hand toward me. "Dance with me."

I stared at Cylas's outstretched hand. It'd been weeks since I'd seen him, thanks to the lockdown because of the attack. But I missed how carefree I felt around Cylas. I could flirt and have *fun* with him. After my argument with Khel, I wanted to be daring tonight. The exciting, pulsing energy inside the bar from the flowers' aphrodisiac probably helped my resolve.

Still, I hesitated.

"I won't bite." Cylas leaned into my ear, and I shivered. "Unless you want me to." He pulled back and winked, making heat crawl up my cheeks, which I was sure he could see, even under the low lights.

I rubbed the back of my neck and took a breath, moving slightly away from him.

Taking his hand didn't have to mean I was giving him the power to take our flirtations further. But I was here with Nera, who had poured her heart out to me moments ago, and I was a girl's girl. I was going to stay by Nera's side.

I gave Cylas our empty glasses instead of my hand. "Let's start with you helping us get drinks." I smiled.

Cylas groaned.

"It's a girls' night, Cylas," Nera told him. "She's not interested."

Cylas leaned into me again, and my skin broke out with goose bumps. I closed my eyes as my body responded to Cylas. It always had.

Cylas offered uncomplicated flirting, and I was tired of feeling suffocated by Khellios. I was overcome with the music, his eyes, his low voice, and the darn aphrodisiac flowers that were everywhere.

"I'll come back for you," he said against my shoulder, his lips hovering over my skin tortuously, sending a delicious tremor down my spine.

I nodded slightly, my body responding in a sigh like a wanton woman, and I couldn't help but watch as he sauntered away toward the bar.

"I'm not drunk enough for this," Nera said. "Let's go dance." She pulled me out of the booth. "This is turning out to be some twisted alternate universe I have no plan for."

I furrowed my brow but just nodded, letting her lead me to the dance floor, where we found a little corner next to the bar. We could see Cylas off in the distance getting us drinks.

Moving our bodies to the beat of the music, we began to dance.

A beautiful woman with long black hair that reached her waist like black liquid velvet came to stand next to me, leaning her long, elegant back against the bar. "I don't think you're being satisfied," she whispered to me with a smirk.

Her eyes were wide with hunger as she surveyed the bodies on the dance floor, swaying to the beat. Her eyes glittered as she took them in. She licked her lips.

"Excuse me?" I was confused.

"You haven't been properly fucked." The woman turned to look at me.

She raked her light purple eyes down my body, sending a shockwave of sexual awareness through me. My nipples responded to her probing stare, and I, too, daringly looked at her body. She had a tight red mesh dress that revealed her bare breasts, which sat high on her chest, dark nipples erect, while a red thong covered her tan skin below. She was beautiful.

"And how would you know that?" I said, tilting my head.

"My dear," she chuckled as she came closer. "I make it my business to know how good you're being fucked. Like the people here." She gestured to the dance floor. "They would not come here if they were satisfied. I provide them a high they won't forget."

"Misha," Nera said behind me.

"Kitty cat," Misha cooed at Nera. "Am I glad to see you." She smiled. "And you brought a guest,"

Misha ran a red manicured fingernail down my arm, and my nipples ached for attention against my dress.

"Welcome to you both," Misha smiled.

"Thank you," Nera said shyly. "I'm glad I was finally able to make it."

"I'm glad too, kitty cat," Misha said, winking. She gave Nera a once-over. "You've always looked smashing in leather. But aren't you hot?" Misha leaned closer to her with a mischievous smile. "You could take some of it off, you know."

Nera turned crimson red, and she squirmed under Misha's intense gaze.

Sensing her discomfort, I cut in. "This is a beautiful establishment."

"Thank you, dear," Misha said proudly, looking around her bar.

Misha zeroed in on a couple swaying to the beat, hands and legs intertwined. With glittering eyes, she brought her hand to her lips and blew pink dust toward them. It traveled like stars, dancing through the air, and settled around them. The couple immediately stopped dancing, and the man led his lover off to a dark booth.

She leaned back against the bar. "Taria has been great for business."

"I couldn't imagine a nightclub in downtown Taria." I

laughed, knowing the sleepy town of Taria was too slow-paced for the metropolitan life on the outskirts.

"I couldn't agree more. *All this*," Misha said, gesturing around her, "the souls who come here, enjoying themselves, loving, worshipping, *fucking*." She whispered the last words against my ear. "Their energy fuels me."

"How so?" I breathed as I wondered if the aphrodisiac was making me want to touch Misha.

"Their lust, I get high off it," she said with a small laugh. "I take their energy and give it to those who ask for my intervention in their own love lives."

My eyes widened.

"It's exhausting being the goddess of fucking," she joked. "I've learned to siphon energy. Reuse and recycle." She winked. "I used to fuck nonstop to obtain energy to give to others. Quality began to wane as I went through several partners. I have now turned it into a business."

I was speechless at Misha's fearless embrace of her sexuality.

"Speaking of fucking," she said after a few minutes. "I can tell who is getting maximum enjoyment between the sheets based on basal energy." Misha swung her gaze to me. "That sweet spot between your legs has been neglected. *Badly*. Your energy almost reads like you are being denied full pleasure."

I thought of my dream with Sethos—the last one I had with him before he left me.

"However," Misha said, "I know a good opportunity when I see one." She looked pointedly into the crowd.

I turned to where she looked and saw Cylas emerge, his eyes on me.

"Don't disappoint me, little Renna," Misha whispered against my ear, her wet lips brushing my skin, making me shiver.

I turned to look at her. Our lips were close. My breaths came faster, shallower. I could move toward her and kiss her. I had never kissed a woman before . . . Would I dare? I met her eyes, and she smiled wickedly before pulling away from me, as if she was teasing me.

"Kitty cat," Misha called while maintaining eye contact with me. "Want to step outside?" she said with a smirk.

Nera was dumbfounded by her offer and automatically let Misha lead her away.

"*Do* fuck . . . this up," Misha said to me with a wink and smile as she walked away.

"Hi," Cylas said when he got to me and handed me my drink. He placed Nera's drink at the bar.

I downed the elixir in the glass and took a steadying breath. "Hi," I said while holding his stare.

Cylas leaned closer to me. "I want you," he said against my neck while rubbing my bare arm, "*and* this dress . . . to dance with me."

"*Cylas* . . ." I heard myself say. "Everything is so complicated right now."

"It's just a dance." He smiled in earnest, holding out his hand.

Seeing him waiting for me to take his hand reminded me of Sethos asking me to join him in Daya. I smiled to myself and mentally went there as I took his hand, imagining it was Sethos's. It was ironic that the only man I felt the most peace with was unavailable to me.

As if he could see my warring thoughts, Cylas grabbed my glass and put it on the bar before leading me to the dance floor. We settled in the middle of the dancing couples, and he brought his hands to my waist, tugging me close. I draped my hands over his neck and let him part my legs with his knee as we danced close, my chest against his as we moved to the music. In that moment I could imagine Sethos's body against mine, and I clung to Cylas. I suspended all thoughts and closed my eyes, feeling the music thrum in my veins as the heady atmosphere of sex and sensuality entered my system, making my skin hyper-aware of every touch, every move, every brush of his body and that of other couples around us.

"I could have died for you," Cylas suddenly whispered against my skin.

"Hmmm?" I said, my eyes still closed as I moved against him in a haze.

"I didn't want you to leave without knowing that," he said, holding me closer. "I would have given you the world. I could have unmade it and regifted it to you."

I pulled away slightly to look at him.

"I would have made a place just for us to exist, far from all of this."

One second his expression was serious, etched with deep sadness, and then it was back to the regular nonchalant Cylas.

I stood still. "You can't say something like that and expect me to ignore it," I said with my hands on his chest, searching his face.

Cylas held me close again and whispered, "I'm not expecting you to ignore it. You deserve to know the truth, Renna. You are more than you know. You are *everything*."

My eyes went back and forth between his. "What are you saying?"

"The truth." Cylas's words were ominous, and I shivered.

Suddenly, the night sky beyond the glass dome became darker. It was as if the moon had left the sky, and the world was plunged into darkness with only the light of the skyscrapers to illuminate the night. Even the stars hid.

The people around us shifted nervously, noting the change.

"I've had enough of this lie, Renna. I refuse to play his game."

"What are you talking about?" I tried searching his expression for a clue as to what he was saying.

Cylas lifted his eyes from mine and looked behind me. I turned.

A pair of amber eyes stared back at me.

Khellios.

I skipped a breath as Khel stood feet away from me, regarding me with an unreadable look.

"Khel," I whispered as his powerful body moved through the crowd, the magnetism he exuded causing everyone around him to turn and look at him.

He stood before me and leaned down. "Hi," he said against my cheek.

"I—" I stuttered. "You're here" was all I could say.

"Don't look too upset," he said, running his knuckles down my back.

"I'm supposed to be mad at you," I said, trying to clear my head, which was always difficult when I was around him.

"Not any angrier than I should be at the moment," he growled against my ear.

I jumped slightly, but Khel held me to him.

"I smell him on you." Khel's tone was accusatory.

"Khel, you have to stop," I said, looking at him, my pulse racing.

"I've been watching you all night from The Watch." Khel pointed to the sky. "You left me no option but to come down to you."

"Khellios," Cylas said behind me, unimpressed.

Khel and I turned. Khel wrapped his arm around my waist and pulled me to him as we faced Cylas.

Cylas looked at Khel's arm around me and shot his eyes to him.

"Fancy meeting you out," Cylas said mockingly. "Shouldn't you be somewhere?" He pointed to the sky.

"You would like that, wouldn't you?" Khel said, his tone deadly.

"Oh, just me and the rest of . . ." Cylas said, tapping a finger against his chin, feigning deep thought. "Ah, yes!" he said, shooting a finger up in the air. "Me and the rest of this part of the planet would very much appreciate it if you left." Cylas snapped his fingers. "Get to it, *moon boy*."

Khel stepped forward, and I held him back, my hand on Khel's chest.

"Please don't," I said.

Cylas zeroed in on my hand on Khel's chest, and he looked toward me. "I don't take back any of what I said, Renna," Cylas said, his voice hard. "You deserve to know the truth." Cylas then looked at Khel. "You know I'm right."

Khel fell silent, his body tight with tension.

"Khellios is lying to you."

My heart stopped. *No.* I had asked him not to lie to me anymore. *Please just let this be a misunderstanding.* Even if we didn't know what we were to each other, I didn't want to be lied to.

I looked to Khel expectantly.

"You're out of line, Cylas," Khel gritted out.

I swallowed hard. *He didn't deny it.*

"You know . . ." Cylas pursed his lips. "I don't think I am. I think you're just an overcontrolling asshole. You cannot claim to care for someone while blatantly lying to them. Imagine if you actually fucked her. Now *that* would get complicated."

Khellios reached past and grabbed Cylas by the shirt. Stepping away from me, he slammed him to the ground.

I brought my hands to my mouth as my eyes widened in horror.

The dancers around us immediately moved away, and a large circle formed, caging us in.

"Stop this!" I yelled, stepping forward, unsure how to break up their fight.

"He's lying to you, Renna!" Cylas managed before Khel pummeled him to the ground. "Tell her the truth!"

"*Khellios!*" I screamed, running to hold him back. "Khellios, stop this!" I kept pulling on Khel until he suddenly pushed me, and I fell back, crashing onto the stools along the bar.

When I scrambled to stand, my anger rose and my body began to boil with hatred. I had promised myself that no one would ever physically hurt me again after my mentor.

"Stop!" I screamed at both men before me. "*Stop!*"

The music stopped then as the patrons formed a bigger circle, their faces horrified as their gods came to blows before them.

As Khellios and Cylas continued to ignore my pleas, with every blow they exchanged, the violence triggered the anger inside me. It felt like black tar moved within me, slowly coiling itself around my skin. I fisted my hands and could feel the magic inside my palms, fighting to be let out.

Cylas punched Khellios in the stomach, and Khellios landed several feet away on the ground.

"Stop this," I said, my voice straining, as I grabbed Cylas's arm and pulled him to my side while trying to hold back the pressure of my magic and the emotions warring and building inside me.

I recalled every push and every violent shove I received as a child. Every time I was pressed against a wall as my mentor screamed at me to perform magic.

How I wanted to protect myself in those moments.

"You picked a good one," Cylas said, wincing as he touched his lip.

"What do you mean?" I asked as Khel got up.

"You picked a good, *honest* man. A real winner. Aren't you, Khellios?"

I looked between both men.

"Did you ever wonder about your tattoo, Renna?" Cylas cocked his head. He gestured to my chest with his chin. "Did you ever find anything particular about the design?"

"My . . ." I touched my sternum on instinct. How could he know about that? "What are you saying?"

That night flashed back to me. The chaos. The uncertainty. Etara fleeing and leaving me with no answers.

"Did you know the symbol you have on your skin is Khellios's symbol?"

My eyes grew, and a wave of dread filled me. "What does he mean?" I turned to Khellios, who was silent, his eyes narrowed at Cylas. "I'm talking to you!" I yelled at Khellios and walked to him. Only when I was in front of him did he look at me, his eyes suddenly soft. "*Say something!*".

"I can say something," Cylas said, and I spun to face him. "That"—he pointed to my chest—"is no coincidence. Khellios used it to track you. You summoned him, in blood. He knew all about you before you even knew about him."

"Did you do that?" I asked Khellios. "Tell me he's lying."

When Khellios remained mute, fury raged inside me. I pushed at Khellios's body. "Why won't you speak to me? Defend yourself if it's a lie."

Khellios tried to grab my hands, but I backed away from him.

He looked at me pleadingly. "It's not what you think. I had no idea you would summon me—"

"So many lies. One after the other." Cylas scoffed and shook his head.

Khel raged, hurling himself toward Cylas once more.

I quickly placed myself between both men with Cylas at my back.

"Please!" I yelled. "Both of you, stop!"

Both men breathed heavily, glaring daggers at each other.

"Are you going to tell her?" Cylas challenged. "She's practically yours now. Afraid she'll vanish?" He laughed at the last phrase.

Khel stayed silent.

"Khel?" I urged.

Khel's shoulders slumped, and his chest rose with a heaving breath. The light in his eyes slowly dimmed from amber molten gold to a dull bronze.

"Were you ever going to tell her?" Cylas asked, all mocking gone. At Khellios's silence, Cylas cursed. "Fucking, gods, Khellios." Cylas shook his head.

"Fuck! Yes!" Khel yelled and looked at me, gripping the back of his neck. "Yes, I was going to tell you," he said, pleading with me. "I wanted *this*"—he gestured between us—"to be your choice. I didn't want you to feel like you owed me anything. I never wanted your love to be forced."

I stepped back, bringing my hands to my mouth.

What was he saying?

"Am-Re," Khel began. "He is—" He let out a frustrated yell and gripped his face. "Fuck! You and I—*This* is not the first time we have lived a life together," he said, reaching for me, but I kept my hands pulled tightly against myself. "You must know that I love you, Renna—"

"This is not love," Cylas interjected.

"You can stay quiet!" Khel pointed to him.

Cylas crossed his arms and glared back.

I whipped my head between both men.

Khel looked like a caged animal, wanting to be anywhere but

here, and I still found myself wanting to reach out to him and hold him.

"Your father," he began.

"My father?" I said, my eyes widening.

"Renna!" Khel pleaded, gripping my arm.

"You know nothing of my past," I said, searching his face. When Khellios closed his eyes, my heart began to beat faster. "Do you? And what do you mean this is not the first time we have lived this?" My heart painfully thumped behind my ribs, dreading his response.

This was too much.

"Renna," Khel said softly.

I saw a man, a being, who was broken.

"Talk to me," I begged.

"Renna," Khellios tried again, pulling me to him. In my shock, I let him. "I have loved you forever."

Suddenly, the scene around us began to rapidly change as a revolving blanket of haze filled the room with sparkling greens and blues and whites, enveloping everyone. I jumped as figures began to take shape within the haze, and Khellios tightened his hold on me. Patrons began to speak nervously and back away while Cylas had his arms crossed and his eyes narrowed.

My eyes widened at the scene before me. "What are you saying?" I whispered, looking up to Khellios, and he gripped my wrists.

"I loved you when I met you when you escaped your father. I loved you when the old city fell," Khellios stated desperately.

And that's when I saw them. Ghostly apparitions began to fill the space as if a scene was playing out before us. My heart stopped when a figure came close to us ... It ... it was *me*.

I shook my head and swayed. *What was happening?* "What is this ..." I breathed, looking around, my jaw falling open.

"You were to be my consort then. I love you now. I love you still. I never stopped loving you."

My heart pounded in my chest as a younger version of myself came into focus, dressed in a long gown, laughing while holding her hands out to someone in the distance. Her eyes glittered with mirth as she said something I couldn't hear. I followed her gaze, and an apparition of Khellios stepped forth, his arms stretched out toward her. He was laughing at whatever she said, and when they touched, he brought her to his chest in a passionate embrace. Time seemed to slow down for me as he lifted her off the ground and kissed her. She draped her arms around him, letting him.

"These are my memories of us," Khellios explained, drawing me closer. "You don't remember," he said bitterly and shook my wrists. "I don't know why your memory has not been triggered, but if you let me, I intend to help revive what we had."

Tears welled up as the scene changed multiple times, each time featuring Khellios and me. When an apparition of Nera came into view with the younger version of me, I began to sob. They were picking flowers in a field while Khellios approached them with a grin and held out his arms to me in greeting.

It felt like I'd been stabbed in the gut. They all knew. They all knew about my past. They all lied to me.

I shook my head and balled my hands into fists.

Screaming, I pushed Khellios off me. He waved a hand, and the haze and apparitions disappeared.

Even though the images were gone, they swam in my mind. My chest heaved with heavy breaths, and I scrubbed my hands down my face.

Khellios stepped toward me, cautiously stretching his hand out, like I was in danger of fleeing. "You have reincarnated to this lifetime. I do not know how. But it is you—*you* are my Renna. You have returned to me, and I love you."

"*This.*" I shook my head as tears slipped from my eyes, and I wiped them angrily. "This is not love. You have"—furious magic swelled within me—"betrayed me. You lied."

"I did what was best for us both. But I am done with the lies." He advanced toward me, ignoring the space I kept putting between us until I bumped into Cylas, and he stood in front of me to face Khellios.

Khellios held his palms out. "Renna. Am-Re is your father. You hailed from a sea siren and Am-Re," he said softly. "You come from him still."

I covered my ears and closed my eyes as my stomach roiled. My breaths sawed in and out of me. I shook my head. "No! You're lying."

I had been worried because my magic was similar to this awful enemy, and now? Now I learned my magic wasn't just similar, it *was* his magic. It had to be a mistake.

Memories of my childhood flooded my mind. Glass shattering, fear, cold, hunger. Cigarette burns. And the taunting. The taunting that would not cease. What father would hurt their children?

"I am speaking the truth."

"Enough!" I opened my eyes and rushed to Khellios and hit him with all my strength.

He barely moved, and it furthered my anger.

"Why are you telling all these lies? You're deliberately trying to hurt me. I know nothing about my parents. Now you expect me to believe he is the one attacking Taria?" Even though my mouth denied the truth, my mind roared with the possibility of his words.

I attempted to hit him again, but Khellios gripped me and hugged me to his chest. "I'm not trying to hurt you. I love you."

I broke free to face Cylas. His arms were crossed, a solemn

expression on his face. In his eyes, I saw pained, raw honesty. He nodded.

I spun back to face Khellios. "It's all true, then?" I demanded.

Khel looked lost. "I wouldn't lie to you, my love."

My face contorted in disgust. "I am not your love," I gritted out.

Khellios flinched.

"So, the whole time I've been in Taria"—I gestured around me—"you've been keeping me here from my father, and you lied to me about who I am, and . . ." I pointed between us, words escaping me.

"I wanted to protect you from Am-Re. Telling you about our love would only complicate everything. You and I were to be married. You were to ascend as my consort. You died on the night the old city fell. You and our child." Khel shook his head. "You've come back. I cannot explain it. I wanted to tell you who we were to each other, but *fuck*!" He began pacing. "I did not want you to feel obligated to love me in this life."

"So you lied to me?" I said, backing from him, and when he pursued me, I put my hands out to create a boundary.

"No!" he yelled, advancing toward me, ignoring my boundary and gripping my shoulders. "Can't you see that I love you? I would never hurt you—"

"You knew who I was this whole time. I told you never to lie to me!"

"Yes, but—"

"And you knew how painful it was for me to grow up the way I did—"

"Would you listen to me?" He shook my shoulders.

When I tried to break from him and he refused to let me go, my arms began to burn with magic as if the power inside me would explode from my chest.

"You knew!" I screamed. "You knew who I was! You didn't think to tell me—"

"Renna!" he said, his hands locked on me while I struggled to get away. "Stop this!"

"You knew! Even while you seduced me, you knew why I responded so easily to you, you knew why I was drawn to you, and you preyed upon that!" I screamed, and Khel dropped his hands from me. "You-you tricked me!" I spat, horrified, trying to scrub his touch from my skin as my heart broke in jagged splinters.

"He killed you, Renna!" Khel said, rushing to me, once more ignoring my boundary, and I felt like I was suffocating.

"Don't touch me!" I screamed, pushing against him.

"Please! You love me! You must feel it—underneath every-thing—that your soul is mine and I am yours. You belong to me!"

In that moment, a dark emotion moved like thick tar from my chest through every inch of my body. "Nobody owns me," I said with a deadly calm I didn't feel.

Khel stepped back, looking at my body, which I could feel was now wrapped in flowing ribbons of energy.

"Renna," Khel said carefully, reaching for me again as if I was a scared animal. "I'm sorry. Please, let's move forward. We have so much to live for. Let us start anew. I love you. You are all I ever wanted."

"Renna," Cylas stated, his eyes pained. He shook his head. "You deserve better than this."

Khel screamed in rage and launched himself at Cylas once more, and I stood motionless, watching everything play out in front of me like a slow-motion film. My breathing was the only thing I could hear.

Suddenly Misha and Nera arrived and ran toward the men.

Nera tried to tear them apart with her magic, but their magic blocked her from getting near.

My eyes zeroed in on Khellios, who grabbed Cylas by the collar, and the energy of that wounded child within me exploded inside. I screamed as my body burned with the magic spilling from me, my hands now open as I doubled over from the pain of so much energy coursing through me.

Patrons around us began pointing at me, their faces white as black shadows slithered from my body like serpents. The shadows covered every visible space of the ground, encasing us in a cloud of black mist. My magic entangled the legs of those around me like the tentacles of a sea beast.

Panic took over the crowd as everyone began screaming.

Is this what it meant to be the product of a siren and the monster that was Am-Re?

I was a monstrosity.

Khel stopped his assault on Cylas, his eyes frantic as he observed the shadows around him. He looked to me, his mouth open as I crashed to the ground.

The last thing I remembered was Cylas and Nera rushing to me to break my fall, and then the continued screaming as people pointed to the dome above us before it shattered.

30

KHELLIOS

"K hel!" Nera screamed, holding Renna in her arms. "The wards," Nera yelled, looking at the sky, tears streaming down her face.

Emerald light filled the sky, and violet lightning began to strike Taria like bombs.

Am-Re had come at last.

I looked down to an unconscious Renna. "Take her back to my house. I will come for you both."

When Nera began to refuse to leave my side because she wanted to fight, I grabbed her by the arms. I would not lose Renna. Not again.

"Listen to me," I said, bending so I was eye level with her. "I cannot help you both. You are the best chance Renna has. Protect her with your life. Tell her I love her and that I'm sorry for everything."

"Khel," Nera cried, pulling me to her with one arm. "Please stay safe."

I nodded and stood as Nera opened a portal with her free arm and hoisted her and Renna through it. Dread filled me then. I wondered if that would be the last time I would see Renna. She would live. But would I?

I walked out to the rooftop, dodging human soul patrons who ran inside toward the elevators and stairs. None of them questioned why I walked to the danger outside. They had counted on me and the rest of the enclave to protect them. We had failed again.

Outside, my cousins and other gods stood facing the sky where a swirling portal of fire and lightning opened into the terrace, bringing with it chilling cries of primordial beasts not known to humans. Chaos had come at last.

"Nice of you to join," Cylas yelled, his face contorted in rage as he crashed into me like a boulder, sending me flying.

I scrambled to stand as Cylas stalked toward me again.

Ukara flashed toward Cylas, arriving in a clash of colors to hold him back. Her gold wings were extended behind her as she hovered above us, donning gold armor. A dozen of her female warriors hovered at her side, spears ready for her command.

"You led him to her!" Cylas screamed, spit flying from his mouth as he resembled a furious beast. "You left your post on The Watch and directly dropped into this portion of Taria. Did you not think *he* would think it suspicious that a god—that *YOU* —would descend into this portion of the planet where there is nothing?!" Cylas spit at my feet. "You practically served her to him on a platter, you fucking scum."

I charged at Cylas, pushing him and Ukara, who still held him, with all my might. Ukara let go before the impact, and Cylas crashed onto the rooftop's railing.

"Says the lowlife who was taking what was not his." I charged at him again. "You think I could just stand by and watch you with her?"

Cylas stood, shaking off his body from the crash. "I did not plan to take what was not freely given."

I saw red at that moment as I replayed every touch and look they had shared. I had seen them from The Watch tonight, which was why I came down to Taria.

"She's mine," I growled, feeling the anger swirl in my veins as I called on solar energy to charge toward him if he decided to attack me again.

"Enough!" Ukara yelled. "None of this will help Renna, us, or the citizens we have vowed to protect. We cannot fail them again." Ukara turned to me. "Am-Re is *here!*" she yelled. "Wake up, both of you. *Enough!*"

Her words cleared the haze of madness that had overtaken me.

"Don't you see this is what he wants you to do?" Ukara yelled at Cylas and me while the other gods watched. "He's creating chaos within our hearts. He is dividing all of us!"

"I agree with Ukara," Calyxa, a minor Goddess of Stars, said, stepping forward. "Tell us what to do, General." She bowed her head to Ukara.

Other gods around her nodded to Ukara.

"We stand together," Ukara commanded, looking at the nine gods on the rooftop. "No more division. Am-Re will not be defeated in one night, so let's repair the shield and try to understand the energy Am-Re has so we can fight back. We have not encountered Am-Re for hundreds of years. His energy has changed." She shook her head. "This feels different. We need to siphon our energy to push him out and close the shield."

"Why take a chance? He will try again." My mother arrived in a mist of cobalt-blue fire, her brilliant white hair suspended in the air in waves. "Expel Renna from Taria. Her presence poses too much risk for our people. He is all she wants!"

The gods present broke into various arguments, some agreeing with her and some siding with me.

"Son." My mother placed her hands on my shoulders. "Renna's presence here cannot continue. We are breaking the vow to protect the souls we were entrusted with caring for," my mother argued. "If Renna were meant to be yours, her presence in your life would be easy. Nothing connected to her has been easy. She has brought chaos into our lives. Let her go." When I tried to cut in, my mother shook her head. "Am-Re will only come back." She continued. "Renna is not yours. You keep forcing her presence into your life like an obsession. She is not a prize to be had." My mother gently cupped my face. "Son, you have to stop."

I remained speechless, staring back at her, my chest heaving.

I knew the risks in bringing her to Taria when she summoned me that night. Renna and I were supposed to be together. And I failed to save her.

"Khellios," Ukara said quietly. "We need to close this gap. *Now*."

My mother's eyes searched mine. "It never had to be this way. Let her go. Exile her from Taria now. She is all he wants. You don't have to fight him. There can be a different solution."

"Khellios," Ukara repeated, her voice now firm. The war commander in her had taken over. "Now."

I turned toward the other gods assembled, each staring back at me. I broke from my mother and stepped in front of them. "I brought chaos into our lives, into our homes. I will right this," I said, not waiting for arguments.

There was one way to close a shield gap. A god needed to siphon the energy of seven gods and transmute the energy into their body, combine it with their own power, direct the energy to the gap, and seal it with divine fire. We had designed it this way to ensure the magical traits and elements of various gods could strengthen the wards.

Closing a gap in the shield was risky. Closing a gap in the shield with a foe like Am-Re was suicidal.

My mother immediately began to claw toward me, begging me not to go. Calyxa gently held her back. I nodded toward Ukara to indicate I was ready.

Cylas was the first to step toward me to deposit his energy into me. He glared at me as he placed his hands on my shoulder, his skin glowing with the power beneath the surface.

Depositing power was draining for a god. Power took time to replenish, and a god needed a full day to recover. It left gods vulnerable as the ability to fight back was unlikely. The benefit we had was that Am-Re did not know how the wards in Taria were strengthened, so he could not know that there would be several incapacitated gods on the ground open to attack.

I could not fail.

Receiving power from a god was not pleasant either. My body felt like it was on fire, as if molten thick lava had entered my blood system, burning everything inside me.

I squeezed my eyes shut as each god placed their hands on me. A god began to chant a spell in our old tongue to enchant and bind the energies to me for this sole purpose.

I mentally left my body then to block out the pain. I focused on Renna and her face in our last lifetime together, when she had arrived in the old city all those years ago and I found her.

My mind was brought back to the present when the seventh god, Ukara, stepped from me, having deposited the last of the energy needed for me to ascend to the shield and seal the gap.

Ukara stood close to me and touched my arm lightly. "I know you can do this on your own," she began, "but I will not let you go alone."

I began to protest. "It is up to me alone to ensure the safety of Taria, and you are weak, having just given me your magic."

But Ukara shook her head. "I can still cast magic even without my full powers," she said. "I am going with you to support you and to show Am-Re we stand united."

I took a deep breath and nodded. With my newfound strength, we shot up into the heavens to the edges of Taria's shield.

As we approached the barrier, I could see the shield's brilliant lilac hue now tarnished to a moldy, brown, charred color where the gap was. The brown color seemed to be spreading as the gap became wider, created by Am-Re's fiery chaos.

"I cannot understand it," Ukara yelled at me, shielding her face from the blinding fire in the gap with her golden-armored forearm. "This magic feels different."

Different indeed. Although our enclave had not dealt with Am-Re for thousands of years, one could not forget how his energy felt. We could feel the essence of Am-Re, but it was difficult to understand the power he wielded. The energy was faster, sharper, stronger, and more vengeful. There was rage and pain in this energy where pure apathy had existed before.

In the middle of the fiery chaos that pierced the gap was a black vortex with green electricity. The chilling, shrill screams from the void continued. The sound was like hearing the destruction of stars as they were violently ripped apart and disintegrated into dust.

Am-Re was nowhere to be found.

"Let's close the gap now!" Ukara yelled. "Let's not wait for him to appear."

Rage filled me at Am-Re's absence. The memory of Renna's bloodied body when she died blinded me with anger, and the energy inside me demanded I seek restitution for everything done to me.

"Coward!" I screamed at the vortex. "You hear me?!" I screamed, flying closer to the gap.

Ukara immediately flew toward me, pulling me back. "You idiot!" she cried desperately. "What are you doing?"

"Do you hear me?" I screamed at the chaos. "She's mine! You will *never* take her from me again!"

"Do you want to die?!" Ukara shoved me back, but I fought against her and flew back up to the gap. "Khellios!" she screamed. "Stop this!"

The energy in the air suddenly changed and became erratic. Lightning shot from the vortex, barreling straight for us. We darted out of the way as black mist oozed from the void, darkening the sky.

"We have to close the gap. Now!" Ukara pleaded. "The people below are in danger!"

I gritted my teeth and nodded. Blowing out a harsh breath, I called on the magic inside me, summoning it into my hands to heal and seal the gap. Ukara began to recite spell chants, her palms facing the gap.

And then a voice echoed through the sky.

"You have something that is mine," the voice growled.

It was a male's voice, but it was not Am-Re.

I had heard it before, but I could not remember where . . .

I dropped my hands, and the ball of energy dissipated. Ukara had stopped too and now looked up to the vortex with wide eyes, hands suspended in midair.

From the black void, a fire-breathing serpent beast emerged, its body taking over the sky like a goliath. Its emerald and black body, adorned with horns, slithered closer to the vortex, its gruesome body coiling as if the beast would attack at any moment.

Ukara turned to me; her eyes were full of questions.

Am-Re had chosen a deadly gold serpent as his spirit animal, but this was something far more gruesome and terrifying than we had ever seen. And we had lived for as long as the universe existed. What type of demonic beast had Am-Re created?

"We meet again, God of the Moon and Stars." The beast's

jaws remained closed while his voice echoed from him, ringing loudly through the sky.

I was still unable to place where I had heard the beast's voice, but it rang true to my ears. I would have remembered meeting a beast such as this. Not remembering made me feel a fool.

"Who are you?" I demanded, inching closer to the beast. "Where is Am-Re? Has he sent you to do his bidding?" I spat. "Is he too important to show his face so he sent his *beast* instead?"

Ukara gasped and quickly held my arm to prevent me from moving closer to the gap.

The beast chuckled. "Am-Re is no more. Seven years ago, I scattered his remains across multiple universes."

My heart stopped.

The beast had destroyed Am-Re. Am-Re was an immortal—like us. We were difficult to kill.

"What are you?" Ukara demanded.

The beast's voice vibrated throughout the skies. "I am chaos like my teacher before me. I am darkness. I am Sethos. And I rule in the place of my father." The beast slithered closer to the gap. "You have usurped my place, Khellios."

Sethos. The adopted son of Am-Re while in exile.

Ukara gasped and looked at me, the white in her eyes showing in terror.

If Sethos had killed Am-Re, then that made Sethos more powerful than him. Sethos's magic was nearly identical to that of Am-Re's, and this attack left no doubt that Sethos would continue Am-Re's war against us. He had attacked Xhor and was looking for Renna.

But with Am-Re gone, Renna posed no value to him. Why did he need her? For leverage against us? She was innocent.

"Speak plainly," I yelled.

"The daughter of chaos does not belong to you."

"Leave Renna out of this," I gritted out. "Am-Re is dead. She means *nothing* to you!"

The beast laughed, and bolts of fire shot from the vortex toward Taria, targeting the land below.

As fire rained down on Taria, Ukara flew to me. "Khellios," Ukara pleaded. "Finish this!"

I gathered the energy once more between my palms, and Ukara screamed her enchantments.

The fire continued to rain on Taria, and Ukara turned to me. "On the count of three, you have to launch the sphere at the gap!"

I gave her a curt nod and focused on reinforcing the power in my hands. It surged to the surface effortlessly, my body vibrating with the struggle to contain it.

Ukara paused in her chanting to shout, "Three!"

I lifted my arms, chest high.

"Two!"

I pivoted my torso in preparation.

"One!"

Grunting, I pulled back and, with everything I had left, I catapulted the magic toward the chasm. It arced through the air, aiming true.

But Sethos was ready. The crackling ball of energy reached the beast, and it was as if time itself had stopped and noise had canceled out. My heartbeat was the only thing I could hear.

Any chance of the siphoned magic working to stop Sethos died when the beast opened its jaws and consumed the ball of energy, countering it with fire built from its belly. The fire moved out toward the world below, like a deadly fire in a forest, trapping all goodness in its clutches until there was no more.

I shoved Ukara out of the way with the little magic that was left in me and shielded my body against death.

An inferno encased me, trapping me in the flames of

destruction Sethos had wielded so easily. I thought of Renna and Taria and my responsibility to both.

I would not fail either.

I pulled my sword from its scabbard and propelled my body against the beast. I would injure it before it could destroy Taria.

As I approached it, firelight glinted off his black and emerald scales, and his horns were larger than any beast I had seen. It was unnatural. Only hatred could create such a monstrosity when left to fester. Only a monster such as he could kill a god.

I raised my arms and plunged my sword into the beast, and a guttural roar vibrated from his fiery throat through the night. The beast recoiled before plunging back toward me with hatred in its eyes. I felt the magic around the beast reach out to trap me, as if the black vortex itself was sucking me in, trying to rip my body in half. My atoms, my soul, began to split apart until the pain was overwhelming, silencing everything around me, and it was like I had left my body as I watched my arm, with my sword, in the mouth of the beast.

The shock of seeing my body charred and maimed made the world spin, and I felt my body begin to fall. The wind did not cradle me. Instead, my body thrashed as it fought gravity and the inevitable pain that awaited me. I would survive as I had many other times, but I did not know what the magic of Am-Re, wielded by Sethos, would do to me. Am-Re had not survived it. I had not experienced pain like this in any lifetime.

Out of the corner of my eye, a flash of gold ripped through the skies toward me. The last thing I saw was a pair of golden wings.

31

RENNA

Quiet voices woke me up. It was night, and I was lying in bed, alone in my room. My bones and joints and muscles felt like they were on fire. My throat was parched as I tried to swallow.

I groaned and held my head, wondering why I felt like this.

And suddenly it all rushed back to me.

Khellios's confession.

I was the daughter of a monster.

I was a monster.

And Khellios's lost love.

Rage began to course through me at his lies. He claimed to love me but lied to me repeatedly, even after I trusted him not to.

And I had used magic.

It had not been a small amount either. The amount of magic that was expelled from me mirrored the magic that surrounded my mentor whenever he worked with energy.

I had never been able to call forth that much energy before. Had I been able to summon that much power in the past, perhaps I would have had a different fate and my mentor would have respected me.

I would not have been hit as hard.

I could have fought back.

It didn't matter now.

My mentor had won.

I exploded with power in response to anger.

Still, I wondered how my mentor would have looked at me if I had produced that much magic. Would he have looked at me in shock, like Khellios had done? In fear as the patrons had with their gasps and fingers pointing at me accusatorily? Or would he have looked at me in awe, like I was the most incredible being to exist, like Cylas had looked at me? Or perhaps how Sethos would have.

My hands felt odd.

It was too painful to move, as my bones felt like liquid, but still, I tried to wiggle my fingers and found them encased in a thick liquid.

Cold, viscous liquid.

I craned my neck to look down my body.

I stopped breathing.

Black liquid was pouring from my hands, like blood, pooling onto the bed. I wiggled my toes and could feel the same liquid . . .

It was almost like my body was bleeding magic.

How was this possible?

The quiet voices in my study continued, and my heart sped up. What would they say if they saw me like this? Would I be feared like Am-Re?

I bent my elbows and gritted my teeth, quietly screaming as I propped my body up. The black liquid was pooling under my legs. I had no way to turn it off.

Before, I had been able to suppress my magic and hide it deep within me so I could forget about it for a time. Now? No matter how much I tried to relax, breathe, and divert my mind, it remained just below the surface of my skin, active, waiting to be called upon. Was this my new normal?

I was a monstrous thing.

I vaguely recalled Nera's fear earlier as she helped me settle into my room, careful not to touch my skin too long or stand too near.

What if I hurt someone? Did I hurt anyone? Clearly I could not be trusted to control my magic . . .

Would I be chained up like a beast, labeled as a hazard to all? There were so many gods in Taria who already opposed my presence in their land. I wouldn't welcome someone like me. I had no doubt Khellios would step up security around me.

I had to move.

I bit into my fist to muffle a scream as I managed to sit on the bed and swing my legs down.

If this is what fully integrated magic did to my body, I didn't want it.

Something made me look to the side of my bed.

On my nightstand was a black and gold vial.

The vial that would quell my magic.

I hadn't put it there.

It became clear to me that it was placed there for me to take.

"Renna . . ." a voice suddenly whispered.

I looked at the door.

The quiet voices continued.

My eyes returned to the vial. I stretched to reach it, pushing past the pain, and took it in my palms. The glass was cold to the touch. Such a small dose to take to do away with the pain running within me.

"Renna . . ." the voice called again.

I paused, shifting my eyes around the room while my body stilled.

The mirror.

It stood to the right of my bed, propped up on a corner next to the balcony doors.

I hadn't taken it out. How had it moved?

"My sweet Renna..."

That voice.

Tears clogged my throat.

Sethos.

My eyes zeroed in on the mirror. His voice was coming from there. Adrenaline pushed my body up, and I tensed in fear, only to immediately double over in pain.

And then the surface of the mirror changed from black obsidian to dark emerald cosmos. Millions of stars, galaxies, and stardust dotted the expanse.

Suddenly I felt cold at my feet. I looked down, and my magic bled from me while black tendrils extended from the mirror to my feet and legs. My magic and the smoke intertwined, combining into one. The smoke coiled its way up my legs, making me shiver.

It whispered against my skin as it continued to wind its way up my body.

"Sethos," I whispered, looking down at my feet and back up at the mirror.

While my heart beat in a staccato, the rest of my body was frozen. Focusing on the smoke, I couldn't move even if I wanted to.

"Wh-what's happening?" I trembled as the smoke continued to coil up my skin, like a serpent, ever so softly and gently, barely touching me.

"Your magic..." the smoke whispered.

"I didn't mean to," I said, panicking. "It happened so fast, and I didn't know that I could—"

"Shhhh..."

"I'm afraid." I lowered my voice. "What will happen to me? And how are you here?"

The smoke paused.

"Are you afraid, mejtah?"

His words sent shivers down my spine. "Not of you," I said quickly, to which the smoke continued to slither its way up my legs.

My lower half was now covered in black smoke, like a translucent veil.

"Put the vial down, Renna," he whispered.

I looked at my palms.

"Don't do it, *mejtah*."

"This is a painful existence, Sethos."

"Let me help you, but don't extinguish that which makes you, you."

"I'm afraid of what I am. What will become of me?"

"Come to me," he whispered.

The smoke pooled around me but made no move to push me in the direction of the mirror.

He was making this my choice.

I looked to the door leading to my study and noticed the voices had stopped. I whipped my head to the mirror.

"Renna," he spoke. "We don't have much time. Come . . ."

"What will happen to me?" My voice broke.

I was afraid of the magic that I knew awaited me if I stepped through the mirror.

"It's time to come home."

Home.

Livina's promise came back to me. Her promise that I'd go home before the equinox.

Tears blinded me as the implication of what this moment meant for the trajectory of my life. I knew deep in my heart that if I followed him, my life would never be the same.

Suddenly the door handle to my room began to move. Whoever was coming into my room would catch me. And then what?

I took a deep breath and nodded to the mirror. The smoke gripped me and carried me closer. The black dripping from my hands and feet mixed with the smoke until both were bound as one.

"Come to me, Renna, my *mejtah* . . ."

I reached out to the mirror's surface, and when my fingers touched it, they went right through. It was liquid.

And then I heard Nera's voice behind me. "Renna!" she screamed. "Don't!"

I looked behind me one last time and saw my beautiful friend frozen to the spot in terror, the whites of her eyes like the full moon. She reached for me.

The vial slipped through my fingers, and then I stepped through.

32

SETHOS

Visiting Renna in her dreams had never been my plan. I looked for Renna after her death. I looked every second of my existence.

Unlike the man who claimed to love her, the so-called God of the Moon and Stars Khellios, I never let up the search.

I looked for the girl with hazel eyes and wavy ebony hair who always had a shy smile for me.

The girl who always laughed at inappropriate jokes in private when her father, Am-Re, was not around.

The girl who had been like a little sister to me for many years until one day she grew up, and I could not help but notice . . .

The young woman who watched as I trained with her father's soldiers, her eyes wide, lingering a little too long on my body, making me self-conscious and even falter in my steps as I was molded to become a tool of death and Am-Re's right-hand assassin.

Renna was seven years younger than me, and I tried to shield her from his abuse as much as I could.

With my body, I took blows intended for her; with my mind

and words, I comforted her when living under his roof became too much. And with my love, I arranged her escape from her father's clutches.

Only I didn't know when she escaped that she would run to Arios's enclave.

I didn't know she would fall in love with Khellios.

I didn't know she would agree to become Khellios's consort after three months. Why did she do it? For protection? Did she truly love him?

The Renna I knew had always developed a young girl's crush on me. Out of respect for our age gap, even when Renna became of marrying age at sixteen in Am-Re's kingdom, I never made a move or set my hopes on her.

To me, sixteen was much too young. Renna was sheltered. I was the only protector she truly had. I wanted her to see the world and experience life before I took her longing gazes and blushing smiles seriously. What did she know of love between couples?

Then she turned eighteen, and overnight, she became alluring to me. Her gazes became more daring, the corner of her lips lifted just so—playfully, mischievously—making my chest tighten, and she began to wear more fitted gowns. Renna had grown into a woman, and I could not help but notice. And the glances she sent my way told me she wanted me to notice. The way she managed to brush past me just so that our bodies would touch.

I found myself wondering about pursuing something with her and knew that any future with her would need to be away from her father.

I knew that I wanted more for her because living with her father was no life.

And so, I arranged an escape.

I wanted her to travel to Sirius galaxy where I had contacts.

I promised I would come for her.

However, in transit to Sirius, Renna never made it to her destination. Somehow, she went to Arios's enclave and sought asylum.

Her father killed her three months later.

I always knew Am-Re hid her soul, and I vowed to find it for the rest of my days. I never forgave Am-Re, so I plotted to topple him. I became stronger, smarter, and developed my magic in ways that challenged my mind, body, and spirit.

My commitment to magic impressed Am-Re, and he began to train me more and more, never knowing he was training me to kill him.

Then Renna reincarnated, and I found out Am-Re was abusing her again.

That's when I killed him.

Visiting Renna in dreams was never my plan.

Touching her, doing everything short of actually fucking her, and feeling myself fall for her was never my plan. I couldn't. Not now. Renna going to Taria was my way to find the gods and exact revenge on all they had done . . .

And now that she trusted me, my revenge could begin.

ACKNOWLEDGMENTS

This book and series would not be possible without the support of my husband, child, family, and friends.

To my husband: thank you for the countless jalapeño margarita mocktails you made me as I wrote this series every night after we put our baby to sleep. While you were washing baby dishes and getting the house ready for the next day I was writing this book. You checked on me, brought me drinks, snacks, and blankets. You are an incredible father and husband and my very own MMC.

To my child: I hope you see this writing journey as an inspiration to follow your own dreams. Never stop learning. Always ask questions. Be curious. Know that in life you bring your own seat to the table.

To my extended family: thank you for cheering me on and listening on and on and on about the plot. For being excited for the character art. For just, everything. Mom- remember when I would miss out on family events by locking myself in my room to write my novels? You would bring me food because I refused to go downstairs to join the party because I needed to write "one more chapter." Yeah, so that paid of- love you! Ps. Please bring more food.

To my friends:

Molly Tullis: You are the OG. You have led the torch for so many writers in the last 4 years. Thank you for being my unofficial mentor and for cheering me on. Thank you for being a part of my family.

Mariah Oller: You were there when Khellios was born. You were one of the first people I told about my sternum tattoo and this story. Thank you for being in my life. You are magic.

Danny Santos: Our heart to heart in Jamaica will always stay with me. Thank you for cheering me on and confirming a lot of my thoughts about my characters running through my mind.

Angelina: Remember when you told me the story was not a coincidence? So, yeah, you were right! Thank you for the sisterhood.

Sarah Jaeger: THANK YOU. For your honesty. For the real-ness. For the fierce friendship. It is an honor.

Jeanine Harrell: You are the best. Thank you for editing this goliath. You might be a wizard. *(sorry I did not run these back of the book sections by you).*

Kelsey Schneider: Sarah wasn't kidding when she called you the chaos coordinator! Thank you for helping my story shine on social platforms. You are a PR genie.

Val: MY BOOK GODMOTHER. Thank you for believing in my writing. You rock!

To my university friends: you know who you are and I love you. *13 really is a lucky number...*

ABOUT THE AUTHOR

Mina Brower is an American citizen who immigrated from Mexico and aims to inspire other immigrants to chase their dreams. A wife, a mom, and a lawyer, Mina is proud to live a life long dream adding author to her many list of titles. If you were to ask Mina how she balances it all she would give you a diplomatic legalese answer of "that depends."

A fan of Fleetwood Mac and ghost hunting shows Mina most enjoys books where the morally gray villain gets the girl. A God of Moonlight and Stardust is Mina's first published book and part of the series Daughters of Chaos.

Stay in touch with Mina on social media at https://www.insta gram.com/minabrowerauthor/.

AFTERWORD

In 2021 the muse for this story visited me in a dream. Draped in a cloak made of stars, my muse appeared to me in my apartment much like Sethos appeared to Renna. In my dream, the roof of my apartment was blown open to reveal the cosmos. He brought me the stars. My muse did ask me if I was happy to see him and I replied yes, that I would always be happy to see him.

The dream with my muse and my conversation with him will always stay with me and was adapted for this story. My muse gave me the courage to take a childhood hobby of writing seriously as a way to cope with infertility. I owe him this series.

The idea of Khellios came to me when I got a sternum tattoo in early 2022 with an early version of Khellios's sigil. The tattoo design was all my own and getting the tattoo felt magical (sad to report that no lights exploded and the tattoo artist was not Etara).

I connect with Khellios as he is still healing from loss. He reminds me grief is not linear. Sometimes people have good days and sometimes they have bad days. It's okay to not have it figured out. While I do not agree with how Khel withheld information from Renna, I can understand his fear of her vanishing from his life and of feeling too happy. When I got pregnant after years of infertility and loss, it was hard to stay positive and allow myself to look too far into the future because I was scared of going through loss again. Therapy helped immensely.

Livina is my homage to oracles from ancient civilizations. She is at the helm steering the story. Like the character Pemira, I know how the story ends for Renna Strongborn but Liv likes to be difficult about disclosing the exact steps Renna must take to get to the finish line. Liv, why must you be difficult?

Lastly, Renna's journey as she processes anger and trauma is my own way to explore topics of domestic violence in my own life. All survivors are champions. Like Renna, I studied classical civilizations at university. It was a lot of fun to imagine what magic would have looked like on my own campus. Renna's last name "Strongborn" is also personally significant. Her last name is inspired by my child who was premature but strong and healthy.

Made in the USA
Monee, IL
18 August 2024

63500101R00194